Born in Manchester, England, Charlie Hogg has been writing for television, radio, magazines and newspapers for a number of years. He has written scripts for many comedy performers. *The Funny Assassin* is his first novel. He attended Salford University before becoming a professional entertainer and writer. His profession has taken him all over the world and he, with his family, is currently living in Tampa, Florida in the United States.

Charlie Hogg

THE FUNNY ASSASSIN

AUSTIN MACAULEY PUBLISHERS™
LONDON * CAMBRIDGE * NEW YORK * SHARJAH

Copyright © Charlie Hogg 2024

The right of Charlie Hogg to be identified as author of this work has been asserted by the author in accordance with sections 77 and 78 of the Copyright, Designs and Patents Act 1988.

All rights reserved. No part of this publication may be reproduced, stored in a retrieval system, or transmitted in any form or by any means, electronic, mechanical, photocopying, recording, or otherwise, without the prior permission of the publishers.

Any person who commits any unauthorised act in relation to this publication may be liable to criminal prosecution and civil claims for damages.

This is a work of fiction. Names, characters, businesses, places, events, locales and incidents are either the products of the author's imagination or used in a fictitious manner. Any resemblance to actual persons, living or dead, or actual events is purely coincidental.

A CIP catalogue record for this title is available from the British Library.

ISBN 9781528993043 (Paperback)
ISBN 9781528993050 (Hardback)
ISBN 9781528993074 (ePub e-book)
ISBN 9781528993067 (Audiobook)

www.austinmacauley.co.uk

First Published 2024
Austin Macauley Publishers Ltd®
1 Canada Square
Canary Wharf
London
E14 5AA

Chapter 1
A Comedian by Any Other Name

The room was pretty much crowded with hookers and guys from the oilrigs, very few of whom were interested in the comic's show or any show for that matter. Why would they be?

The Karlson Club was a late-night pick-up joint. It was rough. It was smoky and dirty, but to Billy Doyle it was an extra income.

This night, his set had felt longer than it actually was. Such is the way when the audience isn't interested in the performance. Relief from his ordeal was almost in sight as he neared the end of his bit. That was until a group of rowdy guys staggered in. Oblivious of Doyle's predicament, they took it upon themselves to have a go at the comedian with some insulting banter:

"Hey, what time does the comic come on?"

"Don't you give up your day job!"

"Son, you want to save your breath. You're going to need it to blow up your date later!"

It wasn't a reaction that Doyle wanted but at least it was some reaction. He stopped his show and breathed at the loudest of the louts: "You know, sir, I have to admire your father for building a shit house like you with one screw!"

Ordinarily, the line might have subdued a lesser person or at least someone lesser intoxicated, but the man staggered forward towards the stage. "Hey, you! Don't you be talking about my father like that!" the lout spouted.

"Your father!" Doyle said, "The best part of you ran down your father's leg and if your mother hadn't been there, to lick it up, you wouldn't be here now. Fuck off! Goodnight everybody." With that, the comic left the stage and made his way to the back door where two bouncers were waiting to escort him to his car.

Also, in the doorway was the customer who he'd just verbally reviled. He looked at the guy. He hadn't looked that big from the stage, but now? He was big! He was well over six and a half feet tall and close to 300 pounds. The customer raised his massive clump of a hand. It was almost as if the scene was in slow motion. The big man grabbed the comic's hand, which was miniscule in comparison:

"You're the best fuckin' comic I've seen in a long time, Son."

Billy's face was ashen. Not sure if it was fear or confusion or both, he uttered, "Than…thank you, sir."

He and the bouncers scrambled quickly through the doorway and away to his car in the car park.

"Did you see the size of his hands?" said Billy.

"We did," answered one of the escorts.

"I thought he was going to kill me."

"We did too."

"What?"

"Yes, I thought he was going to kill you. We couldn't do anything until he hit you though, or at least till he tried."

"He only had to hit me once. Did you see the size of his hands?"

Billy was still shaken, even trembling as he drove away from the club. He was thinking what might have happened if the heckler hadn't taken to his repartee. What was he thinking? He obviously had little or no protection if the guy had taken offence to his jibes. He thought the bouncers didn't want to get involved and why should they? He'd brought the situation upon himself. He'd not had a good set and it was almost over when the men came into the room. It would have been much easier for him had he just waited out the last few minutes of his act and then just disappeared.

Perhaps it was comic instinct that made him lay into the drunkards. Perhaps it was just sheer stupidity or even a lack of experience as a comedian that meant he didn't know when to draw the line. Either way, he was resolute he would never come at a customer that strong ever again. *Easier to climb out of the back window and disappear than get your head kicked in*, he thought.

Billy had only been working as a comic for a few months. He'd been at it, pretty much since he'd left the special services in the army. After six years of service, he felt he had little to show for his time in the military. He'd done a couple of tours in Afghanistan but didn't feel he had gotten much out of his service despite his military training. He'd gotten some self-defence training, bomb disposal and military manoeuvres to his accomplishments, but felt his time had just been a rigmarole of general fatigues.

Working places like late night sleaze rooms wasn't quite what he had planned to do after leaving the services either but it was a start. He did know a little about comedy performance and getting laughs, but the Karlson Club was not the usual type venue for a young comic. It would be a long time before he'd take on a late night gig like this again, he told himself. It was time to move on and find other work in the entertainments field. A couple of gigs at local clubs which would take care of his bills for a week or two but after that he had no idea what was in store for him.

Contemplating what he would do for a career, the clear night gave him time to think about his future as he pulled up to the traffic lights. They seemed to take a long time to change. He switched the radio on and some cool jazz played in the background, then the lights changed. He lifted his foot off the brake pedal. He was about to pull off and head for home when a young woman, carrying a large shopping bag and pulling a young girl of about five or six behind her, ran in front of his car.

They were in a hurry. The young girl slipped. He slammed down on the brakes and put the car into neutral. He jumped out. "Are you all right?" he asked.

The woman didn't answer. She picked the girl up and the shopping bag and awkwardly tried to run away.

Billy recognised the woman as she lifted the girl up off the road. It was Margaret, his friend's wife. She was battered. Blood was gushing from her lip.

"Margaret," he said, "what's wrong?"

"Nothing. Got to go!"

She was distraught and Billy knew it.

She hadn't noticed who Billy was. "Wait! Let me give you a ride. Where are you going?"

"Nowhere. It's okay. Got to go."

"Margaret. It's me. It's Billy, Tom's friend. I was best man at your wedding."

Billy had been at their wedding a few years earlier when he and Tom had joined the army together. Unfortunately, while in Afghanistan, Tom and a few others in his unit had been ambushed and lost their lives. He hadn't seen Margaret nor heard from her since Tom's funeral.

Margaret's carrier bag burst open and clothes scattered on the road. She clumsily tried to pick up the clothes. He knelt down to help.

"You're hurt. You're bleeding. What happened?"

"I told you, I'm fine."

"No, you're not. Get in the car. I'll take you home or to wherever you are going."

"No!" she screamed.

"Well, where do you need to go? You're not in a fit state to be running around at this time of night. It's after one. Get in the car."

Margaret relinquished and pushed the young girl into the back of the car then she got in the front. Billy jumped into the driver's seat. "Where do you want to go?"

Margaret suddenly broke down in tears. The little girl was frightened. So too was Margaret.

Billy pulled into the roadside and left the engine running. "So, what's wrong?"

"Nothing! There's nothing wrong. There's nothing anyone can do," she said.

"I'm sure there is. Where are you going?"

"Anywhere. I can't take it anymore… It's Jimmy… He beat me."

"Jimmy? Who is Jimmy?" he asked.

"Jimmy Schmollen."

"What are you doing with him?" Billy was shocked at her situation.

"We kind of shacked up together. A couple of months back. It would've been while you was in the army. It seemed fine at the time. He wasn't always, he isn't always… It's when he's had a drink. He takes it out on me. I've got to go."

"Where to?" asked Billy.

"I don't know. Anywhere! I don't care. I'll get out of this town. That's what we'll do. We'll get out."

"No, no. I'll tell you what we'll do. I'll take you to my place for a while. It'll be fine there. I'll do you some supper and you can sleep on the couch for the night. It's safe for you. You need to clean up anyway. Don't you?"

"I don't know, Billy. He'll get really mad. We can't be seen …"

"Calm down. I only live a few blocks away." Billy turned the engine up and drove for about ten minutes. He took the girls to his house. The street was dark; no street lights but that wasn't uncommon for the Staleybrook area. The moon was bright as he opened the car door for them to get out. The young girl looked in a state of shock. Billy had been shaken up at the club, but that was nothing like the state Margaret and her daughter were in. In the moonlight he could see blood on her dress and bruises were beginning to form on her face.

He opened the door to the house and switched on the light as he led them into the kitchen.

"Here, sit down. I'll do you a cup of tea. Do you want some supper?"

"We're fine, thanks. I'm sorry. We shouldn't be here, Billy," she sobbed.

"Look, no one is going to find you here. Relax." Billy looked down on the young girl and knelt in front of her. "And I've not seen this young lady in a long, long time. I bet you've forgotten me."

The girl looked dumbstruck and couldn't speak.

"I know you're Angela. You're growing up to be a real beauty." Billy signalled for the young girl to sit down on a chair by the table.

"And how old are you now, Angela?" he asked.

The girl wouldn't speak. She was too frightened to.

"Angela's six. Aren't you, dear?" Margaret grabbed hold of her hand. "It is okay, Angela. Billy is a friend. He's going to take care of us for now."

"Is she hungry?" Billy opened a cupboard door.

"We're fine, thanks."

"How about some cereal, Angela? Would you like some cornflakes?"

There was no answer.

Billy put the kettle on and then poured Angela a bowl of cornflakes.

"I don't know what we're going to do," wallowed Margaret.

"Well, we'll have a cup of tea first. That's what we'll do." Billy put the bowl of cornflakes on the table where Angela sat. Then put out some milk and sugar. The girl was hungry and devoured the cereal as if she hadn't eaten for days.

"Margaret, sit down a while." He handed her a pot towel to wipe the blood from her face.

"Give me a minute and I'll have a look at that." He ran some warm water into the bowl in the sink, then took it to the table and placed it in front of Margaret. He took another towel and bathed her wounds. The kettle boiled a few moments later. He handed Margaret the towel to finish cleaning herself up while he went back to the stove to brew the tea.

"Listen, you can't be wandering around at this time of night. You can both stay here the night and we'll work out what we'll do tomorrow. Angela looks exhausted. Well, you both do. You can both sleep in the bed in the spare room tonight."

"It has been a long night," relinquished Margaret.

"Drink your tea. I'll just get some towels and stuff and you can clean up in the bathroom and put Angela to bed."

"We can't stay." She had changed her mind.

"Yes, you can. Angela is almost out of it now. In fact, let's take her to bed now. She's finished her cereal and is almost asleep on the table." Billy led them towards the guest bedroom and left them there to get situated.

Margaret came back into the kitchen about ten minutes later. She was wearing a pair of Billy's sweatpants and a shirt.

"I took some of your bandages from your bathroom cabinet. I hope you don't mind." Her face was somewhat hidden by bandages. Fortunately, it didn't look like anything was broken but she was sore. She was hurting.

"Angela is asleep," she said.

"Good. Okay, sit down and have another cup of tea and tell me all about it."

"No. I can't."

"Yes, you can. Here's your tea. I've done you another cup. I've done some toast for you too."

Margaret's saddened face really told the tale. "Well, it's the old story. I should have known."

"Well, tell me."

"There are times when he's had a drink, Jimmy that is, and he gets out of his depth. He gets very angry and takes it out on me."

"And how long has this been going on?"

"A few weeks now. We didn't have anywhere to go."

"And you've stayed with him?"

Margaret nodded. "We kind of got hooked up in the situation. It was all supposed to be temporary but it just went on and continued going on."

"What about the police?" he interrupted.

"That's easier said. The police don't want to get involved with domestic problems. Some things just happen. You know how it is." Margaret was sobbing. "I didn't know his family were, like, you know."

"I'm sorry. Jimmy and his brothers have a bit of a reputation for getting into a few fights. Way of life to them. I wish I'd known, Margaret. Then again, how would I have known? I wasn't here."

"But, tonight, when he came back from the pub…I was asleep…I heard Angela scream and ran into the bedroom. And…and…Jimmy was in Angela's bed. He was… I hit him with… I don't know what I hit him with. I don't know after that. He got so mad and threw me against the wall and then he tripped down the hallway himself and passed out. I grabbed some things and we left and…"

"Where were you going?"

"I don't know. We were just looking for a hotel or something. I don't know where we can go. No. I don't know. I have to leave him though. It's a very bad situation and I'm frightened for Angela more than for myself. I don't know what we'll do. I don't know where we'll go."

"Hum. Is this all your stuff, in the bag?"

"No. There are still some more bits and pieces at the tenement apartments. My suitcase is still there and my money's there too. I got paid yesterday. I left it on the kitchen table. We were in such a hurry to get out."

"Well, listen, you need to rest up tonight and we'll work out what we're going to do tomorrow. What else is there at your place that you need?"

"There are a couple of dresses, a sweater and Angela's clothes. Not much really. We could do with a change of clothes though. My passport and like I said, my money are there. I can't go back. Billy. I can't!"

"What's the address?"

"You can't go there. Jimmy's there."

"Don't be worrying about that. I'd like to get your money and your passport before Jimmy discovers them. What is the address?"

Margaret gave Billy the address and told him where her stuff was in the drawers and again reminded him her money from work was on the table.

"Listen. You get some rest tonight. We'll plan something in the morning."

"We can't stay here," said Margaret. "He'll come looking for us. He'll send his brothers, I bet. We need to get away. I don't know where we're going to go but we have to get away. What are we going to do?" She was getting excited again.

"Calm down. I told you, we'll sort all that out. For now you'd better get some sleep. It'll be okay. I'll go and get your things."

Billy didn't feel in the mood to go to the tenements to get the rest of Margaret's things but he was now very much awake. With the heckler at the Karlson Club and now this incident, he didn't think he'd get any sleep for a while anyway. "You get up those stairs and get some sleep with Angela now," he said.

Billy knew Jimmy Schmollen from his school days. He and his family were not the most reputable. Last he heard, one of his brothers was doing time in Strangeways Prison and his two younger brothers thrived on fights most Saturday nights.

Around two thirty, Billy climbed the steps to the third floor of the tenements. It was derelict and certainly not the most luxurious of places. He got to Jimmy's apartment. The door was open. For the most part, Billy knew he was able to handle himself even though he hadn't thought much of his chances with the guy earlier in the evening. The tenements were dark. Some of the windows were boarded up. The stairwell was dirty and smelly. It was disgusting.

Not wishing to cause any unnecessary trouble, he knocked on the open door. There was no answer. Perhaps, Jimmy had gone looking for Margaret. He went inside and saw Jimmy. The slob was passed out on the floor.

Billy found his way to the bedroom and picked up some of Margaret's things from the closet. He folded them quickly into a couple of bin bags. He also saw her wage packet and the passport on the table which he put into his back pocket. He picked up the bin bags and the suitcase that Jimmy had tripped over and then made for the door. It looked as if he wouldn't have to deal with Jimmy. That was wishful thinking.

"What are you doing?" said Jimmy. To get away without confronting Jimmy had been too much to ask for. Jimmy was still in a stupor as he tried to get up from the floor.

"Hello, Jimmy. Just came by for some of Margaret's things." Billy hesitated.

"What?"

"You heard."

"What are you doing in my house?"

"Heard you like beating up women and playing with little girls."

"Fuck off, you bastard. I'll fuckin' kill you."

"I don't think so!"

For a moment, Jimmy seemed to sober up. He crawled round the couch and picked up a half-empty bottle of scotch from the floor. Billy dodged out of the way as bottle hurtled towards him. The drunk slid against the wall and took a swing at Billy. Jimmy missed again and Billy hit him hard in the stomach then smashed his fists into his opponent's face, knocking him backwards.

Jimmy clambered back up and ran towards Billy with his head down. Billy jumped out of the way of the onslaught and jimmy went headfirst into the doorway wall, knocking himself out cold.

He lay on the floor. He was motionless. Billy looked at the heap. This was no way for his friend's wife to live. How had she gotten caught up with such a person? Billy felt Jimmy's neck.

He was breathing but out cold. He was mad at Margaret for getting herself into this situation. He was mad at the night. He was mad at everything and wanted to take it out on somebody. There was no use for Jimmy. He was a complete waste of space. He had to go.

Combat in the military might be a lot different to any confrontation at home. The enemy in the battlefield is a stranger, a complete unknown. *This so and so, right here lying on the floor, is just a piece of crap,* he thought. *He'll only come sniffing for his friend's wife again. Oh, sure he'll apologise, and they'll probably make up. BUT, then he'll do it again later,* Billy's mind was ticking. Margaret should have taken care of this situation. But the moron had assaulted the young girl, his friend's daughter, Angela. He had to go.

Billy unfastened the belt from Jimmy's pants. He went to a wardrobe and found another belt. He also took a pair of gloves off the shelf. He mustn't leave any fingerprints. He didn't want any trace leading back to him. He tied the two belts together, putting one loop around Jimmy's neck. He started to drag the body outside. Someone was coming up the stairwell in the distance. Billy slowly stepped back into the apartment as the person's footsteps came closer.

The man staggered past the apartment, almost falling over Jimmy. "What? Oh, it's you Jimmy Schmollen. You passed out again? You drunken bum. That's what you are. A drunken bum." The man stepped over Jimmy's straggled legs. Billy waited a few moments till the man disappeared into an apartment a few doors down.

He secured the end of the other belt around a bar to the railings outside the apartment.

Then he hooked it to the one that was tied around Jimmy's neck. He struggled awkwardly to lift Jimmy's body over the railings. Jimmy, the slob, was coming around. As he did, the slob realised what was happening and began to struggle. He tried to fight Billy off, but his struggle only tightened the belt around his neck and his sheer weight pulled him down over the railings. He jolted his neck and hung there.

Billy stood back. No one was around. And no one came out to see what the disturbance was about. Billy made his exit quickly. He descended down the back steps of the tenement building and shuffled out to where he'd parked his car. He looked around.

Continuously looking around, all the time. He expected someone to just appear at any moment.

Luckily, no one did. He got to his car and threw Margaret's stuff onto the backseat. He switched on the engine and drove away.

Driving back home, he felt a little discomfort, just as he had earlier when he'd left the Karlson Club. This time he wasn't shaking though. It was different this time. This was the first time…the first time he had ever murdered anyone, and he realised he had enjoyed it.

He felt he should be shaking, but driving home, he almost felt elated. It was almost a nice feeling. He told himself he'd rid the world of a bad sort. He felt he'd done some good, but it was more than that. What was the feeling? It was almost exhilaration. He'd killed somebody. And it felt good. And he'd gotten away with it too. Well, for the moment he had gotten away with it…

Or had he? That was exciting too. How long would he get away with it? What does it matter?

"Still, I would like to get away with it," he said to himself.

He smiled as he parked his car outside his house. He opened the back door of the car and took out the bin bags filled with Margaret's and Angela's clothes. He'd left nothing at the tenement apartment that could be traced back to him or back to Margaret. He had done away with Jimmy.

Not a bad night's work, really.

Chapter 2
Everything Starts Somewhere

Was that the night when it had all started? Was that the beginning? Billy lay on a rough mouldy bed, looking up to a damp dirty ceiling. He wasn't sure how long he had been locked in this dingy cell which he guessed was somewhere just outside of Panama City. He didn't recall where his captors had taken him after they had hijacked him from the airport just after his arrival there. He'd had a few hours of solitude to contemplate what and why he was in his present circumstances, and nothing was making sense. He recalled getting into a taxi as he left the airport, then a cloth going across his face, and that was all he could remember. It wasn't the first time he had been abducted or drugged, but a routine trip to Panama to join a ship didn't add up.

Why was he there in this dingy room now?

It had been some time since Doyle had worked the seedy Karlson Club. His confrontation with the drunken hecklers had been all but forgotten. But that was the night that Billy Doyle had decided he would no longer work the late-night sleaze bars and clubs for a living. He would find himself easier places to perform even if it did mean less money. Surely, elsewhere, audiences would be easier to handle and he would get laughs. No comic enjoys being paid just to fill in time. Laughs are a comic's breadline. The only reason a comic was hired at the Karlson Club was so that the club could keep its license. Food and entertainment were merely legal requirements from local authorities to keep a club licensed in business.

Once he'd quit his job at the Karlson Club, a series of events had occurred but none could explain his present predicament. He lay back on the scrappy bed thinking about some of the things that had happened. Some had been quite amazing. Some had been very mundane but many had been dangerous, even life threatening. Certainly, he had found himself performing in some wonderful venues and for some wonderful audiences. Though he had been very well rewarded for his troubles, he was fully aware though that entertaining was only part of what he was about. His entertainment schedule was now more of a 'front' for his main business. But who else knew that?

He wondered, had his cover been blown? Was that why he'd been kidnapped? Who'd taken him? And why had he been taken? Did someone know who he really was? How would they have found out why he was travelling through Panama? He reached to his wrist to see what time it was, but his watch was missing. His tie and shoes had also been taken. He looked over to an old wooden chair in the corner that was empty. His jacket was missing too.

He'd been alone for some time. Much as he thought about it, nothing seemed right. He was supposedly on a routine trip to Panama to meet up with a ship in Gutan Lake. It was nothing unusual for an entertainer to fly into Panama and later join a cruise ship in Gutan Lake just through the canal. To all intents and purposes, that is what Billy was to do. It wasn't possible for anyone else to know that he had other reasons to be joining a ship there. Or was it? Obviously, he was concerned.

It didn't look as if he'd have to wait long now to find out. The door opened to the dingy room. He got up from the bed to see a rather smart-looking man of medium build walk in. He was accompanied by a shorter but much heavier man. He looked like he might be the smarter man's 'heavy'. Billy looked as he saw the man was holding his jacket. The heavier man looked as if he was trying to force an air of authority into the proceedings but really, he was ineffective.

He reminded him an MC he'd met at a club a few weeks before. On that occasion, the MC thought he was more important and necessary than he actually was. He remembered that evening at the Boiler Maker's Club.

Chapter 3
It's All a Show

Billy was dressed and ready to perform but the show was the farthest thing from his mind. Normally, he would have been focused, but his thoughts were somewhere else. He knew where they were too. It hadn't been twenty-four hours since he had hung Jimmy Schmollen over the tenement railings. Last night, he had killed someone. Murdered him no less, and no one had inquired about it. The police hadn't questioned him. No newspaper reporters, nothing. It had been all too easy.

True, Jimmy Schmollen was a complete waste and society was better off without him, but he was still a human being. Somebody should have been asking about his demise. But no one was. The only mention of the murder was when he picked up some milk and the Sunday newspaper at the store. One person happened to say that someone had hung themselves from the railings at the tenements last night. The body was no longer there. The police had taken it away early morning. It was another cold Sunday morning in a quiet neighbourhood where no one seemed to know or care about anybody or anything.

Billy knew though. However, he wasn't likely to hand himself over to the police. Sure he'd done it and part of him felt remorse for the killing. Part of him also felt good for getting rid of such a piece of garbage. And, part of him was experiencing a huge rush. He still had that high.

The exhilaration of doing away with another person was a ride to him. It was something he'd never experienced. He was high from the thrill of it. There was a frustration too, in that it was his secret and of having no one to share it with. But he could live with that. Well, for now at least.

Was it really so easy? How long could he get away with it? Could he do it again? Could he get away with it again? Could he keep doing it? Was there something wrong with him? Is this what serial killers do? Keep asking themselves questions about a murder? He hadn't set out to be a murderer; it just happened. It hadn't registered at the time, but he knew he had enjoyed it. There was no financial reward or any emotional gratification for his actions, but, no doubt, he had enjoyed it. And he knew he could enjoy doing it again. Billy was a killer.

==========

The MC came into the room:

"Okay. Are you ready?" he said to Billy. "Now, listen, young man. I have to tell you. This is a decent club and Sunday night is like family night. So, I don't want any swearing or any bad language. Now I knows you is a comics and I hast to tell this to all the comics, but it is a respectful club, so we wants a good clean show. Okay?"

"You don't need to worry," said Billy. "Everything will be fine."

"That's what all youse comics say, and then youse goes on and does a dirty show." The MC wiped his nose on his sleeve.

"It'll be okay."

"I sure hopes so!" The MC looked at himself in the stage mirror and straightened his beer stained tie. "Now I've got a couple of announcements to make and then I puts you on. But don't forget, no dirty stuff or swearing. Got it?"

The MC opened the door to the stage and left to go on. He picked up the microphone and blew into it to make sure it was working. He turned to Billy again, "Okay, I'm going out now. No dirty stuff!"

A loud scuffle was heard as the MC tripped and fell over, dropping the microphone on the floor, "Which fucking cunt placed that box of wires there? There's some fucking twatty bollock brains around this place. I could've brokes my fucking neck! The bastards! They fucking are! Good evening, ladies and gentlemen, how you all doin'?"

So much for family night! thought Billy.

"Well, we have a great show for youse this evening, ladies and gentlemen. We 'as a comedian. Well, it says he a comedian on his contract, but we'll see. They say 'e's good, but so was Hitler they said. But then Hitler was no comedian." And neither was the MC. How about killing the MC?

Billy neared the door that led from the dressing room to the stage as the club's compere made his announcements and then began his introduction:

"Ladies and gentlemen, it's time to start the show. To open this evening's show, we 'as a wonderful comedian. He needs no introduction. So, I won't give him one. He's had a long run all the way from the men's room. Ha ha." The compere loved himself. "Please welcome, Willy Small!"

"Willy Small?"

The play-on music sounded out as Billy walked on stage and he forgot all about what had happened the night before.

"Wow. What an introduction! Is he still here? A round of applause for your Emcee tonight, please. Good evening, ladies and gentlemen. Nice to be with you tonight. You look like you're in a good mood. Actually, I'm in a good mood. I've just heard I've sold my house. I'm pleased about that… Mind you my landlord isn't too happy about it…but I'm happy about it." The audience returned him some mild laughter as if to invite him on and show them what he had for them.

"It's a good-looking group tonight. I was at a club down in Cumbria last night and there were some ugly people there!" Making a reference to a nearby club or town always gets a laugh.

"And I was reading in today's paper that one in every three people is ugly. Yeah. So, I want everyone to turn to the person on your left and have a look." Billy walked slightly left on stage and pointed to the other side and then he walked over to that side of the stage. "If they're okay, turn to the person on your right and have a look." Billy paused a moment as he walked centre stage. "If they're okay, guess who it is!" They gave him a big laugh. He had the audience.

The old joke had got them and he knew he could go anyway he wanted. He might even get a few new jokes in his routine tonight.

The act went well and forty minutes sped by. The audience loved him. They thought him fresh and they liked his youthful persona. A couple of the young girls in the room fixated their gaze upon him. They were probably unaware of anything he was saying but just enjoyed watching him. All he had to do was smile at them. The older folk enthused over his humour and his energy.

Billy settled into a routine:

"You know, I've been wondering about a few things. Like you know: Why don't they lock crying babies in the overhead compartments on an airplane?" The unexpected statement caused a delayed laugh. "I wonder about these things.

Like: Have you ever noticed, if you dropped a piece of toast on to the floor, it always lands butter side down? And yet if a cat falls from a height, it always lands on its feet? I wonder what would happen if you tied a piece of buttered toast to a cat and…?" Billy signalled with his hands as if he was tossing a cat in the air. "I wonder about these things I really do.

"Like: Do you ever wonder: Who was the first person to ever discover that you could get milk from a cow? Do you ever wonder what on earth they were doing at the time?"

Another big laugh. The tried and tested formula of threes worked again. "Yes, I wonder about these things," Billy faded.

The comic began to wind down his show when he saw the MC creeping down the room towards the stage.

"Well, I have to leave you now, ladies and gentlemen. I have another engagement to go to in…in September! Yeah, that's when it is." The audience roared.

"I tell you I'm leaving because a lot of entertainers go off stage and wait 'til the audience cheers and shouts for more and then they come back and they do an encore. I don't do any of that. No! Once I've gone, I've gone. No, I tried it once. I went off stage and then came back and the audience had gone. So, I don't do it no more."

Big laugh again and the audience applauded.

"No. I have to go backstage now and find that box of cables for the Emcee to trip over again. Maybe he'll teach us some more swear words."

The MC grimaced at him but faked a laugh as the spotlight shone on him and Billy said, "You have to be careful you don't trip and break your neck." Memories of last night were recaptured.

"Thanks for your time, everybody. Goodnight." Billy left the stage to a thunderous round of applause and cheers.

Still he hadn't been apprehended for the murder.

"Billy Doyle, ladies and gentlemen." Billy Doyle, the Emcee got the name right this time.

"We're going to take a short break and then we'll be on with our next entertainer." Billy was already in his car and driving home by the time the MC got back to the dressing room. Angela was asleep on the bed in his spare room. Margaret was busy in the kitchen making her some supper.

============

A few days passed, by which time, Margaret and her daughter had settled into Billy's place. Angela had started a new elementary school, Margaret had taken a job at the market and life seemed as if all would be well. There certainly were no signs of any retaliation or retribution from Jim Schmollen's family and no one was searching for Billy. Yes all seemed well.

"I have an audition for BBC Television in London today and a couple of gigs coming up this week. Also, I have a couple of after-dinner shows to do, too, so, I'm going to be in and out of here for a while. Will you be okay?" he asked.

"We'll be fine," said Margaret "I'm going to look around for a place for Angela and me too."

"There's no need. You're more than welcome to stay here as long as you want. I'm not here that much anyway."

"Thanks. We'll see."

Just then, a taxi pulled up outside the house. Billy got up from the table, put his breakfast dishes in the sink and grabbed his coat and bag. "Okay, I'm off to catch the train to London. Expect me when you see me."

"Be careful," said Margaret.

Billy almost said, "The same to you too," but thought better not to in view of what had transpired over the weekend. He did manage to mutter a "take care and see you soon".

Chapter 4
Trains and...

The London train from Manchester was busy. *As it probably always is*, thought Billy.

Billy had found himself a window seat on the London train. It would be a few hours before it would get to Euston. His audition at the BBC wasn't until 1:30 pm, so he would have plenty of time to take a taxi over to Wood Lane studios when it arrived. He read his daily newspaper. As he always did, he started with the sports page and worked his way backwards through it. So, it didn't take him long to finish the periodical.

He noticed a lady working at her computer at the tabled area across the way from him.

Sitting next to her was a very heavy-set guy. Billy assumed the two were travelling together as the man got up to bring down a large briefcase to her that was rested in the luggage rack.

Opposite them was an elderly couple. No one spoke which was strange and caused Billy to wonder what everyone's story was.

He wondered why no one said anything, especially the old couple. After about an hour, the train began to slow down as it pulled into the station at Crewe. He watched as the old couple got up to leave. The old man reached under the table and picked up a briefcase similar to the one the woman typing held on her seat next to her.

The train guard passed by after the disembarking passengers left and changed the reserve tickets on back of the vacant seats. All the time the lady in the tweed suit kept typing on her computer and checking figures against a sheet of paper. Billy was curious. He was more intrigued when another couple entered the tabled area and sat down opposite them.

Very strange! he thought. *Now why did this gentleman, who had just boarded, put his briefcase under the table? It was exactly the same type as the one the couple who just left had taken with them except the new one looked to be full.* A mystery was developing and Billy's attention was gripped to the attaché cases.

Now why did the stout gentleman swap the empty briefcase from the luggage rack with the one that the new passengers had deposited under the table? It became even stranger when the woman working on the computer took the 'new' briefcase from him.

Billy stood up to try to see what was going on. He didn't want to draw attention to himself so he made it look as if he was going to the bathroom. He turned and saw the woman empty wads of envelopes from the 'new' briefcase and stuff them into a carrier case. She then handed the empty briefcase to the stout gentleman who then pushed it under the table to the man opposite.

It was obvious that some sort of transaction was going on. He took his time to return to his seat to try and to find out more. The stout man looked at him. He had a menacing look. His nose was large and slightly bent. It could have been a boxer's nose that had been broken some time ago. He scurried back to his seat. What was going on?

The lady continued typing on her computer. He had noticed that the screen looked like some sort of data-entry sheet page and that she was entering figures into different columns.

Perhaps, the stout man and she were making pick-ups and she was keeping a tally in the computer. What sort of pickups? Money? He couldn't think what else the envelopes could hold.

When the couple left the train at Stoke and an elderly gentleman took one of the seats and he too exchanged a full bag for and empty one, Billy was convinced something was afoot.

Twice more such exchanges occurred on the journey. At each station, passengers got up from their seats and left the train, then other passengers boarded and sat at the same seats and an exchange of briefcases was made. It was more than likely the rotating passengers were delivering something. They were doing this by leaving full briefcases full of envelopes and disembarking with empty ones. But what were they dropping off to the couple? All the time the woman kept typing, except when she took out the envelopes from an arriving briefcase and returned it to her stout companion. It had to be money. What else could it be?

His curiosity was raised to a pitch. He felt he had to know what was going on. The train was ten minutes early when it arrived in Euston at 11:15 am. He had plenty of time to make the audition and decided he would follow the woman and her companion for a little while. The stout gentleman stepped back to let the lady out into the middle of the train to leave. He carried the now two large bags, presumably now full of money, while she carried her attaché case and computer off the train.

The two trundled out of the station with Billy in close pursuit. He summoned a cab to follow them after they had gotten into one already waiting for them. It was only a few minutes journey and he saw the couple leave the taxi to go into some sort of office complex. He followed close behind them. A receptionist stopped Billy. "May I help you, sir?" she said.

Billy didn't have time to answer. Her phone rang and she was distracted while he jogged after his train companions who were boarding the elevator.

He caught up with them. "Which floor?" said the stout man.

A light for the fourteenth floor indicated that was where they were headed.

"Fifteen please," said Billy as he shimmied his way to hide behind others in the elevator.

The elevator stopped once at eight and all the passengers except Billy and the couple had gotten out. He hoped that they wouldn't notice him. Billy was aware that the stout man had seen him earlier on the train journey, so he pushed himself almost into the back of the elevator. It reached the fourteenth floor and they exited. Luckily, they didn't turn around and he thought they hadn't noticed him at all.

At the fifteenth floor, he found the stairwell and descended cautiously but quickly to the floor below where he caught a glimpse of them going through a doorway marked 'TRANSIT CARRIERS' with the numbers 315 in the centre. The door closed slowly.

He was tempted to just go in but held back. What would he do if he did go in, he thought. He almost did decide to cast caution to the wind and enter but was stopped when a young lady opened the door and the two walked into each other.

"Oh, I'm sorry," she said. Billy did get a glance of a few young ladies that were sitting at desks and counting money and typing as they did.

"My fault, ma'am," apologised Billy.

"Ma'am? Well, I've never been called 'Ma'am'," the girl giggled pulling the door behind her.

"Either way, I do apologise. Er, er." Billy looked at the plate on the door. "I believe I may have come to the wrong floor. I was told Room 315 for marketing. This is Transit Carriers. What is Transit Carriers?" he asked.

"Ooh, I'm sure if I don't know. I just brings up any mail from downstairs," the girl had a strong south London accent. "I do knows it is one of Lord Carmthen's businesses. But I don't know what they does in there. What floor are you supposed to be on?"

The elevator rang and a portly gentleman wearing a Stromberg hat and expensive coat strolled out. The young girl recognised the man. "Oh, Lord Carmthen, sir. How are you today?" she simpered.

"Fine. Thank you," the man replied in a pompous manner. "Are they in?"

"Who? Miss Henkins, sir, and her companion?" Billy assumed that to be the name of the lady from the train.

"Yes. Who else?" grouched Lord Carmthen.

"Yes, I'll walk you through there, sir."

The pompous ass looked at Billy inquiringly and smiled.

"Do you know where you is going, sir?" the girl returned her attention briefly to Billy.

"Yes. I'll be fine. Thank you." He knew the girl had to attend to Lord Carmthen. She smiled politely at Billy as she took His Lordship to the door from which she had just come and they both went in in together.

Time was now moving on. Billy had to make the BBC for one o'clock.

He sneaked out of the building and left to taxi to Wood Lane to do the audition something Billy hadn't thought about too seriously. He had other things on his mind but he hadn't received any answers to his inquisitiveness. He was questioning himself right now as time while wasting his time away in a cell in Panama, Central America, no less.

Chapter 5
You Needs a Job?

"Mister Boyle," said the man, "we apologise for any inconvenience we may have caused you, but it was important that I wish to talk wid youse."

"Did you have to knock me out and kidnap me to do that?"

"That is of no consequence, my friend, only to say, we wished to 'ave a private conversation and this seemed the best place to do it."

Doyle looked at the man, puzzled as to why he wanted a private conversation.

"We 'as a proposition for you. You are to join the Starlight of the Seas, cruise ship tomorrow morning, are you not?"

"Yes, I am or rather I was supposed to be."

"Why iz dat?"

"Don't you know?"

"Yes, I do."

Doyle was nervous to say anything to the man. He had no idea if the man or anyone else knew the reasons for passing through Panama and onto the cruise ship. He wondered if his identity had been revealed and what was to become of him. Was he about to disappear soon in Central America? Then the man had said he had 'a proposition' for him. That didn't sound like they intended to do away with him, at least not just yet.

"Well, why don't you tell me?" asked Doyle.

"Oz course." The man turned and walked to one side of the room. "I believe you are to pick up the cruise ship tomorrow morning and you 'as been hired to perform your show for zee passengers on board zee ship. Correct?" He looked at Doyle. "And you iz scheduled to sale to Cartagena, Columbia wid da ship before it moves on to Miami where you are supposed to disembark. No?"

"So, you're a mind reader?" Doyle said sarcastically, wondering where the conversation was leading.

"No. I am not a mind reader, senor. I have all your information and your papers."

"My papers?"

"Yes, we 'as you papers, documents, your passport and things. Give him back his things," the man said to his assistant. "And give him 'izz shoes too. Why you take 'iz shoes? Ay Caramba!"

It didn't look like he was going to be done away with in the immediate future, otherwise there would have been no need to return his things to him, which the assistant did as ordered.

Doyle checked them through. He put them in his jacket he took from the grease ball holding it.

"So, you have a proposition for me?" said Doyle, trying to get the situation moving.

"Yes, I do. We are giving all your papers and passport to you. Also, here is your belt and tie." He reached over to his assistant and handed them to Doyle. "Your baggage is in your hotel room."

"Why have I been kidnapped and held here?"

"I vill tell you." He looked right at Doyle and grimaced. "We 'ad to check you out first, and it appears you are who you says you is. Dat's true?"

Of course it's true, thought Billy. *Who else would I be? What earthly reason do I have to make stuff up? Does any of this have anything to do with the incident at the Karlson Club or me killing of Jimmy Schmollen. What about the people on the train? What about Lord Carmthen?* His mind was rattled away.

Chapter 6

The Train Now Standing

Billy boarded a return train from Euston to Manchester later in the afternoon. His audition hadn't gone particularly well. They were very polite and thanked him for his endeavours and for attending. They even reimbursed him for his expenses, but he didn't think he'd done an inspiring performance.

It wasn't altogether his fault he was thinking as he sat down on the train. How could they tell what he had to offer when he was expected to perform cold without an audience? There was no one to appreciate what he was trying to do, except some other performers attending for audition. *Telling jokes to a panel of critics and not an audience can be quite a daunting proposition*, he said to himself. Why should they laugh? They smiled, but they didn't laugh.

Laughter is something a comic cries for but I guess they didn't understand that. Still, he'd given it a shot and now the audition was behind him. "We'll be in touch in a week or two," they said.

That was like saying, "The check is in the mail," and the check never does arrive. He wouldn't be doing a television show in the near future.

It had been a strange day and he felt tired. He soon began to doze off. It was the sound of the train pulling into Watford Station that woke him up. He looked at the passengers who were disembarking. He was sat further back in the compartment on this journey but he noticed a couple leave the train at Watford and another couple board there, just as they had in the morning commute. He recognised them. They sat in the same seats as they had before. He also noticed that the woman with the computer and her minder had the same seating arrangements as before, too. Were they all going to go through the same routine again?

Yes, they were. They exchanged briefcases as the passengers boarded at one station and disembarked at the next. The same passengers took up the same seating arrangements each time. What on earth was this all about? It had nothing to do with Billy, but he wanted to know what was going on. He watched as the whole rigmarole reversed itself. If the old couple, which boarded with him in Manchester, get on at Crewe, which was where they left this morning and go to Manchester, he'll follow them before he heads for home he decided.

Sure enough, that is what happened. And sure enough, when they got off the train in Piccadilly, Manchester, he did, too. He followed them to a bus stop a few hundred yards away from the train station. It was now approaching dinnertime. He shielded himself from view amongst the work crowd. He heard them say to the driver 'to Audenshaw' as they boarded.

Audenshaw was a small town, about thirty minutes out of the city. Billy new it and paid the same amount of change when it came to his turn in the line to pay.

He sat in a seat behind them and tried to listen to their conversation:

"I'm getting tired of all these trips to London," said the old lady.

"We only do it once a month, Maisey," the man replied.

"It just messes up my schedule. It really does."

"What schedule? I don't know why you're bitchin'. We gets paid for it. And you know we gets paid pretty good if you asks me, too," replied the old man.

"I don't know. I'm just tired of it. All that traipsin' around those post offices and stuff. It just gets old. I'm just tired of it. You know what I'm sayin', don't ya?"

"Look, you're always tired on the journey back. I can't see how you can be bitchin' about it. We only does it once a month. I think it's easy money. And, its good money too. Anyways, you got your Bingo tonight. That'll cheer you up." He looked out of the window.

"I guess so. Yes, you're right. I just want to get home and get dressed. What are you going to do tonight?"

"I think I'll go down the pub." He turned from the window view.

"You drinks too much, Harry, you really do," she nudged him.

"No. I'm going down the pub for the talent show. You know, they have Karaoke Night tonight. Yeah. I'm looking forward to it. I might even do a few numbers myself tonight, too."

"Well, I'm not doing no dinner for you. Don't have time. We should have gotten sommat in London. I told you that."

"I wasn't hungry then."

"Well, I's not cookin' tonight. That's all. Sometimes I think that's all you're with me for."

"I'm with you for a lot more than that," laughed the old man as he gave her a tickle. "It's okay. I'll get myself something at the pub. Woah, 'ere's our stop."

"I knows where we live, you daft bugger!" she grumbled and struggled her way off the bus behind the old man.

Billy followed the old couple off the bus and walked a little behind them.

"Are you going in there now?" asked the old lady as they passed a pub called the 'White House Inn'.

"Naw! I want to clean up first. I'll come home first." The old man glanced behind. Billy quickly ducked into the White House Inn, hoping he hadn't been seen by the old man.

A sign sporting 'KARAOKE NITE TONITE' greeted Billy on his way into the pub.

Entering, he also saw tables set for dinner. He grabbed himself a place at a table and looked at a dinner menu.

"What are you having, sir?" said the waitress.

"I think I'll have a steak and kidney pie, please, miss."

"French fries and peas?" asked the waitress, holding her pencil to her note pad.

"Oh, yes please. And a pint of—"

"You'll have to get your drinks at the bar, sir," she interrupted.

"Okay. Thanks." He handed the menu to the waitress and got up to go to the bar.

As Billy was getting a pint of Guinness from the bar, the old man strolled in. *That was a quick clean up*, thought Billy. "A pint of bitter please," the old man collared the barman.

The two men stood at the bar waiting for their drinks.

"How are you doing?" said the old man to Billy.

"I'm doing well, thanks. How are you?"

"Can't complain. No one ever listens if you do complain," the old man joked.

"Are you eating, sir?" the waitress said as she passed by the bar to the old man.

"Oh, I'll say I am. I'm so hungry, I could eat a horse. Yes. I'll have fish, chips and peas please and some bread and butter too."

"Where are you sitting, sir?" she asked.

"How about there?" he pointed to the empty table. It was Billy's table.

"Is it all right if he sits with you, sir?" asked the waitress.

"No problem. That will be fine."

"Thanks, mate."

"Not at all."

The barman brought the two drinks to the men, "That's six pounds fifty, thanks."

"Here I'll get that," said the old man. "You can get 'em later, Oh, and mine is the pint of bitter, my old cock's sparrow," he said to the barman. "Just put it on my tab."

"Are you sure?" asked Billy.

"Positive. I've had a good day today. It's always a good day when it's payday!"

"Okay, thanks. Let's sit down." Billy pointed to the table with his beer in hand.

Billy and the old man sat down and quickly got into conversation, "So, where you from?" inquired the old man. "Not seen you around here before."

"Oh, I'm from Stalybridge," said Billy. It was not his intention to give away any information that he didn't have to.

"And what brings you to these parts?"

"I was hungry. Saw the sign for food from the bus." Billy wasn't sure if the old man had seen him on the bus or not, so he just went with it. "I missed lunch so this works out just right."

"They do good food 'ere. I'm in here many nights for my dinner. They have karaoke here later too. I think it starts in about an hour. You should give it a go. Have you done that before?"

"No. I haven't."

"Well, you should." The old man was more convivial than Billy would have liked as he knocked back his drink. "Are you ready for another?" he asked, indicating for Billy to drink his drink. "I'll get these. It's my round." Billy got up and left to get the drinks. The waitress brought the dinners to the table.

Billy soon returned with the fresh drinks. "There you go. Okay. So, this is your local?"

"Yeah, the wife and I have. Well, she's not really my wife, we just lives together. Well, kind of, that is. But we've been here for a while now. What about you? You married?"

"No."

"No? How do you manage that?" he laughed.

"Your wife isn't with you tonight?" asked Billy.

"No. Wednesdays is her Bingo night. She's at Bingo."

"And what do you do?"

"How'd ya mean?" the old man said a little suspiciously.

"No, I meant what do you do for a living?" Billy ate into his pie.

"Oh, whatever comes along."

"Such as?"

"Well, today, the wife and I went to Crewe to do some business."

"Yeah, what sort of business?"

The old man lifted his pint pot and drank the rest of his drink that was left in one gulp and lifted himself from his chair. "Let's get some more drinks. I'll be back." He got up from the table. "Do you want the same again?" he turned back at Billy to check.

Billy wondered if he could get the old man to tell him the whole business of why he got on the train and swapped briefcases with the couple taking the same journey. He recollected his thoughts as he waited for his beer and ate into his pie. The old man returned about five minutes later.

"Here you go. I never asked you your name. What's your name?" Billy sensed he might have looked a little too inquisitive for the newly found friend. The two dined on their meals and continued idle chatter.

"Billy." He held out his hand as the old man sat down and shook his hand.

"Well, I'm Harry. Harry Tomkins. Nice to meet you, Son. Are you going to do the karaoke then tonight?"

"Oh, I don't think so. I'm feeling quite stuffed right now. The pie was really filling. It was good but filling. I'm full!"

"Told yer that it was good food in here. Beer's good too."

"So, what is it you do, Harry?" Billy asked again as he pushed his empty plate to the side of the table.

"Told yer. I does a little bit of this, a little bit of that. Whatever comes along."

"Well, you said, today was payday. What was that for?"

"You're asking a few questions, aren't you?" Harry looked inquisitively at him.

"Sorry. I'm just making conversation."

"Just kidding," Harry laughed. "The wife and I go to the post offices around there and we pick up some mail. I'm guessing it's for some company in London. Transition something or other, they're called. And then we have to take them. Well, we're supposed to take them to London but a lady picks them up on the train for us. We get off at Crewe, do the same again in Crewe and then come back home. Nice job. Easy job really and it's cash. That always helps."

"And you do that every day?"

"Goodness no! Just once a month. That's enough. The wife and I are pretty much retired so it's a nice little gig for us. The money helps and today is payday." The old man pushed his plate to the side and the waitress came by to clear up.

"Anything else for you, gentlemen?" the waitress smiled.

"No. I'm good thanks. That was delicious."

"I'm fine too." He reached to his pocket as the waitress dropped the check on the table.

"I'll get this." Billy picked up the check and returned it with three ten-pound notes.

"That's fine, ma'am. Thank you."

Harry sat back surprised. "Are you sure, mate?" he said.

"Yes, I am. Good food and good company. Cheers, Harry." Billy raised his glass.

Thanking Billy, the waitress cleared away their table.

"Well, in that case, I'll get the next drinks. I'm going on whisky now. What do you want?"

"That sounds good. I'll have the same, thanks."

The room had filled, presumably for the karaoke competition and the pub's DJ dropped a book of karaoke songs onto their table. He put one on each of the bar table for those participants who wished to do karaoke.

"So, you're staying for karaoke then?" said Harry.

"Well, for a little while, I can."

"Good. What are you going to sing?"

"Oh, I don't think I'll sing. What about you?"

"I always sing my favourites. You'll see. I do enjoy this karaoke thing."

Harry went up to the stage and gave the DJ a paper with his name on and what he was going to sing. He and Billy were having a good night. Billy sort of wondered why he had stayed but he'd soon gotten into the swing of things. The competition was not unlike any other karaoke competition in a pub. Most of those involved thought themselves better than they actually were.

One or two had trouble keeping time and singing the right words at the right moment. One guy sang a Tom Jones song with a voice that almost shattered the beer-soaked glasses in the bar. And two girls couldn't carry on singing a Kelly Clarkson song because they couldn't stop laughing throughout the rendition. Then it was Harry's turn.

Harry announced he would sing one of his favourites. "You all knows this so how's about everyone joining in. It's called *Side by Side*." Harry smiled at Billy. The music started and Harry went into his rendition of the old song:

"Oh we ain't got a barrel of money,

Maybe we're ragged and funny but we…"

Harry continued like a man possessed and even got the patrons singing and clapping. It came to the second verse and Harry submitted his own version of the song:

"We went to the bedroom together.

My heart was just like a feather

When her teeth and her hair she placed on a chair

Side by side…"

The room silenced as he sang his parody.

"…Then to my amazement, her glass eye it looked so small

She took her wooden leg and her bosom she placed them against the wall

There I stood broken hearted 'cause half of my woman had parted

I said I'll sleep on the chair, there's more of you there side by side."

The audience joined in when Harry reprised the last line:

"I said, 'I'll sleep on the chair, there's more of you there SIDE BY SIDE.'"

He left the stage to a full accolade and joined Billy who'd bought them both more whisky. He too applauded him. "Well done, Harry. Very good. Enjoyed it."

"Ladies and gentleman, our next performer is Billy," announced the DJ. The audience waited in anticipation. Billy hadn't heard the DJ announce his name.

"That's you, tosser!" screamed Harry as if he'd won the lottery. "It's you! Go on up there. You're on next. He's here! He's coming!"

"I am. What am I going to sing?"

"WHITE CHRISTMAS."

"What?"

"WHITE CHRISTMAS. That's what I wrote down for you."

"WHITE CHRISTMAS? In July?"

"Why not? Get up there. Go on!" urged Harry.

The intro to the song began and Billy started,

"I'm dreaming of a white Christmas.

Just like the ones I used to…know.

Where the tree tops glisten and children…listen to hear sleigh bells in the snow…"

"I'll do you Harry for this!" he joked and he saw that Harry was talking on his phone.

"Go on kid! You can do it." He put his phone down.

"I'm dreaming of a white Christmas with every Christmas card I write…"

Harry almost fell off his chair laughing as Billy caroused around the stage. Billy was enjoying the fun too, even though the music volume was coming and going and for a moment, it sounded like it was about to stop altogether. Being a performer, he didn't want to look embarrassed when it ceased altogether. He went into an old monologue:

"It was Christmas Eve in the White House Inn.

Whisky was flowing which was handy.

When in walked a man, known as one legged Dan and his one good leg was bandy.

His false leg was carved from an old oak tree and in summer he would go all forlorn 'cause when April was out, it started to sprout and his kneecaps were covered in acorns."

"Yer music's stopped!" shouted Harry.

Billy continued:

"It was around about then or it could've been ten and a quarter when out of the night came a terrible sight.

It was Rhona, Dan's runaway daughter.

From her neck to her foot, she was covered in soot.

She'd spent fourteen weeks on a whaler.

They'd used her as bait and to settle the fete she was six months pregnant by a sailor."

"Tell the DJ yer music's stopped," Harry yelled again, holding onto his glass for dear life.

"It's okay," said Billy, hoping to pacify his friend so he could carry on with his monologue.

"Dan said, 'Why did you do it,

Why did you go and leave your poor father that day?'

She said, 'Don't shout I beg. It was that wooden leg.

The sight of it drove me away.

Every June, it needed a prune and the foliage grew as thick as thieves.

And I'll always remember, at the end of September, the bedroom was knee deep in leaves.'

Dan said, 'There's hope for us yet, I'm having a new leg created. It's being made in the cellar by this Indian feller and it's going to be all metal plated.'"

Billy wasn't sure if he could remember the all of the monologue and almost froze.

Fortunately, someone jolted him.

"What happened next?" a voice in the middle of the room resounded.

"Now the end of this tale is sad to relate, indeed it is rather quite frightening.

One thing that Indian fellow forgot is that metal's affected by lightening."

Billy took a deep breath and sighed out for the last bit of the verse:

"Dan went for a walk, one wild stormy night, with the rain beating down on each winda' when there was a lightning flash and a hell of a crash and poor Dan was burnt to a cinder... Thank you!"

He had chanced his way through the verse and it had worked. He walked back through the clapping crowd to his seat.

"Where'd you get that from?" asked Harry. "That was real funny."

"An old army buddy gave it to me some time back."

"You was in the army? That was very good."

"Thanks. Listen, I think I'd better be making tracks back home," said Billy, seeking permission to leave the party.

"Nah. I just got you another whisky!" Harry killed any thought of an immediate exit.

Billy hesitated and said, "Well, all right, one more then." One more led to two more which led to how many more? But no one was counting. Whether it was the drink or the atmosphere, the two men were having a good time and listened to more karaoke. The evening moved on. It was another twenty minutes before Harry looked at his watch and said, "Woah. I'm going to have to get back for the missus. She'll be home soon. Hey, they haven't called my name again, have they?"

"No, they haven't. Why are you going to do another song?"

"Yes, I am. It's my big one, too," Harry went up to the DJ to inquire if he had gotten his request ready and after a short discussion, the DJ said, "I forgot folks. Here's Harry again."

The intro to the song, *My Way* started up…and Harry went into his version of the Frank Sinatra favourite. It was his version too as he kept singing the first line of the song. At first, the audience thought he'd forgotten the words until he said "Second verse!", as the music took the tune to the beginning of the second verse and Harry again repeated over again the first line of the song which made everyone realise his rendition was a routine.

Harry grinned his way through the song but finished the number with the correct words which brought a thunderous round of applause from the pub's audience.

"I'll be here all week!" he joked to the crowd and left the stage. The audience loved him. No wonder he liked karaoke. He enjoyed his accolades all the way out of the pub, not forgetting to knock back two more scotches that were almost left on the table.

"Goodnight, everyone!"

"It's been a pleasure, Harry. See you another day…" Billy made his excuse to leave Harry.

"Nah, nah, nah! You're coming back for a coffee. I'll put the pot on for us."

"No," said Billy, "I'd better get back home."

"I insist." Harry wasn't to be argued with. "And anyway, the wife would like to meet you. I'm sure."

The two men staggered down the street and turned a corner, then crossed over to a brick house that was set back from the street. Harry stumbled to unlock the door, then switched on a light and led Billy to an 'almost kitchen' that the house possessed.

"The pot's there on the stove. You get the coffee ready, I'm just going upstairs a minute."

Billy prepared the pot and found the coffee jar on the counter. Grabbing two cups off the counter, he put a spoonful of coffee into each of them.

Harry staggered through the kitchen door holding an old Smith and Wesson pistol. He pointed it at Billy. "Okay, sit down, you little shit!" said Harry, waving the gun at him.

Billy did as ordered. "What's wrong with you? Are you playing or what?"

The hand holding the gun was shaking and so was the gun. Maybe it was the drink that didn't control the hand or the fact Harry wasn't used to holding it. Either of which were both good reasons to do what he was told. Billy was caught completely off guard. Harry's attitude was totally unexpected.

What was this all about? "Why are you holding a gun?" said his karaoke partner.

"Shut up. We're just going to wait till my friends get here."

"Friends! What friends? Who are you talking about?" said Billy.

"You know you've been following us all day," admonished Harry.

"What do you mean?"

"You were on the train this morning and you were on the train this evening. Then you followed us home tonight. You know what I mean."

That was exactly what Billy had done, but he hadn't realised Harry had caught him out.

Now what? And who were they going to wait for – probably the woman and her minder?

"I think you've got this all wrong," pleaded Billy. "True I was on the train, but I was going to London for an audition at the BBC down there," pleaded Billy.

"Yeah, sure you were. What were you going to do there, sing 'WHITE CHRISTMAS'?" he said.

The two men had sobered quickly. No sign of any camaraderie was left. Maybe Harry was smarter than he appeared and the whole evening had been a façade. Maybe Harry had detained him while his colleagues had time to get to his house?

"Look, Harry—"

"Don't move! Sit down! Don't move!" the gun was shaking really wildly now.

Billy sat down as told. They were going to wait. Billy didn't want to wait though. He was nervous of the shaking gun that could go off at any moment. He didn't think Harry could hold that gun much longer either. He would have to do something and do it soon, otherwise someone was really going to get hurt and he hoped it wouldn't be him.

"I don't believe this. Do you always point a gun at a house guest?"

"You aren't no house guest. You're going to get yours soon. They won't be long—"

The kettle began to whistle which distracted the two men. Harry panicked and fired a shot. It went straight through the kettle. Water seeped through the hole that the bullet had made.

Billy took the opportunity and jumped up from his chair at Harry. Another shot fired. Billy had knocked Harry's hand and the gun away from his direction. The room went quiet and all that was heard was water trickling from the kettle onto the floor where Harry lay motionless. Harry had fired the gun but in the ensuing tussle his hand had turned the gun on him. He shot himself. Harry Tomkins was dead.

Billy was stunned but was soon disturbed as a voice from the hallway shouted:

"Harry. I'm home. Where are you?" Harry's wife was home from Bingo. She made her way into the living room from the front door. Billy hid behind the small partition dividing the living room from the kitchen.

She came into the room and screamed. "Oh, my God! Harry!" The wife looked at the motionless corpse lying on the floor. "Shit! Oh God, no."

"I've got to get out of here," she said to herself. "Oh, what have you done Harry?" She tried to step over the blood that was spilling onto the kitchen floor. The water dripping from the stove was making a stream of red flow across the floor. It was running towards a briefcase leaning against a chair. Harry's wife picked up the case and dropped it on the table. "I need to go, quick." She quickly reached into the case and pulled out some envelopes and banged them onto the table. She tore open a couple to check there was money in them. Billy knocked an ornament on the divider as he tried to hide himself.

The woman was scared. She stuffed the money into her pockets, grabbed her bag and made for the front door. But she was stopped as she began to exit the front door.

"Oh, it's you two. It's Harry. And I didn't do it! Someone shot Harry. Unless he did it 'imself. Maybe he did. I don't know." The muffled conversation coming from the hallway could barely be heard.

Billy looked at the briefcase. He knew now it was full of money. He grabbed the briefcase. Harry and his wife wouldn't have a need for it now anyway. A stifled gunshot was heard in the hallway. It shocked Billy. The back door to the kitchen seemed a million miles away but he knew he had to make it before the assailants came into the kitchen. It was almost like another old time movie as he motioned to the back door, turned the latch and opened it. They heard him but he was out in the back yard and half way over next door's fence before the minder had made it to the back door.

The minder scrambled about the backyard looking for Billy but couldn't see Billy, who was now running for his life down the back entryway of the neighbouring houses. Billy ran as fast as he could. He came to a road. Not knowing where to go, he turned into another entry. He had no idea where he was going or what he was doing. He stopped for a breath as he felt a pang in his side from his running. A pang was a lot better than a gunshot. He started running again.

He was now on the main road but he knew it wasn't a good idea to stay on it. The minder would undoubtedly have a car and by now would be in it and looking for him.

Chance was on Billy's side as a taxi rolled its way down the road. Billy waved it down, got into the cab and ushered the cab to take him to the town, Stalybridge. Billy looked out of the back window and saw a Black sedan pulling onto the main road. They were looking for him. He knew it was them. They ran a red light in pursuit of the taxi. Billy tore open one of the envelopes and took out some notes. He was sweating, more from fear than all his physical exertion.

"There's another hundred for you if you lose that car behind." Billy handed the money to the driver.

"I've waited all my life to hear that!" said the cabbie.

The cabbie swung the car down a side street and doubled around the block before the pursuing vehicle behind could get close enough to identify his number. The sharp round turn threw Billy against the rear car door. The cabbie turned off his meter as he hit the road again and made in the direction of the town of Ashton and not Stalybridge.

"I think we may have lost them, but I'll make sure," said the cabbie. "We'll take the long road down to Stalybridge through Ashton."

Billy still was not at ease and kept looking out the back window.

"So who's after you, mate? Somebody's husband? Been a naughty boy, have we?"

"Something like that." What could he say?

"Well, listen mate, it's nothing to do with me and I don't want no police trouble or anything, so, I'll tell you what I'll do. We'll be in Stalybridge in a couple of minutes. Where I'm going to drop you off is just around the corner from a taxi place. I'll drop you on the corner there and you can get another taxi from there. Okay?"

"That's great thanks." Billy wiped his forehead with his forearm. Changing vehicles would be a good tactic to deceive the chasers.

Billy handed the cabbie another one-hundred-pound note.

"Wow! She must have been some shag, mate!"

Billy jumped out of the car and ran fast around the corner to the taxi place and got another ready car to take him home. Billy didn't sleep that night. He kept peeping out through the curtain on his window in case the minder was still searching for him. For now, all seemed well. *What a night! What a night!* he thought.

What had he done to invite such circumstances? Was everything that had happened all his fault? Two more people were dead. That's three in less than a week. Was he keeping score?

Why was he keeping score? "All this was because he was unable to mind my own business?"

The people on the train certainly had nothing to do with him. Why was he compelled to be so inquisitive? Would he run into the woman and her minder again? *God, I do hope not,* he said to himself. Was it his fault that Harry and his wife were no longer alive? Questions just kept spinning and kept him awake till very late.

Billy brewed himself a cup of tea and was having it with a piece of toast for breakfast in his kitchen. At the same time, he was opening the envelopes that he had taken out of the briefcase. He was counting it. It was a lot of money. Whose money was it? All that was on the envelopes was a post office address and a number. A different handwritten number was on each of the envelopes. He was also studying a tote sheet he had taken from the briefcase. It itemised various amounts that had been picked up and from where.

It was obvious to Billy that it was some of the 'pick up' money that Harry and his wife collected at the post office or post offices and deposited in the bags they left on the train. From the train, the woman and the minder would take it to the office in London, Transition Carriers.

He'd seen Lord Carmthen go into that office. What had he to do with the transactions? Billy was getting inquisitive again. None of it had anything to do with him. He had almost lost his life from being too nosy.

He must get rid of anything that connected him with Harry and his wife if he was to remain safe. What if someone had seen him with Harry at the pub? No one knew him there. It would be unlikely that anyone would remember or recognise him. The pub was busy. He was just another character in the pub on Karaoke Nite. No one would remember him, would they? He will burn the envelopes with the cash though. "No. You don't burn money. I'll just burn the envelopes and throw the briefcase into the garbage dumpster outside."

He took a cigarette lighter and set fire to the envelopes over a garbage can. There were a lot of hundred pound notes, almost 15 grand, he counted. That's a lot of money and it's only a fraction of it. Imagine how much was collected in the full day and by a number of people. "It's nothing to do with me, though. Still, it's a lot more than I'm making being a stupid comic!"

Margaret walked into the kitchen. "Morning," she said.

"Morning."

"You're up early?"

"Er. Yes. I didn't get much sleep last night."

"Are you working tonight?" Margaret asked.

"Oh damn!" Billy suddenly remembered he had an after-dinner function in Rugby, in Warwickshire, that he was to perform that night. "I'd better get ready." He gulped his tea back and put his dishes in the sink.

"Just leave them there. I'll clean them up later," Margaret said.

Chapter 7
Just Another Show

Margaret would clean them up. He would get a shower and hit the road for Rugby. This time he would take his car. It was going to be a late night. Grabbing his tuxedo and shirt from his closet, he put them with the rest of his stage persona he needed and threw them into a clothes' case. He showered, shaved and headed out.

He was driving and glancing through his rear-view mirror to see anyone was following him. He was still looking over his shoulder until Manchester was behind him on the M6 Motorway. He felt he was beginning to breathe easier and not in so much of a panic mode the further south he drove on the motorway. What was yesterday all about? He was being unnecessarily nosy again, but he couldn't leave it alone and deep down he was shaking. Probably a little like he was in the jail in Panama right now. He recalled how, he thought, that someone would always be after him, but for what reasons, he had no idea. He knew he had stumbled upon something but just didn't know what.

He had found that money was being transferred but for what reason? The reason had to be worth killing for and he was sure someone was going to kill him, too. No doubt the whole scenario of Harry and his wife dying had unravelled him. It had meant what. He wasn't sure. The situation was extremely dangerous. He did now knew that.

The car ride to Rugby had given Billy plenty of time to think about the events of that week and consider his options. Much as he had been shaken by it all, he still wanted to find out more. He didn't think it safe for him to take train rides to London though. If Harry had seen him on the train, who else? Hopefully, it wasn't the woman or the minder. They wouldn't have seen him last night. Then again, what would Harry have told them when he phoned them from the pub?

He had guessed by now that it was the woman on the train that Harry had phoned and not his wife.

Billy got to Rugby Golf and Country Club, a large grandiose place that seemed to stretch to eternity, a little before five. The clubhouse was located on some very nice grounds. He parked around the back at the staff parking lot and entered the building. Someone showed him to a room to clean up and change. He had a couple of hours to kill before the dinner, so he took the opportunity to rest up and take a nap on a couch for a while. Maybe he felt safer here than he did back home. Maybe he was just so exhausted he could sleep anywhere, even a jail cell in Panama.

Billy's much needed nap time was interrupted by some servers who came into the room to take away some tables and chairs. Apparently, the function was overbooked and they needed more seating arrangements for dinner. Looking at the clock on the wall told him he'd had enough sleep and it was time to get ready for dinner.

Dressed and cleaned up, he was shown to the table of honour where he met the MC for the evening. Soon after, the club captain and the famous golfer, Arnold Sussabecker, entered the room to enormous applause. Sussabecker had pretty much achieved every major honour in the golfing profession that could be given. He was extremely popular and known as a very witty speaker. The MC introduced himself to the club captain and Sussabecker, and then introduced Billy to them.

Most performers, even the most temperamental and sensitive of them, once they enter a stage, would all but forget what had passed before. Billy was no exception. Although it was only a dinner event, he felt all eyes would always be upon him, well, certainly upon the head table.

As such, he was on stage and all that had passed the last few days was forgotten. All that mattered now was that everyone had a good time and his job as guest comedian was to ensure that. If only he could just recall what he planned to say.

Dinner passed and the tables were cleared. Coffee and drinks were being served. It was almost time for the after-dinner speeches. Some of the guests ushered themselves quickly to the bathrooms in order to not to miss the highlight of the evening. Some folks were turning their chairs around in order to get a better view of the top table and the proceedings. High anticipation was in the air.

The MC rose at the table and paused as the room gradually went quiet.

"Ladies and gentlemen, if I may have your attention for a few moments. I am Victor Spalding and I am your host for this evening's festivities. Before we start though, I would like to say a few words."

The host pulled out a piece of paper and started to read from it:

"If you don't leave my wife alone, I know where you live and I'm going to kill you!"

This was a kind of stock opening for a speaker but one that always got a laugh and breaks the ice with the audience.

"Oh, sorry. That was just given to me." The audience laughed and the MC carried on.

"The problem is it wasn't signed, so I don't know who it's from. Anyway, ladies and gentlemen, we are here for a good time. Well, I am anyway. Is anybody else?"

The room responded. They were ready for a good time.

"Well, I'm going to tell you a little about myself in a few minutes but first there are a few people that we need to thank. Did everyone enjoy dinner?"

Again the audience enthused.

"Well, would you mind putting your hands together for the chef and all his staff, not forgetting the waiters and waitresses who are doing a marvellous job tonight?"

The applause was loud and included a few cheers.

"That was wonderful. And if I might add, the chef's, Mister Heinz Maricoldi's, entire life has been is dedicated to his job. This is what really impresses me about that man. He cooks the food himself. He prepares the menus. He does everything. You've got to admire that kind of dedication. I mean that. I mean, if it was you or me and we had hepatitis, we wouldn't even be coming to work." Some of the audience laughed and a few groaned at this humour.

"I'm just kidding, it's a joke. We don't know what he has."

There was more laughter but there were also a few more groans too.

"Ladies and gentlemen, it gives me great pleasure – and it has done since adolescence – to introduce to you someone you all know. Please give a round of applause to your club captain, William Devine."

William Devine, the years' club captain, rose and went into the usual type of speech a club captain would give on occasions such as this.

"Thank you. I'd like to welcome you all here this evening. It is a great pleasure…"

Billy was listening but not really paying too much attention as he looked around the room. He was carefully studying his audience. A little apprehension was beginning to creep in.

He was focused on his speech, and yet he still couldn't recall what he would say during his act.

The club captain's speech was short. He handed the microphone back to the MC to take over the proceedings and seated himself.

"Thank you, Mister Captain, Sir Captain, Captain Captain? I'm not sure how to address you properly?"

"Club Captain is fine," the captain thought he was helping the MC out.

"Thank you, Captain Captain. That's nice. A little understated but nice. Well, ladies and gentlemen, I'd like to be brief. I'd also like to be rich and famous but what can I do?"

"My job is to ensure you have a good time. Your job is to make believe your laughter and your applause for the speakers is sincere and I'm here to make believe they deserve it."

A big laugh came from the audience. They were ready to get the proceedings under way.

"So, I know you didn't come here to listen to me. So, it is a great honour that I introduce to you a really great sportsman. A gentleman who has been awarded every major accolade that the great game of golf has to offer. Ladies and gentlemen, will you please welcome, your guest of honour for this evening, the legendary golfer, Mr Arnold Sussabecker…"

The audience pushed back their chairs and rose to its feet to welcome its guest speaker.

The golfing legend took hold of the microphone and stood tall. "Thank you. Thank you very much. Please, please sit down. That was very kind of you. That was wonderful. I haven't felt that good since I lost my wife's credit cards!"

This was a funny line, more so because there had been a recent newspaper article about his wife's extravagant spending habits.

"Most experts advise that a speaker should open with a joke. But those experts have never heard me tell a joke!"

"Two things happened to me on the way here tonight… Unfortunately for me, I forgot my watch. Unfortunately for you, I remembered my speech."

"In life they say, you have to take the good with the bad, bitter with sweet, speaker with dinner…your club captain with golf."

The audience roared at the joke, especially the friends of the club captain. Arnold spoke very eloquently for over thirty minutes expounding on his early days in the profession and his many and varied experiences of how and when he won so many trophies. His humour was very much appreciated. The audience enjoyed his confidential manner and felt akin to the sharing of his achievements.

Billy was introduced right after him and a courteous applause greeted him:

"Thank you. Wow Arnold! What a speech." The audience clapped again. "You know, Arnold, you talked about winning the American Open, The British Open, The Americas' Cup and all the other trophies and how you broke so many records in the game. That was wonderful, but I've got to tell you I've played a few rounds of golf myself, but I don't feel I have to boast about it like you do."

The audience laughed and he was off and running and recalled his full routine which climaxed with a great ovation.

Most times, this type of sportsman's dinner, where a sport's celebrity was the guest speaker and supported by a guest comedian, were very congenial affairs and fun to do. Billy had gotten a number of these gigs up and down the country. On this one occasion in Rugby, in the Midlands, Billy was packing up his things into his car after his bit when a couple of young drunks, who he had insulted during his show, were hanging around waiting for him.

Unfortunately, the alcohol they'd consumed was doing most of their talking for them.

They thought it would be fun to have a go at the comedian. They hadn't done well trying to heckle him while he'd been performing. Their behaviour was not what would normally be associated with that of golf club patrons but apparently, they had taken offense when Billy zinged them with:

"You really shouldn't drink on an empty head. It's dangerous," and, "Take your hands out of your pockets, you'll go blind," and, "Does your mother know you're here? You'd better go, she's on stage next. Yeah, she's a stripper!"

There were a few other regular put-downs but these two customers didn't find them funny. The audience did though and that was what was important.

He heard a voice as he threw his suit bag into the back of his car, "There he is." He turned to see what was happening.

"We didn't like you saying that you did benefit shows in aid of people like us, Mister Comedian. That infers something not nice, with us," said one of them as they made their way across the car park in his direction.

He pretended he hadn't heard them.

"Hey Mister Comedian! We're talking to you." They were almost upon him.

He turned towards them. "Look, I don't want any trouble. I apologise if I said anything to offend you. It was all meant in fun."

One of the guys raised his arm to smack Billy in the face, but Billy had decked him before he landed a blow. The other man ran at him full force, knocking Billy to the pavement. He then began kicking him. Billy grabbed one of his feet and tossed him back. "You've snagged my suit!" Mister Comedian was angry now.

A fight was about to ensue.

The first heckler had gotten up off the ground. The two then lunged at him but the comedian turned and as he did, he pulled the lapels of one of them and catapulted him into a hedge. The other man jumped Billy from behind and was swinging on his shoulders. The first assailant dishevelled himself from the bushes and getting back to his feet, hit Billy in his face.

Enough of this crap! he thought. Billy lifted the guy behind him up off his shoulders, threw him over the hedge and into the river that streamed by the car park. As the other young man ran towards him again, Billy lifted his arm and swung his fist into the guy's jaw, knocking him out cold as his feet dangled to the water's edge.

"Very good, old boy," someone who had been watching the tangle spoke. "You didn't need any help at all." Billy looked at him.

"You handle yourself quite well," said a very well-dressed gentleman, sporting a very educated type of voice.

"Some people just can't take a joke," said Billy, straightening his clothes.

"Or don't know when to keep their mouths shut," said the stranger.

"True."

"The name's Smythe. James Smythe." The man reached out his hand to shake with Billy.

"I enjoyed your show and this one too," the man nodded at the two ruffians. "I would like to talk to you about some business I may have. I hope you might be interested."

"What sort of business?"

"Here's my card. Give me a call and we can talk in a more appropriate setting. It will be well worth your while. I assure you."

"Again, what sort of business?"

"Let's talk. Where are you tomorrow?"

"Manchester. I live near Manchester," said Billy.

"Excellent. Well, call me tomorrow morning. I will be at this number. I have to go for now. I have a large brandy waiting for me at the bar. See you soon." The man was gone.

There are always people with ideas, gigs, photo collectors and other things that hang around entertainers. Rarely are there people with 'business to offer' though, that do approach an entertainer after a show. Perhaps this was just gook. He looked at Smythe's card. All that was on it was a phone number. No name, just a phone number but he remembered the name. It was Smythe.

The drunks clambered out of the water. He didn't want to waste any more time with them so he got in his car and drove away.

Chapter 8
Let Me Tell You What I Can't Tell You

James Smyth answered the phone, "Hello William. How are you? Good. Are you in Manchester right now?"

"I'm near Piccadilly," he replied.

"Good. That isn't far away. Well, look I'm at a place called Saxon's Restaurant on Broad Street. It is just off Market Street. Why don't we have lunch and talk. I'll meet you in say, thirty minutes? How does that sound?" He hung up.

He had never heard of the Saxon Restaurant, but he knew the area. It was very close to the City Centre. He walked over in that direction. He gave the receptionist his name and said that he had a luncheon reservation with James Smythe. The receptionist showed him towards the dining room. James Smyth signalled to Billy as he entered the restaurant. He felt underdressed in jeans and jacket. The restaurant looked to be one of the finer establishments. Smythe was wearing a very expensive suit and tie, not to mention the gold cufflinks that gleamed at the sunlight that shone through the windows.

The waiter handed him a menu and asked if he'd like anything to drink.

"What are you drinking?" said Billy to Smythe.

"Scotch and soda."

"I'll have the same. Thanks."

"And I've ordered us both salmon. I hope you don't mind me ordering."

"What?" he was puzzled. "Oh sure."

"Good," said Smythe.

"You said you had some business for me."

"And I do."

"Well, what is it?"

"All in good time, dear boy, all in good time. Do sit down and relax." The waiter interrupted when he put his whisky and soda down on the table.

"Why don't you just get to it? What is it you would like?"

"Okay. I represent an organisation. Can't say what it is or what we do or where we work."

"Pardon?"

"Very confidential you see. But before you disappear thinking you're talking to a lunatic, I have to clarify a few things. I know it is all going to sound very strange and suspicious because I have to speak somewhat in circles. I head an organisation that is aligned to the government, but it isn't. In that, it is a separate entity and no one knows, other than a small number of people, of its existence. I want to tell you who we are and what we do but I can't."

Doyle laughed at the outrageousness of the conversation. "Is this a television spoof?" he asked. Billy looked around the room to look for any television cameras. There were none. As he looked around, he did notice there was no one else sat at any of the tables near them but the rest of the room was full.

"It really doesn't take much to work out what sort of an organisation we are. We do work for the government that ordinarily can't be done by government and occasionally, we do work for other governments. And we also do work for ourselves."

Doyle laughed again. "You mean you're a spy!" He thought he was joking when he guessed that. It was a wild guess.

"Goodness no! Although there have been times. We have a small number of employees that do special work for us, and governments that is. It isn't recorded or accounted for in the general sense of government business. I'm sorry I have to be so very vague."

"And where do I come in?" Billy sipped on his whisky.

"It's obvious. We'd like to recruit you. We have to try you out first, but I'm sure you would be suitable. If you were suitable, then we could give you more details of your work."

"I'm not sure if I'm hearing this right?"

"Oh. It is very right, old man."

"There is nothing to stop me leaving here and telling anyone I've been offered an undercover agent's job."

"Well, no. There isn't. Except, no one would believe you. Oh, here's the salmon."

The waiter placed the meals on the table in their respective places. "Is there anything else, sir?" he asked Smythe.

"No. That looks wonderful. Thank you."

The waiter bowed and left. Smyth touched his knife and fork and leaned over,

"Let me ask you: Have you ever killed anyone, Mr Doyle?"

Doyle nearly choked on the bite of food he'd just put into his mouth. Did Smythe know of the Jimmy Schmollen situation?

"Well, I'm sure under the right circumstances, you are very capable of doing so."

"Is that a job requirement?" asked a shocked Doyle.

"Oh, no. Goodness no." Smythe smirked and then his face dropped, "Well, yes, it is actually."

"Look, I've had enough of the games. What is it you're after?"

"My organisation is looking for a new face or two. We need someone who can work independently, under, often, very difficult and dangerous circumstances. They will report directly to me."

"Are you serious?"

"Yes." He was beginning to suspect Smythe might be for real. Almost without him noticing, the room had emptied. The tables had been cleaned and none of the other customers were around. *That's very eerie,* thought Doyle.

"Can we cut to the chase? If what you are suggesting is true. You're looking for an agent."

"Not exactly. We're looking for a killer."

Doyle felt he was being led into a trap.

"We need someone who is very reliable and who, under guise, can do specific work for us. I'll get straight to it. We are looking for a killer to work for us. Any training will be provided where necessary. Although, you were in the special forces in the army, were you not. You—"

"You've done a background check up on me?" Billy interceded.

"Of course we have," said Smythe. He took a piece of salmon onto his fork and looked at Billy before he put it his mouth.

"You have a unique situation in that you are a comedian which I think can serve you well as a cover and you are fully able to take care of yourself. You will work alone and obviously, while all possible assistance will be rendered to you, you will be your own boss. I have to warn you," Smythe went deadly serious for the moment and put his knife and fork down onto his plate. "Should your cover be revealed to anyone, you will be solely responsible for any actions taken during the course of your work.

"All the usual adages go with the job. Just like they say in the movies, *License to Kill, Unlimited Resources* etcetera, etcetera… Unfortunately, those are the only perks of the job. Oh, and in case you're wondering, the pay is very good."

Smythe reached into his breast pocket and handed Doyle a cell phone.

"Here, take this. We will communicate on this. Our phones are untraceable. I want you to think seriously about it before we go into any more details. I will call you in a couple of days to see if you are committed and then we can proceed. Confidentiality goes without saying. For survival, you understand? I have to leave now."

"You haven't eaten your salmon," said Doyle.

"I'm not hungry." As Smythe got up from the table, he reached to shake Doyle's hand. "We will be in touch and hopefully we can enjoy a good working relationship. Good day, Mister Doyle."

And he was gone just as quickly as he had disappeared the previous night.

Billy had lost his appetite too. The waiter cleared away the plates. He was ready to leave.

It appeared everyone else had already gone. Little now appeared to show that he was even in a restaurant. Even the name of the place had been removed as had the receptionist's podium. The waiter, now without his uniform, walked with Billy to the door as he was leaving.

"Good day, sir," he said. Billy was on the sidewalk outside as the waiter closed the door behind him. There was nothing on the door or the windows to show this was even a restaurant.

Wasn't it the Saxon Restaurant a few minutes ago?

Chapter 9

Here's the Deal

"I'm a professional entertainer joining a ship for work," said Billy. He wanted to find out why he'd been abducted. He'd barely landed in Panama when he'd been taken at the airport. He was getting nervous. He still wondered had his cover been blown.

"I sometimes fly from ship to ship for my work."

"Yezz I knows 'ow zat dot work, senor. And you have a contract with dis cruise line, for to join it. I seen dat. But izz not what we izz interested in?"

"Well, what is it you are interested in?" He fastened his shoes. If he was to get into a fight, it is easier to fight with your shoes on. "What is it that you want?"

"We 'as a package for you to deliver to a friend of ours in when your ship docks in Cartagegna in Columbia. He will meet you at a bar near the dockside. Dis is da package. It is $100,000 dollars. We want you to give this to Paulo Gradesci, the barman. He will contact you at da bar dere. Dee Sporting Bar. Dat is what it is called."

"How do you know I won't keep the money and stay on the ship till it gets to Miami?"

"Only a very stupid man would do that. You would be dead before the ship got to Miami."

"So, that's it? I just go to the bar, give the money to Paulo Gradesci, a barman? Nothing else?" It was beginning to look like the man thought Bill Doyle to be only an entertainer and nothing else.

"No, no, no, senor! At da bar, Gradesci will give you two bags. They will look like laundry bags and will have a few clothes in the top to make it look dat way. The two bags, you will take onto the ship and when you leave in Miami you take them off with you. You will be met by two gentlemen in the port dere and they will relieve you of the bags. And dat is it. Done.

"No more. No mas."

They didn't know who he was or what his real purpose was. He began to think this was an independent organisation that had nothing to do with his original intentions for being in this part of the world.

"So, I'm to buy drugs in Cartagegna and drop them off in Miami. That seems straightforward," he snickered.

"Yezz, dat is right."

Doyle stood up in front of the man. "You've got to be kidding me! I'm supposed to do that in broad daylight, in full sight of everyone especially the local authorities and military in Cartagegna, not to mention all the customs officials, their sniffing dogs and goodness knows what else in Miami."

"Youse don't 'ave a choice, my friend. We could kill you 'ere, right 'ere and now."

"Or, I could be killed in Columbia or if I'm lucky spend a lifetime in a jail cell in South Florida?"

"All is entirely up to you, 'owz you do it. We 'as people dat will be watching for you. But hopefully, you won't need any assistance."

Doyle assumed they had some sort of backup to get the drugs through customs in Miami even if he did get caught. "Well, that is all well and good. But again, why should I do this? What is in it for me?"

The man reached inside his jacket and pulled out a pad of hundred dollar bills. "Did is for you." He handed him the money. "It is five thousand dollars. Do you know what is espected of you?" He looked sternly at him.

"Seems I don't have a choice, then?"

"No, you don't. Do this and get the delivery to Miami and we will not contact you again."

"Okay, I guess."

"Good. Get dressed. We need to get you to your hotel. Zee ship's agent will be contacting you in da morning, for to take you to pick up da ship in Gutan Lake."

Why had these people chosen to abduct him at the airport and to do an exchange when the ship picked him up? Did many entertainers get propositioned like this? They would have had to do some sort of check up on the ships itinerary, not to mention the manifest of who was joining the ship in Panama. Still, anyone who wanted a few extra dollars at the customs or immigration could give them that information. It was unfamiliar territory for him. He still wondered if they knew who he really was working for and what his real business in the Americas was supposed to be.

These people certainly didn't have the class that Smythe had and they probably didn't have the same expertise. His introduction to Smythe had certainly been a lot different to what he was experiencing with these Central American racketeers.

Chapter 10
Something of an Urgent Matter

Like he said he would, Doyle phoned Smythe on his personal phone a couple of days later. The first meeting had been strange to say the least but it did arouse his interest. Other than getting Margaret and her daughter situated at his house, Billy had nothing else in his book for the next few days. Smythe asked to meet with him at the same place or rather same address in Manchester. It no longer held the façade of a restaurant. In fact, it was hard to say what it was. It could have been a business, a storage centre, anything. From the main entrance, it appeared to be an office or a place of business.

He knocked on the door and a man led him through a corridor to an office where Smythe was sitting.

"Ah, good morning, Doyle. Glad you could make it."

Before Doyle could say anything, Smythe delivered his reasoning for calling in Doyle.

"So, I am assuming you have decided to work for us. Good."

"I, I, I—"

"Now listen, Doyle, This is very important."

"But, I haven't—"

"Yes, you have. We have something of an urgent situation on hand and we need your assistance in the matter. And as soon as possible."

"But I haven't agreed—"

"Doyle, stop interrupting and anyway, the fact that you are here now means that you have accepted the situation."

Is this really how recruitment works in the secret service? thought Doyle.

Smythe continued: "As I said, we have something of an urgent matter. Ordinarily, we would have taken you to training and such, but a situation has arisen and we need to deal with it as quickly as possible. The fact that you are new to our organisation is to our advantage and because you are an unknown. It shouldn't link us to what may transpire over the next few days."

"And what is going to transpire?"

"Do you know who this man is?" Smythe handed Doyle a photograph.

"Er…"

"Well, his name is Lord Carmthen." Billy remembered bumping into him at the offices in London.

"He is a member of the House of Lords. He is a prominent public figure. To the public, he appears to be a very upright sort of person. In reality, he is as crooked and as devious as the worst of mankind."

"Sir, if I may interrupt?"

"I told you not to."

"But, sir, I have seen this gentleman. In fact, the other day when I was in London, I bumped into him."

Doyle explained the circumstances of his meeting. He also told Smythe of his encounter with Harry and the woman on the train and her minder. He handed Smythe the paper, the tote sheet, he'd taken from the envelope from the briefcase at Harry's house. Smyth looked at it.

"I see," said Smythe.

Smythe pressed a button to his telecom machine. "Miss Dobbs. I have something here that I need you to get to headquarters ASAP. They'll know what to do with it."

"Yes, sir. I'll be right in."

A young lady knocked on the door and entered.

"Here you are, Miss Dobbs." Smyth handed her the paper. "As quickly as you can please."

Smythe waited till she had left the room.

"Well, Mr Doyle, it seems you have stumbled upon the very case we are working on right now."

"I'm sorry. I don't follow," said Doyle innocently.

"Let me explain again. For all the honourable appearance that Lord Carmthen may present to the public, he is a despicable sort of person in many ways. For some years, he has been running a blackmail scheme and it is just getting way too out of hand. As you saw the other day, his organisation hires ordinary folk to collect his money from various post office boxes throughout the country. Most of it is in cash and money orders collected depending on how people find it best to pay their blackmail fees."

"The money is collected and then delivered to his offices in London—"

"Transit Carriers?"

"Don't interrupt while I'm speaking, Doyle. It's very annoying."

"Sorry sir."

"You're right though. One of his companies is Transit Carriers. It's a shell company. The offices in London are not what they seem. Supposedly, it is supposed to be a charity concern but it is more of a place to count and collect his blackmail money. Lord Carmthen makes a lot of money from blackmail, notably paedophiles who are pleased to pay for his silence and avoid prosecution. We have been ready for some time to close down this blackmail business. It is a disgusting thing and this is where you come in, Doyle."

"How is that?"

"We wish for you to make His Lordship disappear."

Doyle almost fell back on the chair.

"We don't care how you do it and we must not be implicated in any way whatsoever. We can't prove it yet, but we believe Lord Carmthen is using the blackmail money to finance some drug operations from South and Central America and other parts of the world. The money he picks up is massive and we can only assume he is dispersing it with other dealers or cartels or whatever, abroad."

"So, why get rid of him before you know who he is working with?"

"We have reason to believe he may be planning to close-up shop and disappear. If he sets up someone else in Britain to carry on his work before he does disappear, we may have to start our search all over again. What you almost learned in a day's work has taken us almost two years to put together. Although we would have been happy to close-up this blackmail business and slam all those deviants into jail, it does look like we've opened up something even bigger that might even be a threat to our national security."

"And how do you want me to make His Lordship disappear, Mr Smythe?"

"I told you we don't care how you do it, but he has to be 'done' away with and there has to be no trace as to who is responsible for it. We cannot afford to have anything lead back to us. I repeat, nothing must come back to us!"

Doyle knew exactly what was expected of him but had no idea how he was to accomplish such a challenge.

"Do you have an address for His Lordship or do you know when he'll be in his office in London?"

"Lord Carmthen lives in Surrey, in Knightsbridge at Willow Gate Estate, to be precise. It shouldn't be difficult to find but be careful. He has a number of security people on the grounds.

"There may be a couple of dogs, too, as well as a security system. Charles Carmthen, as well as being a big noise in Knightsbridge, is also a member of several private clubs up and down. One in particular is the Senseless Den in Soho, London. It is an underground gay club that operates through the late-night hours. It is an invitation-only and members club and secluded in Peel Street, Soho, London. It is a very difficult place to get into. Having said that, this Saturday, there is a fundraiser and there is a good chance it may be one of the nights when His Lordship will be attending. Anything to make him appear to be doing good works, I guess."

"You want the job done this weekend?"

"By Sunday, please. I do apologise that we couldn't give you any training before your assignment but we hope that your work in Special Services will serve you well. Is there anything else, Mr Doyle?"

"I don't think so." Doyle knew he had to kill Carmthen but didn't know how he was to go to do it.

"Good. Miss Dobbs will issue with a gun should you need it and a reservation for a car. The sooner you get started the better. Good day, Mr Doyle."

Doyle felt he had been dismissed. He left the room. He picked up his gun in a case with a silencer, from Miss Dobbs. Carrying a gun was something that he had been used to in Afghanistan and Iraq but not in his home country. Miss Dobbs also gave him a set of car keys. It all seemed very efficient and organised and now he knew Smythe was not a gook. This was for real.

Miss Dobbs said, "There is a tuxedo, a regular suit and shirts and other clothes that you may need in the back of the car. The car is the Jaguar Six that is parked outside."

"What, no Rolls or even a Lexus?"

"We don't want you to attract attention to yourself, do we, Mister Doyle?" she sarcastically answered.

True to her word, the car awaited him outside. A wallet sporting a couple of credit cards and some cash was on the passenger seat. So far, his wages as an agent – he was an agent now, wasn't he? – far surpassed his earnings as a comedian. With nothing immediately scheduled in his engagement book, he had little else to do, so he drove off and made for Surrey. According to the GPS, it would take him around three and a half hours to get to Knightsbridge from Manchester.

Chapter 11

It Seems Like a Nice Place!

It was still daylight when he got down to Knightsbridge. He drove around Lord Carmthen's estate as much as he was able to, that is. The main gate was closed but he knew he could climb over the walls into the grounds if he had to. As he drove up the hill, he was able to get a wider view of the place. It wasn't something he ever saw himself living in but who knows?

He saw a groundskeeper running with some dogs, possibly three, but he wasn't sure. He might be able to outrun the groundskeeper but he knew for sure he could never outrun the dogs. The groundskeeper and the dogs disappeared as they raced around the back of the house.

On his way back down the other side of the hill, he saw a supermarket that was still open.

He pulled into the car park and went in the store to buy himself 10 lbs of best chuck and a bottle of Dramamine tablets.

Parking his car a few hundred yards from the main gate and amongst some other cars parked on the road, he grabbed his purchases in the plastic bag and strolled over towards the gate area. There were no guards on the closed gate but he did see two cameras located either side of the entry archway. Presumably, there would be some security guards in the main house with a camera system monitoring the grounds.

He was able to climb up and descend the wall on the other side quite easily, something he'd had plenty of practice at in the military. He scrambled his way through the bushes onto the greens and ran quickly towards the house.

It was a very large house. Dodging up and down and along the window frames, so as not to be noticed from inside the house, he got himself to the back of the building, near the stables, where a dog was stirring in the courtyard. Doyle emptied a few Dramamine tablets into the meat and threw some steak over for the dog. He did the same when another dog came running out from behind a garden shed and devoured another couple of steaks that he'd thrown over the gate.

It seemed forever before the Dramamine kicked in and the dogs fell asleep. It was beginning to get dark.

The lights had been switched on inside the house. He climbed up and jumped over the gate and past the sleeping dogs towards the back door. It was locked. Doyle took one of his credit cards and sliding it between the doorpost and the catch on the lock was able to prise the door open. Fortunately, someone had neglected to lock the dead bolt.

"All right," a man's voice said, "I'm off then, Charlie. I'll see you Monday then. I've checked everything so you should be okay for a few hours."

"What time is His Lordship coming back tonight?" replied another man's voice. Doyle assumed the men to be security guards.

"I don't think he is coming back tonight. I think he's staying in London for the weekend. The girl is here though. She's staying the weekend."

"Oh, okay. So, there's just the four of us with the woman here tonight?"

"Yep. That's right. Bob and Alf are doing their parade around the grounds now. See you Monday morning."

"See ya!"

The conversation, although they didn't know it, gave Doyle all the information he needed. Three men and a girl were his only obstacles to searching the building. But it looked like Carmthen wouldn't be seen that night.

Doyle jumped back as he saw one of the guards, probably the one leaving his shift, move out of a room. He waited quietly till the man had left and he could hear his car pull away. Slowly, he moved to what he assumed might be the observation room. The door was open as he quietly moved in and found the other man watching television screens and operating dials to view close ups and switch room cameras.

Doyle wasn't quiet enough. The man was disturbed and turned around. One strong karate chop to the neck knocked the man unconscious. Luckily, Doyle hadn't forgotten all his military training. Who would have thought it would come in handy in Civvy Street?

He pushed the guard to one side and studied the cameras. He wanted to see where the other guards were on the grounds. He saw them on one camera and they were taking their time.

They were carrying guns, though, and that concerned him. He had left his gun in the Jag. Now, were there any other men on the property and where was the girl? He found her on the TV monitor. She looked to be sleeping in a bedroom.

Thinking he had about twenty minutes to survey the house before the guards returned, he began to make his way room by room. First he made for the library which led him to Carmthen's office. He went straight for the desk. He used a metal envelope opener that was on the desk to 'keyhole' the locks to the drawers. He opened the drawers but didn't find anything. He even pulled them out to see if anything was hidden underneath them but in vain. The top drawer held a diary. He opened it to find some tickets for the function at the 'Senseless Den' Club for the following night. He thought he might need one and took it and put the others back in the diary.

He still had no idea what he was looking for. There was nothing of any consequence in the desk. He crept over to a bookcase. He searched through the books and pulled out a couple.

Then he found some books that didn't move. He tapped on the books on the shelf wall. A hollow sound returned as he did. Something was behind the wall. He felt around and one of the books suddenly gave way and then the one next to it. The wall began to open up. This was almost like a television detective show, he thought, where a secret compartment was discovered.

The entire shelf case moved backwards and then to the side, revealing a bedroom of sorts.

There was a large bed in the centre of the room; chains and harnesses and shackles hung on the walls. This was a torture bedchamber. Doyle had never seen anything like it. It was a chamber for kinky sex pleasures. "Chains and whips what is this?" Was this where Carmthen would bring his special guests?

Doyle was stunned for a moment as he viewed the room.

"See anything you like?" a woman's voice said. She was holding a colt .45 at him. He knew the woman but it was the first time he'd heard her speak. It was the woman from the train.

Did she recognise him from the train?

"I expected you would show up eventually," she said.

His question was answered.

She entered the room holding the gun directly straight at him.

"Get on the bed. What is your name?"

"It is Doyle." He did as he was ordered.

"Keep your hands above your head! And move over to the back of the bed."

Before he realised it, his wrist was locked in a metal cuff chained to one of the bedposts.

She cautiously moved around the bed. Her hair was down. She looked very different from her appearance on the train when she wore the beige pencil skirt and jacket. Right now she wore a robe, a pink satin robe and she looked very, very, sexy.

"No, don't try anything or I'll shoot you cold dead now. And we don't want that, do we?"

She cuffed his other wrist to the chain that was anchored to the other bedpost.

"No, we want to have some fun before I kill you."

"Some fun?"

"Don't you like to have some fun, Mister Doyle?"

"Well, it depends what you have in mind."

"I have a few things in mind. Are you comfortable? I'd like you to be comfortable."

The woman placed the gun on a table at the side and leaned in toward her adversary.

Doyle watched away.

"Now don't struggle, my friend. You see there are two Norman axes that are resting either side of the bedposts?"

Doyle hadn't noticed, but he looked above his head and there were indeed two large axes that stood up again the inside of the bedposts looking like decoration but they were very real.

"Yes, I see them."

"Well, if you were to try anything foolish, I might just release their catches and they would undoubtedly just fall and decapitate you. Not only that, under the bed is a large spinning wheel that would send a sharp blade down the centre of the bed that would do nasty things to your manhood? Do you understand what I'm saying?"

"Yes. Yes, I do."

"Good. Well, let us have some fun, shall we? I'm sure you must realise by now that I do like to be pleased. This is my private room." She laughed. "So, shall we let the fun begin! Let me ask you again, do you want some fun, Mr Doyle?"

I hadn't but I do now, thought Doyle.

She stood up from the bed. Doyle was afraid she was going to get her pleasure watching him being mutilated. Fortunately, she just dropped her robe to the floor and stood before him naked. She looked good. She climbed back on the bed and straddled him. She unbuttoned his shirt and began to caress his chest with her fingers... She slipped her tongue down his chest and to his waist. She looked up at him and smiled.

He smiled back but didn't know why he smiled. He was scared. He faced imminent death, a painful imminent death. Why would he smile? There didn't appear to be any way out.

He had to keep her interested to keep himself alive. The longer he kept her interested, the better.

His life depended on keeping her interested.

She undid his belt and then slipped his pants down his legs, stopping only to remove the shoes and socks. Soon he was naked except for his shirt. He was getting aroused as she got on top of him moving her soft firm body over his. She was beginning to enjoy herself.

How would he get out of this situation? He was locked on the bed. He looked at the axes.

He saw the catch. If he could get further down the bed and released the catch, maybe the axes would miss him. It was highly unlikely that would happen. What if he got her head in front of his to shield him?

Possibly the axes would cut right through her and him if he tried that. No, that won't work either. He knew he was trapped but he had to do something. But what could he do?

Her body was moving with his and the two were enjoying the threatening moment. She thrived on controlling him. She climbed above him to straddle face. She didn't want him inside her yet. His mouth caressed her slowly as she grinded on his face. He knew she was about to pleasure. He also knew, whether he was inside her or not, the axes soon would fall and curtail any pleasure he may be getting from the experience. What was he to do? She knelt over him and he was going to die.

He slipped his hands under her knees and with all his strength, he lifted her up, at her knees, knocking her head against the crossbar of the bed. It stunned her for a moment. By the time she came back down to the bed, he had slipped as far as he could underneath her.

Acrobatically, he swung his leg sideways and kicked the lever for the axes. They were released from their brackets and collapsed downwards. As they dropped, they severed her head. It lodged between her legs, inches from his own.

Still he was trapped. How could he break the locks to the cuffs? Where were the keys?

Were there any keys? Was he stuck there?

He tried to reach for her gun on the table. The cuffs were cutting into his wrists as he tried. Stretching his foot, he touched the gun. He was careful not to knock it off the table. Then he lifted the gun between both of his feet. It didn't feel heavy. He carried the gun carefully with his feet to the bed. He wouldn't be able to fire the gun with his feet. He couldn't. He would have to put the gun into one of his hands to fire it. How on earth would he direct the gun at the cuff latch without blowing his hand off? He balanced the gun on one of the woman's feet. He pointed the barrel towards the chain. All this he was able to do with one hand. It was an incredible balancing skill and he knew it was unlikely to succeed. Blood was gushing all over the bed from the dead woman's body. He pulled the trigger. Some sparks flew at the woman's feet as the gun released a bullet that flew at the chain. For a moment, he wasn't sure if he'd shot himself or not, but the chain suddenly dropped loose. He pulled at it and the chain came apart.

He took the gun and fired at the other chain and freed himself from the bed. He saw the woman's decapitated body. He sure had given her the heads up. A moment of levity crept into the situation.

Quickly, he left the bedchamber and ran through the office. He wanted to be out of there quickly, but...

"Charlie! Are you okay?" It was the other guards returning. They were coming in the back door. Charlie rustled into the hallway. "We heard gunshots. What's going on?"

The guards had their guns drawn. There was going to be a gunfight. This was something Doyle hadn't experienced for a couple of years. The last gunfight he'd had was during an ISIS attack in Kabul. He didn't want to be fighting an attack right now either. A gunshot was fired in his direction and forced him back into the office. He got under the table to check if the woman's gun had enough bullets. There were only two bullets in it but there were three assailants. He was under the desk and heard footsteps enter the room. He saw the legs of a man when he was under the desk. Immediately, he fired a shot at the man's legs. The guard let out a shriek and dropped his gun and himself to the floor.

Doyle banged his head on the desk, causing a hidden drawer to open. Inside there was a booklet. He grabbed it. If it was in a secret drawer, it had to be important. He jumped over the screaming man and ran for the front door. He leapt through the doorway and into the yard where he saw a golf cart. It was better than nothing he thought. He got in it and buggy drove down the roadway toward the front gate. Gunshots were firing after him.

They guards chased after him. Luckily, the incline of the hill caused the golf cart to gain a little speed. It neared the gate. He jumped out of the buggy and let it free wheel on its own and into the gate. Quickly, before the guards were in view, he ran through the bushes and all but leapfrogged over the wall. "Thank God, I can still run!" he said to himself.

"He was in his car and driving to Soho, London, moments later."

Chapter 12
A Daffodil by Any Other Name

By the time Billy had checked into a hotel in London, it was getting late. It had been an exacting day. Nothing like anything he had expected. He had his car valet-parked, went to his room, showered and ordered room service to bring him dinner. He was half way through a bourbon and ice when his phone rang. It was Smythe.

"Doyle, where are you now?"

"I'm in London."

"Oh good, so am I. Where are you in London? I think we need to talk. I didn't know you were going to Lord Carmthen's estate this afternoon."

"Well, I had planned on just checking it out but things got a little out of hand."

"I'll say they did. I wish you'd told me. Anyway, we managed to get in and get the place cleaned up a bit."

By 'cleaned up', Billy assumed Smythe's people had managed to get rid of the woman's body and 'quieten' the guards. The 'clean up' team had gotten there fast too.

"Lord Carmthen wasn't there," Billy told his boss.

"I know. He's going to be at the Senseless Den tonight."

"Tonight? How do you know that?"

"I've just spoken with him. I'll be there too."

"Just a minute. You've come down to London? You could have given me a ride," he joked.

"Well, listen. I don't think he knows his place was ransacked this afternoon, which is good for you. Also, there will be a show at the Senseless Den tonight. I think it starts around twelve thirty give or take an hour or so. Drag queens aren't the most exact when it comes to time keeping. There is a stage door that you can enter from Shakespeare Street. You have to go down some steps to get into the place. I think that would be the best way for you to get into the place.

"Assuming that is, that you might be planning to go there for any reason tonight. I think that you would have less chance of being noticed going in that way."

"You know I did tell you we need to get His Lordship's business taken care of this weekend, didn't I?"

"Of course." Was Smythe inferring that Billy had been wasting his time in Knightsbridge?

"Oh, I do have something for you. I got it this afternoon. It's an address book. I don't know any of the numbers or names in it. I got it from Lord Carmthen's desk. You might—"

"Well, give it to me when you can. I'll see you tonight. Why are you here in Lo—"

There was a knock on the door. It was room service with his meal.

"I've got someone at the door. I'd better go. I think it's my dinner. See you later…"

Billy hung up on Smythe and opened the door. He was certainly ready for his dinner. He was also ready for an early night, but he wasn't going to get one.

========

Billy got to the nightclub around eleven thirty. He found the stage door on Shakespeare Street. He was early and the door was unlocked. He made his way into the dressing room. A doorman entered behind him a moment later and was about to question his presence. The phone on the wall rang and Billy picked the phone up off its holder to make it look like he was meant to be there.

"Hello, this is Rosa Titsup."

"Rosa Titsup? Who the fuck is Rosa Titsup? This is Donny," a voice on the other end of the phone replied.

"I'm sorry," said Billy. "Oh Donny. How are you, dear?" Billy faked an effeminate manner. The bouncer looked at him closely as he walked past. "What can I do for you, Bitchy Poo?"

"I'm going to be late, so I can't open the show, can you put La La on for me? Be a dear and say yes for me."

"For you, anything, darling," said Billy. The bouncer had gone out the front door to the dressing room. Billy put the phone down in the receiver.

A young man entered from the same door that the bouncer had just left through. "Hello, sweetness, who are you?"

"Oh, oh. I'm Rosa. Rosa Titsup. Donny just phoned and sent a message."

"Oh, well, I'm supposed to be the stage manager, why didn't she phone me?"

"I don't know."

"What is the message?"

"She's gotten held up and won't be here in time for the opening."

"Oh, fuck!" said the young man.

She said, "Could you put La La on in her place?"

"La La? La La won't be here for another fucking hour! What the fuck am I going to do?"

The young man was in turmoil.

Billy hadn't planned on doing a show but went with the moment. He thought it would keep him in the club and maybe work out something about the Lord Carmthen situation.

"Well, I could open if you like." Billy wasn't sure what he was getting himself into but the young man jumped at his saving grace.

"You could? Oh, you are a dear. But we start in thirty minutes. Can you be ready by then? Where's your stuff? Oh, never mind, you can help yourself to anything that's back there."

He pointed to the walk-in dressing room that was hung full of stage dresses and wigs.

"You don't have much time to do make up and stuff. Can you do it all in thirty minutes?"

The stage manager didn't wait for an answer, "Oh you are a dear. Thank you. Thank you." He was enthralled. He started to leave the dressing room but turned around, "Oh what's your name? Ro Ro?"

"Rosa."

"Oh yes, Rosa Titsup," he laughed. "Funny name. I'll be back." He started to leave again, then turned back, again then turned around to Billy.

"Oh, what about your music?" The young man looked a bundle of nerves.

"I haven't got any. I didn't bring any. Didn't think I'd be working tonight."

"Well, don't worry, sweetness, I'll find something for you. How about 'If They Could See Me Now' for your play-on music. Do you know it? It's the old

Sweet Charity number, but I'll play the Linda Clifford disco version of it and er er."

"That would be fine," said Billy, trying to help out.

"And what about your play off?"

"How about the same?" said Billy.

"You mean, like you'll lip-sync say two verses to start and then lip-sync a last verse to finish?"

"Yes, that's perfect." Billy was beginning to get overwhelmed with the panicky DJ.

"Oh, how do you want me to introduce you?"

Before he could answer, the other 'gurls' and show performers entered the dressing room. They were already dressed and ready to show. *Maybe one of them could open the show*, Billy thought but the young stage manager put an end to that when he said, "Oh, 'girls', this is Rosa. She's opening the show. Donny is going to be late."

"She's always late, that girl. It's not right, it really isn't. Well, okay dear, but what do you do?"

"The drag queens stopped cackling amongst themselves to hear Billy's reply. Before he answeredm the stage manager interrupted them."

"How do you want to be introduced?" he questioned. Again before he answered, he opened the door to leave and said,

"Oh, girls, could you help her get ready, we've got less than thirty minutes." The young man interrupted himself, "I'll call you just before we start."

The DJ/stage manager then rushed out of the room in a flap and then reopened the door, "I'll leave the microphone centre stage for you. Where's your dress?" He'd left the room not waiting again for an answer.

"Er. I'll be back," muttered Billy and made an exit to the lounge.

Billy had no idea what he was going to do. Hopefully, he wouldn't have to do a show. He hadn't done any drag, other than one time for his army buddies, one Christmas and that wasn't really a drag show, he told himself.

"I'm just going to get a drink first," he'd told the cast. Billy wanted to size up the room and see if Smythe and Lord Carmthen were there yet. He was also hoping he could disappear from the place.

"Well, you'd better hurry. Only thirty minutes; you're leaving it very last minute," someone shouted.

Billy ordered a scotch and soda from the bar. He saw Smythe and Lord Carmthen were sat in a corner booth. Neither acknowledged the other. Standing behind Carmthen was the minder from the train. Would he recognise Billy? What was he going to do? Again he was in a situation where hopefully 'winging it' might save him.

He turned when it looked like the minder was transfixing his gaze in his direction. It was only for a moment because another gentleman entered the fray and sat with the group. Who was that guy? It was time for Billy to go backstage and get ready – into what? He didn't know yet, but time to be backstage.

Billy was left alone backstage even though the rest of the cast were bouncing themselves all over the room. Backstage, he looked into the stage closet to see what might be available to disguise himself and present a suitable stage persona. He found a bushy red wig and large green dress. That will be perfect he thought as he opened it up to find a foam frame set inside the dress.

Billy removed his jacket and tie. He rolled his trouser legs up above is knees and put the dress over him. Borrowing some lipstick and rouge, he painted his face before putting on the wig.

Billy was not one that could exude glamour and the drag queens made a point of letting him know that fact as they entered behind each other to view him in the mirror. They had obviously spent hours preparing themselves before arrival.

"Oh, bitch, you look hideous!" said one of them.

Another said, "Is that the look you're going for?"

"Here let me smooth out that rouge for you," a kinder queen jumped in. "You look like you just threw everything together. You poor thing!" The helpful drag queen used a damp sponge to smooth out the makeup. "There, that's better."

The DJ called on the intercom. "Okay, five minutes and we start, bitches. Is everyone ready? Ro Ro, you're opening still, Right. I'll introduce you and I'll play 'If They Could See Me Now?' It's the Linda Clifford version, the up-tempo rock song. I'll fade it out after the second verse and then you're going to do about ten minutes patter and I'll bring back the song when you cue me for you to finish on. Does that work for you?"

Billy said, "That's fine, thanks." Now he was nervous and hoping he could remember some of the lines from his army show. It's hard enough to try out a new joke, but to try a new routine in a very strange setting played havoc with nerves. He didn't have time to think about that.

"Okay," said the DJ. "And then, girls, you're straight on with your floor show and hopefully the Bitch Tess Tickle will be in by then." Billy assumed he was referring to Donny.

"Okay, here we go. Have a great show everyone."

The lights dimmed in the concert room. The DJ played a recorded medley of show tunes. Billy made his way to the stage entrance and waited for the introduction. It was a small stage but he would work the dance floor in front of it when needed. Nerves were abundant now.

The music medley of show tunes suddenly ceased and the DJ announced from his booth:

"Good evening, ladies and gentlemen, and those who aren't sure still, welcome to the Senseless Den Night Club, the only club of its kind in the world. Well, in our world that is. We hope you're all going to have a wonderful time and that you're going to laugh and drink a lot.

"Because remember, the more you drink, the better the 'gurls' look. We remind you to leave your reputations at the front door. I think most of you did that before you even got to the front door.

"To open our show, here is the delightful, the delectable, the dainty Ro Ro. Oh fuck! I've forgotten her name. It's our own Row Row."

The heavy beat music started up and Billy entered the stage. He hadn't even started to lip-sync when a doomed voice over the speaker system boomed, "What the fuck is that! God, that is ugly! That is one ugly bitch up there!"

Billy heard it and instantaneously went to the mike and said, "Thank you darling, you're not so bad yourself!"

The DJ hadn't realised he'd still got his microphone on. It didn't matter. The ice was broken and the audience laughed. Billy went into the song:

"If they could see me now, that little gang of mine…"

He strolled up and down the stage as he pretended to sing. The audience may have been disappointed with his lack of beauty, but they sure enjoyed his performance and they responded with huge applause when the song faded out.

"Thank you, ladies and germs." Some women at the front of the room were giggling so loud. "You're laughing at my looks, aren't you, dear? Well, you shouldn't; it could happen to you… No don't get me started you'll make my massacre run.

"Well, how about a nice round of applause for John, our disc jockey." Billy raised his outstretched arm to the DJ booth. "He seems like a nice boy. One day he'll know when to turn his fucking microphone off!" A stage light was shone on the DJ in his booth.

"He's a real Don Juan. Yes, girls, after one, he's done… Is one enough for you girl?" he returned his persona to the audience.

"You saw him set up the stage and the microphone. He's a dab hand at handling men's parts.

"Well, it is nice to be with you this evening. If I'm not on form, you'll understand. I've been feeling a little rough all day, isn't that right, John?

"No, I have a little frog in my throat. No, don't laugh. It's the only meat I've had all week."

Billy scoured the room and watched as Lord Carmthen swung around in his chair, "Well, what a job I had getting here tonight. The trains were so packed. Honestly, they're so crowded now. They're crowded to the point where it's fun.

"It's a job to hold your own…it really is.

"It was so crowded when I got off at the station, I was holding someone else's."

Billy pranced the stage but all the time kept an eye on His Lordship, thinking how he might get closer to him…

"No, I'd been to the health club. It was wonderful. Now I feel like a new man. You'll do." Billy pointed to a gentleman sitting on the front. "Yes, I'll feel like a 19-year-old, I do. But I don't think I'll get one, so you'll have to do." The man in the audience laughed loudly.

"I had to get a cab from the station. I had a really fresh guy drive the cab. He let me sit in the front with him. We'd hardly left the station when he put his hand on my knee. Well, I went all hot and cold. Then he put his hand just under my skirt. Well, then a few minutes later, he pushed his hand up to my thigh, I thought Heaven's above! What's next?

"Then he said, 'If I raise my hand a little higher, I can give you a little surprise.' I said, 'If you raise your hand any higher, you'll get a bigger surprise.' He felt a prick. He really did."

Billy pranced around the stage another time.

"I don't know if John told you but we're having the usual raffle drawing tonight. It is for a very good cause so please give generously. Give your all. It's for the home for retired Girl Guides of which I am vice president. You can have your choice of prizes, a Dover sole, a parasol, a camisole, a rissole or an Artisan tea set."

Billy awkwardly adjusted his dress. "This dress is like a cheap hotel. No ballroom."

The audience responded as they should… "If my father caught me in this dress, he'd kick my ass. It's his dress."

He strutted more as he became more at ease, "You know, people have asked me what kind of a family is it that I come from? Well, I came from a very theatrical family believe it or not.

"My mother was a cover girl for the magazine SPORTING LIFE magazine and Daddy did bird impressions. He made his last appearance at Bow Street Courts in a ginger wig. He looked vile. He really did."

Each time he made a turn, he looked to see what might be going on with Smythe and company. On the return, he would study the room hoping to find a way to complete his mission.

So far nothing was coming to him.

"Then there is my brother, Phil. We had trouble with him. He thought he was a crocodile.

"Honestly he did. We took him to the psychiatrist. He said, 'You'll have to have him put away.' I didn't have the heart. So, I had him made into a handbag with shoes to match.

"And then someone wanted to know what I did before I took up this life. Well, I've known lots of interesting positions in my time." He paused for the words he'd just said to sink into the crowd.

Billy was doing well with his show but not having any success in planning his mission.

He had taken the gun that Miss Dobbs had given him to the nightclub. He did think he could do a crazy bit and shoot Lord Carmthen later, but there was the DJ the bouncer and goodness who else. Too many had seen him without his stage garb. No. That would not be an option.

"I first started as a photographer's assistant. I hadn't got a clue what to do. The first day, he took me into the dark room just to get the feel of things. The second day, he taught me how to touch up and develop. The third day, he showed me how to make a good enlargement. We started off with postcard size and ended up with whole plates. The fourth day, I broke his tripod and he kicked me out."

Billy felt this material wasn't particularly funny, but it did suit the environment and it was being well received. He was getting comfortable with the audience. The more comfortable he became, the less femininity he afforded to the act. How would he do away with Lord Carmthen? He saw Smythe and the group at the table there laugh. He thought he saw the minder laugh in his own way too. Who was the other gentleman sat with them?

"Then I went on the buses. I lost that job because I let a fellow go all the way for fifty pence.

"From there, I went into menswear which didn't suit me at all.

"And you do get some funny questions when you dress up like this. A woman asked me, 'How do you keep it up night after night?'

"I said, 'It's not easy. I've had it hard in my time.'"

Again, Billy gave a longer pause.

The crowd roared at this innuendo which encouraged Billy to keep going. All the time he was performing, he was planning a way to take Lord Carmthen out.

"She was the worse for drink. We pushed her head between her knees. She screamed, she was smoking a cigarette. We didn't know that.

"Well, ladies and gentlemen or should I say 'Breeders' and 'Non Breeders'? We've had a request for Blossom, Petal, Fern and Tulip and all the rest of the guys at the Watch Stream Army Barracks.

"I've had some requests to do a version of Mack the Knife. It's called Dick the Chopper!

"It's a favourite of my boyfriend's – Dropsy Denis from Davenport... He said, 'Will you love when I'm old and bent?'

"I said, 'You know I do.'

"I was engaged to an Eskimo, You know? I was, I was engaged to an Eskimo but I broke it off... Yes, I put it in the hands of my solicitors, Mssrs Hunt, Blunt and Cunningham... They said, 'It'll never stand up in court!'"

Smythe's table were enjoying the show. His Lordship was slapping his thighs on each punch line the comic delivered. Billy still had no idea how he was going to achieve his objective and he would soon be ending the show.

"Well, this is the part of the show where people have come to see me to ask a few personal questions about myself... So, if you've got any questions just shout them out."

"Do you ever go out with a married man?" someone shouted from the audience.

"Do I ever go out with married men you ask?" Billy replied, "No. I never go out with married people...unless it is with both of them! We had four guys down here the other night," said Billy. "They wanted me to go home with all four of them. Isn't that sick? I made one of them leave. I did."

"How long have you been doing this?" another question came from the audience.

"How long have I been doing this? Since 11:30, dear."

"How old are you?" this one came from Lord Carmthen. Billy was a little shocked but knew he was now into the act. *There might be something here,* he thought.

"Wow! The man said, 'How old am I?' I manage quite well with one asshole thank you.

"... What a rude question, how old am I? I believe the only old people are dead people." He looked in the direction of His Lordship. "You're not looking too well. Shall I call for the undertaker?"

Billy moved towards his Carmthen's table. "Are you in show business?"

Billy said, "You know I always wanted to be in show business. I remember all the boys wanted to join the football team. I wanted to join the ballet class. I told you in bed, didn't I?" Billy looked at His Lordship as he played the aside... "He came to visit me. Didn't you? He said, he was up for anything, didn't you? ... Well, me too... I'll try anything once...twice if I like it!"

Billy was getting closer to His Lordship. "What is your name, darling?"

Lord Carmthen replied, "Charles. My name is Charles."

"Charles," said Billy, "Well, Charlie, I don't know if you know this, but the devil has sent you his favourite daughter – Me!"

"What are you doing later?" said His Lordship.

"What am I doing later? Well, I think I'm doing you, you sweet talker."

"What will you do?" said Lord Carmthen. He was really getting into the act. Billy didn't miss the opportunity.

"What will I do? Well, I'll take you back to my place. I will. I've had a new carpet installed there. I'll show it to you if you like. Yes? I like a nice shag in the bedroom. Don't you like a good shag? I like something you can sink at least two knuckles into when you're down on the floor!"

Billy wasn't aware that the audience were loving his ribaldry. He was aware something was afoot with Lord Carmthen though. He was also aware that the minder was watching him closely. If he was to do anything, he'd have to get His Lordship alone. Pulling a gun in public was out of the question.

"No, I'm sorry, Charles, but we cannot have a fling. I'm married. I am. No, like you, my husband is a sceptic. It took me years to convince my husband that I was straight. Gosh, is my jaw sore?

"Do you have children, Charles? You know it's hard to find that birth control that you feel comfortable with. It really is. My primary method of birth control is to swallow. What about you?"

Billy was really playing to His Lordship now, "So you want to keep me on the side, Charles? Yes? You'd like me as your sidepiece, would you? A bit on the side? Which side would you prefer – this side, that side, inside, outside? I know. You like the backside! Well, maybe later, darling. We'll see.

"You know, you'll never find another like me." The audience laughed at the ridiculousness of such a situation. "I do admit, though, that everything is geared towards a woman these days. You can be fat and have a lot of sex. You can be ugly and have a lot of sex.

"But you cannot have a small dick and have a lot of sex. Isn't that right, John?" Billy looked up to the sound booth to see if John was paying attention.

"And that's my cue." The DJ was quick enough to pick up the song where it had left off.

Billy returned to the stage and mimed the last part of the song. He left the stage but not before he took a curtsey and lifted his skirt a little to show his shoes and socks. As he did, he got another laugh. He would make himself known at the table and try to get Lord Carmthen alone.

Chapter 13
Bye Bye Carme

Billy was glad it was over. It was not his favourite way of performing, but the show had gone well and it certainly didn't feel like he'd been on stage alone for thirty minutes.

"Thank you, Miss Row Row Row Your Boat," said the DJ from his booth. "And now it is on with the show. Please let's have a thunderous applause for our regular showgirls the 'Fabulous Trollops'."

"A wonderful show darling."

"Yes, it was marvellous."

"Will we see you later?"

And other nice comments from the chorus line as he walked past them leaving the stage. The music struck up and they entered the stage to do their bit.

Billy left the stage but found the door to the dressing room was locked. He sneaked down the side of the stage and down the corridor and into the dressing room. Lord Carmthen was waiting on the other side of the stage door. It was obvious he had locked the door from the stage.

"A spiffing show, my dear! I'm Lord Carmthen, but my friends call me Carme. You can call me Carme."

He knew what Carme was after. And although it would have suited Billy to revile the character, Billy would have no better time than now, to do what he had been hired to do. He pulled Lord Carmthen into the small rest room and pushed him onto the commode. He pulled down his jacket over his shoulders to limit the movement of his arms.

"Oh, I say. This is all a bit quick. It is all quite, quite, well, quite." Billy saw a pair of tights hanging on a rack and grabbed them. Before Lord Carmthen had a chance to know what was happening, Billy wrapped the tights around his neck and began to choke His lordship. At first, His Lordship didn't object. In fact, he was quite enjoying it and went along with it. Perhaps it was his thing. But Billy pulled tighter and tighter. He was beginning to get a thrill from His Lordship's strangulation.

He was getting more excited the tighter he pulled the noose around his neck. His feelings of the excitement were arising just like they had when he hung Jimmy Schmollen. Billy thrilled as he roped the tights close around Carmthen's neck and choked the air from his body.

The killer had almost killed his victim but wasn't ready to stop. He got excited as he pulled tighter and tighter on the stockings. Holding someone else's life in his own hands was such a high to him. It was an ecstatic moment for him.

Billy tightened his grip further. Lord Carmthen couldn't speak. His legs were kicking weakly as he was being strangled. His face turned blue and he felt his eyes were about to pop out of his head. Suddenly, he suddenly gave way and gasped his last breath and slumped down.

Carme had stopped breathing.

The killer had and done his worst. The victim was dead. Billy was satisfied.

He sat the dead man upright on the commode. He took a deep breath and surveyed his work. It might be possible that it could look like a suicide? Billy thought. He tied one leg of the tights to the towel rail to make it look more convincing. He put the other leg around Carmthen's hand so as it would look like Carme had done himself in.

Quickly, he disrobed and put the dress and wig into a bin bag. He grabbed a jar of cream off the mirror table and wiped off his makeup with a towel which he also put into the bin bag with the cream.

He could hear the chorus line setting up to finish their routine. He had to hurry. Was there any other evidence that he'd been there? No. He put on his tie and dinner jacket and started to leave. He felt his phone in his jacket pocket and quickly sent a text to Smythe:

JOB DONE!...SEE YOU BACK IN MANCHESTER.
ADDRESS BOOK IN CARME'S POCKET...DRESSING ROOM.

Taking the address book out of his jacket, he went back to the bathroom and put the notebook inside Lord Carmthen's jacket. He dropped the catch to the door. It dropped down as he closed the door. He knew Smythe would take care of the rest. Billy exited the dressing room.

There was less chance of him being seen going through the back of the audience crowd that were entranced by the show. He carried the bin bag with him being aware that CCTV cameras could catch him carrying the bin bag on the main road, so he threw it in a dumpster down an alley to the club. His night was finished. He wanted to get away from London as quickly as possible but he was exhausted. It had been a long, long day. He would have to settle for a nightcap at the hotel and hopefully a good long sleep before he'd head back home in the morning.

Chapter 14
Welcome To Panama

The man sat next to Doyle in the back of the car that was taking him to his hotel in Panama City. The driver roamed the car through the bustling traffic. Pulling up in the front of the hotel, he got out and opened the car door for Doyle to exit. Billy straightened his jacket and made his way up the steps to the hotel.

"Goodbye, Mister Doyle," said his passenger companion. "I trust you'll have a good trip."

The driver took the car back onto the road and it was gone.

"Hello. My name is Doyle," he said to the receptionist. "William Doyle. I believe I have a reservation?"

"Er, let me look, sir." The lady looked at her computer screen before she pushed a few buttons and said, "Yes, Mr Doyle. Room 533, sir. Your luggage has been taken up to your room. Here is your room key." She handed it to him and pointed down the hallway, "The bar is right through there and the restaurant is down the corridor to your right. Have a nice stay with us, Mister Doyle.

"Oh, and the ship's agent will pick you up in the morning for to take you on your journey to the ship in Gutan Lake. And, if I may please make a suggestion for you, sir? That is, please that you don't leave the hotel at night. I am sorry but this is not one of the safest places at night for strangers to our city." She smiled again.

Would she smile while I was being killed? he wondered.

"Thank you." With that, he departed and made towards the elevator to go to his room. He felt quite uncomfortable about the whole situation that had transpired. It was a relief for him to arrive in his hotel room. Sure he was glad to be alive, too, and more so because his cover hadn't been blown and he hadn't been discovered. For now, he would forget everything that had passed and even the lady's warning. The thought of a nice shower seemed quite appetising.

Once he had freshened up, he decided he would go for dinner at the restaurant. But, all the time it was on his mind how he would manage to transfer the money off the ship, pay for drugs, move the drugs onto the ship and then offload them in Miami when the ship arrived in a few days' time. It was a difficult task and one that had a number of variants, all of which could go very wrong and he could find himself in real trouble, if not jail. He hadn't even boarded the ship up yet.

Maybe he should skip dinner and just make for the bar.

Chapter 15

Job Well Done, Now For Your Next Assignment!

Doyle was driving north on the M1 when Smythe phoned him.

"Good job, Doyle. We were able to tidy things up after you'd left and so far nothing has got to the papers. I got the address book, thank you. We're having it studied as we speak. Let me ask you, Doyle, have you ever performed to American audiences?"

"No. I haven't. Why do you ask?"

"Oh. It is just a thought. We might need you to go abroad shortly."

"So, what was the outcome last night?"

"Well, to all intents and purposes, if it does eventually make the papers, it will read that Lord Carmthen died of a heart attack due to stress, probably caused from overwork and exhaustion."

"What about the bodyguard fellow? Lord Carmthen's companion at the show."

"Oh he's being questioned in London right now. I believe he's too frightened to have the murder hanging over him so is very ready to talk about the operations they had going. There should be quite a few arrests soon. You know of people who have been using post office deposit boxes of late. There might be some big name figures involved, too."

"Who was the gentleman sat with you, last night?"

"Oh, yes. Well, that was Terry Johns. He's my, well, you could say, my counterpart at MI5."

"And what is his connection with all of this?"

"Don't worry about Terry Johns for now. You'll have chance to meet him soon enough.

"At the moment he doesn't know anything about you. I think it might be a good idea to keep it that way."

Billy's natural curiosity was getting the better of him. "So, MI5 are looking into this blackmail thing too?" he said.

"Not really, but they will be in on the follow-up soon. Look, I've known Terry Johns for some time now. When I say follow-up, I'm talking about the investigation as to where Carmthen's money has been going and who is at the helm of things. There is a good chance that we may be of need in your services very shortly in that matter."

"And he doesn't know who I am?" asked Billy.

"No, I don't think he does. Certainly, he didn't see you last night, or rather he would never associate you with 'Rosa, Row Row Row Your Boat, Titsup.' Where did you get a name like that? Good show by the way. Okay, I'll be in touch. You have a rest for a few days." Doyle sensed Smythe was unwilling to talk to him about Terry Johns or MI5 and couldn't get off the phone quick enough.

For the most part, Doyle's first job for the agency had been successful. Over the next few weeks, many of the deviants suffering at the hands of their blackmailers would be rounded up and many of them would be convicted and sent down to prison. *That would certainly make the media in a big way,* he thought.

"The problem we have," said Smythe, when the two met a couple of days later, "is, and, I briefly mentioned this before, is where is the money. Who has it and what are they doing with it? We do have an idea what Lord Carmthen was using the money for but we also believe that the funds may have been secreted for a bigger purpose or purposes. We need to get involved to find out as soon as possible. From Carmthen's address book that you got for us, we were able to identify some of the names of several big drug dealers. Some are in the UK, but most are living abroad."

"I'm at your disposal, sir," said Billy.

"I know you are, Doyle. That is why I've called you in today." Smythe looked seriously concerned as he confided with the young Billy. "As we feared, the business 'Carme' was dealing in is much grander than we at first thought and it isn't just limited to the UK. For all we know, it may even be worldwide. We do know that 'Carme' was using money to bring drugs into this country and was involved in some human trafficking too. Hopefully, now that he is gone, all this business will close down, too. But, we also know we have to work fast to make sure it does close down before any replacements for him are put in his place. For that reason, we have to know exactly who and what are behind his operations."

"How can I help?" inquired Doyle.

"Well, for a start, we have you booked to perform on a trans-Atlantic crossing this week on the S/S Britannia Aries. The ship leaves Southampton in two days and sails for Miami. From there, you are scheduled to sail on the S/S Meridian Star Cruise Ship out of Miami for a month.

"You are booked as one of the headliners on both ships."

"How are you able to book me a gig like that?"

"It doesn't matter. I just can," replied Smythe.

"Well, okay then. I know my gig will just be a cover anyway. What is my purpose for it?"

"I'm glad you asked. We have been working with MI5 and Terry Johns in particular. He knows a big noise in the drug industry and hopefully, he will be cruising on the Britannia Aries when it does the crossing. If he does take the cruise, we want you to get as close as you can to a Raul Corologne. He is a very strong character that we know had close dealings with Lord Carmthen. If he isn't cruising, we will need you to do some work for us in the US."

"He's a drug dealer?" asked Doyle.

"It's likely he is more than that. As I said, we want you to get attached to him. We'll see what transpires from your meetings with him. We'll get instructions to you once you're in Miami regarding the rest of your assignment. Miss Dobbs will fill you in with all the details. Good luck, Doyle. Have a good cruise! Oh, you didn't use the gun, please give it back to Miss Dobbs on your way out."

Miss Dobbs did fill Billy in with the details. He was due to embark the S/S Brittania Aries in Southampton in the afternoon a couple of days later. The ship would make one stop, in Vigo, Spain, early in the cruise before it made the crossing to Miami. The cruise was scheduled for eight days. Smythe passed him onto Miss Dobbs to give him the rest of his mission.

She told Billy, he was booked into a Miami hotel for a night once the ship docked there.

From there, he was scheduled to fly to Panama for a night and would then pick up the S/S Meridian Star cruise ship near there the following day. The S/S Meridian Star was in the process of being re-positioned and would be sailing through the Panama Canal. Its destination would eventually be Miami. The ship would then be doing one-week cruises to the Western Caribbean and based out of Miami. He would be contacted, as Smythe had already informed him, as to what his instructions would be once that ship was back in South Florida. He was hired as 'The Comedian' on the ships.

"One other thing, Mister Doyle, and I don't know if Mister Smythe told you, but you have a contact on the ship sailing across the Atlantic. Your contact is Mister Terry Johns."

"From MI5?" Billy asked.

"Yes. I believe you will have no trouble in recognising who he is."

So, as Smythe had told him, he would soon meet Terry Johns of MI5, he thought. *Did they keep all of their agents so much in the dark as to what their plans were?* Doyle wondered.

"No. I think I do know Terry Johns. Is he cruising alone?"

"No. He will have a traveling companion with him. Supposedly, a lady friend," said Miss Dobbs. "Here are all your papers, passport and tickets. Do you have any questions?"

"I don't think I do. Thank you."

"Good. Well, I hope all goes well. Safe sailing and do stay in touch. It's important."

=============

Billy wouldn't have known that the counterpart that Smythe was talking about was actually in the office with him as he was getting his instructions from Miss Dobbs.

Terry Johns was one of the bosses at MI5. He and Smythe had been working together for some time on this case but from different departments. The two men had first met at Cambridge University where they were both studying law and business some twenty years earlier. They had become friends and villains and took great pleasure in playing pranks, mostly on each other.

Some of their pranks, though, were pranks on a grander scale. It was one such prank that had brought them to the attention of the home office some years ago.

A large sum of money had gone missing from the Bank of England on Fleet Street, London, and there was no trace that linked back to them. In fact, there was no trace that linked anyone to the robbery. The police were confused as to who had committed the crime. The underground had no idea either how the crime had occurred. Headlines in the newspapers read:

'Robbery by Invisible Robbers.' There just were no signs of a robbery other than money missing.

No signs of a break in, or how the robbers managed it, just the robbery itself.

What confused the police even more was the fact that about a week after the robbery and after the television people and the papers had made so much of the theft, the money was returned to the vault in the bank. No one had an inkling as to how someone had been able to rob a bank, then returned the money without anyone knowing how it was done? It was a mystery.

A similar occurrence had happened a few weeks earlier in the city of Cambridge where a smaller bank had been subject to a break-in and money stolen, only for it to be returned to the bank a few days later. It was thought that both incidents might have been pranks but concern as to how and why they were done was very disconcerting to the authorities. Well over twenty years later, the crimes had not been solved or anyone apprehended. It was widely believed that both incidents were committed by the same people but nothing could be proved. It was thought that the Cambridge robbery might have been a rehearsal for the bigger robbery at London. No one had been charged in that either.

It was said that job applications had been sent to the home office by the so-called robbers. It may have been coincidence, but shortly after graduating, both Smythe and Terry Johns were hired to work for the government in special affairs. It is said that neither had interviews for their positions, or, rather there were none on record.

===========

"So, who is this Billy Doyle?" asked Terry Johns.

"He's just started working for us," said Smythe.

"Training?"

"Little or none from so far. We haven't had time yet. Fortunately, he was in the army, Special Operations, and they seem to have done a good job."

"And his history?"

"Originally from Northern Ireland, he smuggled his mother and sister out of there to England after his father had been killed by some mobsters. Apparently, there had been a bad drug deal. Doyle hid his mother and sister in a back room at the house while he deterred the villains until he could get his family away to safety. There was a fight too and he killed one of the mobsters and then the three of them made a run for it to England and escaped, obviously."

Smythe topped up Terry Johns' glass of brandy and sat down. "His father would make passports for villains, so I guess Billy did the same for his mother and sister to get them out of the country. His father had been holding some money for a gang. When a rival gang came around searching for it and when the money went missing, they blamed his father and killed him.

"It would appear that Billy and his mother later found the mobster's money after his father's death.

"The rival mobsters knew Billy and went after him in Ireland. So, he changed his appearance as much as he could; you know cut his hair and dyed it, and they had made their escape. A ferry would took them to Liverpool where his mother and sister set up house there. Billy left them once they were safe."

"I assume the mobsters would have been looking for three people instead of just his sister and his mother, together?" said Terry Johns.

"Yes. If the gang ever found him with his mother and sister, they'd all get killed. Now his mother and sister have new identities. He hasn't kept in touch but has watched out for them in other ways. Occasionally, they will receive some money, supposedly won in a lottery or such.

"He hasn't seen them for a number of years now, though. Billy learned to speak English like an Englishman, so as not to raise any suspicions. Being in the army for seven years would've helped him with that?"

"Amazing that you are able to find all this out and the Irish gang couldn't," said Terry Johns.

"You know we have our means, old boy."

"How old was he when his father was killed?"

"Seventeen."

"And so, he has no commitments."

"None."

"Sounds like a perfect recruit for our line of work, Smythe."

"Yes indeed. Cheers!" said Smythe raising his glass. "Cheers! Terry."

Chapter 16
Let's Take a Cruise!

Billy had no idea how Smythe was able to get a gig on a ship for him. Many entertainers would try for years to get gigs on ships but to no avail. Now here he was boarding the S/S Britannia Aries, a first class cruise ship in Southampton, England, to work a transatlantic crossing and then pick up the S/S Meridian in Miami, Florida for four weeks. *Not many jobs like this!* he said to himself as he boarded.

Traffic hold ups had meant he'd get there later than he had expected. It was almost two-thirty in the afternoon. Reception gave him a package holding his room key and details of his and the ships itinerary. He was also informed that he had a rehearsal at 4:00 pm in the showroom as he would be working that evening.

"Where is the sho room?" he asked the young purser on the desk who obliged him by paging for a member of the cruise staff. A very efficient young man who worked on the cruise staff bounced over to assist.

"Hi. I'm Tony of the cruise staff. Can I help you? I'm assistant to the assistant cruise director," he boasted.

"Well, I'm Billy, the comedian. I believe I have a band call at four o'clock?"

"Nice to meet you. Yes. I'll take you to the showroom now. Follow me."

They made their way to the showroom. Along the journey, Tony introduced Billy to almost everyone he passed along the way. "It's a nice friendly ship. You'll enjoy it here," said Tony.

"And do you know what the procedure is this evening?" asked Billy.

"Oh, yes. Tonight is introductions. The staff and the cruise director are introduced then the CD introduces all the concession people. You know, like the photographers, casino manager and shop manager etc. That takes about thirty to forty minutes and then the CD will introduce you. Do you have any music? God I hope not. You don't need the band do you? Please God, I hope not!"

"I haven't gotten my case yet!"

"But do you need the band? You're only doing about ten or twelve minutes. You do like an introduction tonight for your main act later in the week."

"Who introduces me? The CD?"

"Yes, the cruise director does. There are two shows tonight." They made it to the showroom and a young man came rushing up to them. "Mister Doyle, so sorry no one met you when you arrived. We expected you to be here earlier though. Anyway, I'm Nigel. I'm one of the assistants to the assistant cruise director."

"Assistant to the assistant cruise director?" Billy almost queried, but thought better to keep quiet.

"And this is our bandleader, Randy." A man passing by stopped for a moment. He obviously didn't want to stop and wasn't thankful for being stopped.

"You don't need us do you?" said the bandleader.

"No, I guess not."

The bandleader and orchestra disappeared quickly leaving some dancers there to carry on with their rehearsal.

"So, you know what's happening then?" said Nigel.

"I'm not sure."

"I've got a program here. There are two shows?" He handed Billy a daily program.

"I told him that already!" said the first assistant to the assistant cruise director.

"Yes, well, they are 8:00 pm and 10:30 pm. The dancers do their welcome aboard bit.

"Then the CD does his introductions and introduces his staff and then the concession people – the shop manageress, the casino manager, bar staff etc. That lasts about forty minutes and then he puts you on and you do about ten or twelve minutes. It's like a teaser for your show later in the cruise."

"I already told him that!" spited Tony.

"Am I the only entertainer on the ship?" asked Billy.

"Goodness, no," the two assistants almost said in unison.

"Well, why don't they put someone else on tonight? Like someone who is already situated here on the ship?"

"It's the CD's choice. They don't normally put on a comedian on the first night or someone who's just joined the ship or that matter. But he calls the shots. Is there a problem?" asked Nigel.

"No, no, I guess not. I hope my suit case gets here in time."

"It's probably in your cabin now," Tony joined in.

"I hope so."

"Okay, I'll go and find my case and clean up. Two shows then who's..." Without him realising it, the two assistants were gone.

"Yes. Good luck. See you tonight!" was heard as the big swing doors closed behind them.

Billy was left alone. He'd barely arrived on board but had to get ready for his show, of which he wasn't sure what he was yet going to do. Did he ever know?

===========

It was almost eight o'clock. The dancers were 'faffing' around, the concession staff were chattering and the cruise staff were backstage getting ready for introductions. All this meant there wasn't much room for Billy. He still hadn't met the cruise director. He did manage to get his suit on just before everyone crowded into the entertainers dressing room. The cruise director made his appearance. He was dressed smartly, a little over dressed and his manner made him appear more important than he was.

"All right! All right, everybody! I'm here! Are you all ready? Cue the stagehands to inform the sound and light people. Are my assistants here? And what about the assistant assistants?" It was all sounding very important, but no one really knew what was expected of them, especially Billy.

"Where's the comedian?" mumbled the CD.

"I'm here," he said, but his voice was lost in the commotion backstage.

"Not here? Well, if anyone sees him, tell him to be ready for his introduction after my staff have left the stage. Okay, let's go."

And it was on with the show.

"I'm sorry Billy Doyle, isn't it? I'll be the last one off the stage," said a diminutive cruise staff member nudging him. "Once I'm off, he'll introduce you, if that's all right?"

"Thank you," a nice friendly voice, even if it was timid, was a godsend.

"Do I make my entrance from the side of the stage?"

"It's up to you, but you might be able to see what's happening better from the side, where the concession people are right now," she said. "The dancers can be pretty chaotic back there."

"Thanks again," said Billy. He made his way to the side of the auditorium.

It were a long, boring forty minutes of introductions, but it was something that was needed. Who knows when you might need a casino manager in a life raft? Or to want their photograph taken in the middle of the night?

It was all done, or was it. It was time for Billy's bit, but the CD took the moment to try to be funny. He told a joke and then another and then another. Gradually, each joke got less of a laugh than the one before it and once it had reached just polite laughter, the CD decided to call it quits and introduce Billy.

"Okay, ladies and gentlemen. It's show time. It's a pleasure to introduce a very famous comedian and I've forgotten his name already. Here's our comedian..."

"That was it? I've had better intros at the Boilermaker's Club where the MC tripped on stage."

Billy ran onto the stage and grabbed the mic before anyone had the chance to leave.

"Good evening, ladies and gentleman. How about a round of applause for your CD and don't forget his staff and the concessionaires and all the Pilipino room stewards... Did I leave anyone out?

"You've no idea how long I have been waiting to get on this stage...

"So how is everybody? I'm so excited. I've never sailed to Iraq before. Have you?

"What? What? They didn't tell you? I'm kidding we're not going to Iraq. No, we're going to Miami, Florida, USA."

A group of people cheered. "Are you folks from Florida? No, you just recognised three syllables?"

There was no big laugh just a few smiles. It was the first night of the cruise. Most of the audience were somewhat tired from their journey to the ship. Most had been traveling all day and so were very lethargic.

Billy had just begun to get the audience when a group of people walked down the aisle to some empty seats. They were late. "Hello folks. Are you lost? Not now you're not."

He jumped down from the stage, "Let me show you to your seats." Shocked by him coming off stage, the audience laughed at the expense of the late arrivals. "Where are you folks from?"

"Fort Lauderdale," they replied.

"Fort Lauderdale! Really? No wonder you're late. So, we're taking you home at the end of the week, is that right? ... Well, folks you've not missed much, the show started about three days ago. We opened the show with the dancers who sang 'Welcome aboard, we hope you enjoy your cruise'... No, I've never heard that song either. Then the crisis director came on and said,

"'Hello everybody, I'm John Panelli, your crisis director.' John told a few jokes, well he told quite a few really. Yes, everyone was saying, 'Hey he's not the comedian, is he?'

"Then he introduced the shop manageress Sally from Wigan. That is in the North of England. Wigan? That's like Fort Lauderdale without electricity. Then he introduced the casino manager; he's got big hands that fella. And don't forget, our wonderful hairdressers. I have no idea who did their hair. Did you see it! Then he introduced one of our bartenders, Jose.

"He's from the Philippines. I think the Philippines must be empty this week because they're all working on this ship!

"Then he told some more jokes and people said, 'Oh, I'm leaving if he is the comedian! Let's go!' But they didn't because right then, and just in time, he said, 'It's show time. Here's someone you'll never forget, but did, he couldn't remember my name.

"'And he introduced me. I'm Billy Doyle. I'm the comedian. So you didn't miss much!

"Thanks for stopping by, folks."

The audience clapped vigorously for his enthusiasm as well as the humour. Meanwhile, the CD was at the side of the stage, pointing to his watch. He wanted Billy to leave the stage. His time was up.

"I've got to go, ladies and gentlemen. I have to leave you, but before I do, I would like to share something with you. I joined the ship this afternoon, like most of you did. I left home early this morning and I was just putting my little girl to bed. She said, 'Daddy, where are you going?'

"I said, 'I'm going down to Southampton and I'm going to join a ship there.'

"She said, 'And what are you going to do on the ship, Daddy?'

"I said, 'Well, I'm going to do a show for all the ladies and gentlemen in the audience, there.'

"She said, 'And will they be a good audience, Daddy.'"

The audience giggled as they were getting into this bit. "And I looked at her big blue eyes and I said, 'Yes they will, they'll be fantastic.'

"She said, 'And will they all be clapping and cheering and shouting for more?'

"I said, 'Yes, they will.'

"So, ladies and gentlemen, not for me, but for a little girl back home." The audience roared at his sucker punch.

The CD couldn't deny he'd done very well and trying to share some applause, miserly said, "That was Billy Coyle!" How many times would he have to hear the wrong name?

In between shows, Billy hit the bar for a scotch and soda.

"They liked your show," the CD miserly complimented. "You can do a bit longer in the second show if you like."

"Sure, how long?"

"How about an extra minute or two?"

Wow. The CD was generous. "Thanks!"

"I'm going to put you on again on Monday night. That's when we're in Vigo for the day." Billy wasn't sure but he thought, *Five days at sea and I'm on at night after a long day!*

"Doesn't seem this guy is so generous. I don't trust him. Still I'm only on the ship for a week and then I leave."

"Oh, stay away from the ship jokes," the cruise director commanded.

"What?"

"Yes, you'll find everyone else does them. Better to stay away from them."

You mean so you can do them, thought Billy, *but I think I'll do them first because I'm the first one on!*

True to form, Billy's second show went even better than the first. And despite a couple of ship references, everyone seemed pleased.

Billy hadn't eaten since lunchtime, so he decided to dine at the midnight buffet. He sat by himself eating a couple of fish tacos, when a man in his early forties walked up to the table with a lady in her mid-twenties.

"Good evening, Mr Doyle," said the man. Billy recognised him. It was the man who had accompanied Smythe at the Senseless Den Night Club. "I'm Terry Johns and this is my fiancée, Diedre."

Doyle began to stand up to shake his hand.

"Please don't get up. Do you mind if we join you?"

"Sure. Please do."

"We enjoyed your show. We would have liked to have seen more."

"Tuesday night is when I do my main show," said Doyle.

The couple pulled up a couple of dining chairs to the table and seated themselves.

"That's a port day. They're putting a comedian on a port day? On a port day when all the passengers are tired out from walking around in Vigo?"

"I guess so."

"Well, we look forward to it anyway. I believe you know an acquaintance of mine. James, James Smythe."

"Yes, that's right. I do." Doyle wasn't sure how much Johns knew of his relationship with Smythe or if he did recognised Doyle from the show at the Senseless Den Club.

"He suggested I contact you. We sort of have a working relationship together. Actually, I have some information that Smythe asked me to pass onto you."

He was about to go into details when a night steward came up to him and handed him a note in a small envelope. "I'm terribly sorry about this, darling. I've got to go and meet someone.

"I didn't think we'd be meeting till tomorrow. I'm sorry I have to leave you too, Mister Doyle.

"We'll talk sometime tomorrow though, I hope. I'll see you back in the room later, Diedre."

Terry Johns kissed his lady friend and left Doyle to eat his supper and idle chat with his fiancée. She was snacking on some crackers while she stared at the comedian.

"Does he often leave you unattended like that?" Doyle humoured, nibbling a bite of a taco.

"All the time! But, I'm kind of used to it by now," she said, "So, what are your plans for the rest of the evening, Mr Doyle?"

"Well, I haven't unpacked yet. It's been quite a rush today. I thought I might just have a nightcap and crash early. What about you? Do you have any plans?"

"Yours sound quite interesting. Do you mind if I join you?" she asked.

"You mean for a nightcap?"

"Well, that's a start at least," she grinned. Shortly after a quick nightcap in one of the small bars on the ship, Doyle was in bed with Deidre. He later walked her back home to her cabin.

==========

Billy had already done a run around the deck and was back in his room showering as the ship came in to dock at Vigo. He was just getting out of the shower when his cabin phone rang.

"Hello," answered Billy.

"Good morning, Billy. This is Terry Johns. Sorry I had to leave you stranded with my fiancée, Diedre, the other night." Billy hadn't seen Terry Johns or his fiancée since their brief introduction on the first night.

"No problem."

"Anyway, what are you up to today? I would like to talk with you."

"I have nothing planned."

"Well, perhaps we could meet in Vigo later. I would like to talk with you about a couple of things and there is someone I'd like you to meet. I'm hoping I can persuade him to join us."

"Sure. What time?"

"How about eleven o'clock at the Café Renza? It's just off the main street. You can walk there from the ship."

"See you at eleven."

Billy was walking along the dockside and towards the town around ten thirty.

"You want a taxi, sir?" a cab pulled up alongside him.

"No thanks. Er, no, *gracias*."

"I think you do want a taxi, senor," insisted the driver.

"You do? What makes you think that?"

The taxi driver lowered his voice, "A friend of your wishes for to meet with you."

"A friend of mine?"

"Yez pleez, sir. You get in and I take you into da town."

Billy obliged and got into the back seat of the cab. Beside him, there sat an older gentleman wearing a white jacket, Panama hat and cravat.

"You look very English, Mr Smythe," said Billy.

"How are you, Doyle?"

The taxi drove off up the hill. The blossoms were out and formed a nice fragrant view, shielding the hills from the harbour and the ocean.

"I'm assuming that you met Terry Johns?"

"Yes, a couple of nights ago at the buffet. He was with his fiancée."

"His fiancée? Well, I guess that is what he is calling her this week." He grinned.

"Good."

Smythe turned in his seat to face Doyle, "I don't know, if he hasn't done already, he will soon be meeting with a Raul Cologne on the cruise. He is actually cruising after all. Cologne has a number of homes around the globe, one of which happens to be in Miami. We're pretty sure his reason for going to Miami on the ship is to take a large sum of money there. The money would have been picked up from Lord Carmthen last week before his death."

"Blackmail money?"

"Yes. I do not know why Cologne deems it necessary to carry personally a large amount of money with him on the ship. He does have access to a number of boats that he could use to transport his money or let someone else do it. It does seem a little pointless for him to travel with it to Miami. Maybe, he feels safer carrying his money to the US himself. Anyway, we're thinking that Lord Carmthen was financing business with Cologne in the US.

"We weren't sure that Cologne was cruising until the ship had sailed and that is why I'm here to let you know of the situation."

"I thought we'd ended the blackmail thing."

"We have and people are being picked up as we speak, but the money collected from it is probably about ready to be dispersed once Cologne arrives in Miami."

"How much are we talking about?" said Doyle.

"Close to two hundred million."

"What?"

"Yes, and it is cash."

"How the heck is he going to take that off the ship?"

"He has a couple of minders with him. He is very wealthy and I imagine people are paid at the other end to turn a blind eye as to what he carries with him. You might find that out for us."

"And you want me to take the money from him?"

"No, but I would like you to follow the money. There is a good chance that it will be going to connections in the South American market and we need to find out where. So, you are going to have to make contact with him."

"How?"

"That is up to you. You're going to be near him on the ship for almost seven days now. I'm sure you'll find a way. And Terry Johns is there to help you too.

"Okay. I have a plane to catch back to England. Call me when you have news." Smythe signalled to the cab driver to open the door for Doyle to get out of the car. "Oh, don't tell anyone that you met with me today. Not even Terry Johns."

"I'm actually meeting him for lunch at eleven for lunch," said Billy.

"Good. Enjoy it. Okay, I'll see you soon, Mister Doyle."

The taxi driver got back in his car after Doyle had been deposited on the sidewalk and drove off.

Doyle thought it strange that Smythe had come all the way from England for such a short visit with him. *Maybe, he was just checking up on me,* he thought.

Billy began to descend the hill into Vigo and walk back to the town. He saw Terry Johns walking with a Spanish-looking gentleman and a lady. *That was probably Colorogne*, he thought, *but would such a person be walking so unprotected.* Then he saw two gentlemen in suits and dark glasses were walking close behind the group. *Were they guards or was Billy just getting too paranoid?*

Presumably, they were all walking to the restaurant. Billy started to cross the street. Terry Johns saw him and began to wave, but as the party turned to look the other way, a man, who looked suspiciously like the taxi driver who had just left him, jumped between the group. He grabbed the lady's pocket book and ran off up the hill with it. Doyle didn't wait to consider the situation. He ran back up the hill after the man.

Running in pursuit, Billy chased the thief around a corner and followed him down an alleyway. Suddenly, the man stopped and turned. It was the cab driver who had been transporting him and Smythe. He handed Billy the lady's bag: "Here, take the ladies' bag. Don't forget to phone Mister Smythe when you arrive in Miami. Now hit me!"

"What?"

"Quick, hit me! They'll be here in a moment. Hit me and then let me run away!"

Billy saw one of the minders had turned down the alley and was coming in their direction. The driver took out a knife and lunged at Billy, scratching his arm. Billy hit him on his nose with his fist, knocking him backwards. The driver retaliated and when Billy hit him again, he ran off.

The group soon came upon the scene.

"Ma'am, I believe this is yours," Doyle said as he handed the purse to the lady. "I don't think the thief had time to take anything from it."

"Zank you, sir. I do appreciate your azzistance."

"Petty criminals! You can't walk anywhere these days. Well done, Mr Doyle."

Terry Johns turned to Colorogne, "Raul, I'd like to introduce you to Billy Doyle. He has just started working for us." By saying "working for us", he assumed Terry Johns had told him he worked for MI5.

"Pleezed to meet you, Mister Doyle, and zank you for getting my wife's bag back," he then turned to Terry Johns, "Is diss da man you were talking about earlier?"

"Yes it is."

"A grand coincidence you were available at da right time, senor." The man didn't miss a thing. He looked deeply into Billy's eyes as he shook his hand.

"I'll tell you what, why don't we all go for a coffee? I had told Doyle that I would meet him at the Café Renza, which is just up the street from here," said Terry Johns.

"I zinc dat I would like to go back to da ship now," said Mrs Colorogne.

"In dat case, I will come back wid you too, my dear." Colorogne took his wife's arm. "I will see you later. Thank you again, good sir. We will talk a little later I hope."

One of the bodyguards waved down a taxi to take them back to the ship. As Colorogne and his lady got into a cab with the guards, another vehicle drove past them. The driver of that car was covering his bloody nose as he drove by. Smythe smiled and no one but Billy saw him.

"Well, that just leaves you and me. Would you like a coffee now, Doyle?"

The two sat down at a sidewalk table, outside the Café Renza.

"So, that was Raul Colorogne. I would have liked for you to have met him in more normal circumstances, but at least you met him," said Terry Johns.

Billy noticed that Terry Johns covered his mouth with a menu when he spoke. "Just being careful, you know. It's mostly an old habit that I have but I don't want anyone to be listening or watching what I might be saying."

"Taking it a bit far, aren't we?" said Billy.

"Just can't be too careful."

"Anyway, that is who I wanted you to meet. We'll arrange another meeting soon. We have six days at sea yet. And who is Senor Colorogne?

"He is a very important part of the Mesillican Organisation. He has the contacts in America, Europe, China and South America. He is, I guess, a link up man for various money laundering and drug cartels. The reason we want you on this job, Doyle, is that we believe by getting Colorogne's trust, you can get deeper into the organisation and we can find out more about his business."

"Right now, Colorogne's immediate concern will be to disperse funds to some of his business associates and that is where you come in. I've already informed him of your willingness to help and that you could be a great asset to him by delivering funds to the right people in the right places."

"But why is a British agent getting involved in all this, Mr Johns?"

"Indeed why would a British agent get involved with a known drug dealer? And an international drug ring? What are the ties to England? We need to find out for our security. We believe Lord Carmthen was involved in something much bigger than the paedophile blackmail caper. Not only was he buying drugs for distribution in Britain, but we believe he was one of the financiers of a larger operation.

"So the plan is to get close to Colorogne. I've known him a couple of years now. He thinks we're friends, of sorts. It's been an ongoing process and suits the situation for now. I needed a new face in the scene and that is now your place. We've gotten started a little later than I'd hoped but you've met the man, and now, like I said, we want you to get close to him. We'll keep our communication doors open for a few days.

"Right now, I'd better get back to the ship. Don't want to keep Diedre waiting?" He was about to leave Billy at the café. "Oh, Doyle. I had a suitcase of mine placed in your cabin for safekeeping. I hope you don't mind."

That was a strange thing to do, Billy thought.

Chapter 17
All the Nice Girls Love a Sailor

Billy was back in his cabin, cleaning up after his run in with the taxi driver. There was a knock on his cabin door. He wrapped the towel around his waist and opened it. Diedre, Terry Johns' fiancée, stood there. I have something for you. She held out an envelope.

"Come in," he invited. She handed him the envelope as she passed to walk into his cabin.

Billy took the envelope as he watched her approach his bed. He opened the envelope. It was an invite to the captain's table for dinner that evening.

"That's very nice of the captain." He swung the door to close. "I hardly know the man."

"I think it's nicer of Terry. He's the one who thought it would be nice to have your company for dinner." Billy nodded his head. "It's still very nice, whoever sent it. I don't usually get such invitations."

He was perusing the captain's card when he saw Diedre unclasp her dress and let it fall to the ground. She stood there in only her silk panties and enticed Billy to go to bed. Billy dropped his towel to the floor and lifted her onto the bed. She lost her shoes in the process. He kissed her hard on her lips. Her soft breath enfolded his face as she slowly moved underneath him as he got on top.

A soft knock on the cabin door interrupted them.

"Who's that?" said Terry Johns' fiancée.

"I don't know."

"I can't be found here," she said.

"Well, where are you going to go?"

"I don't know." She scampered off the bed.

He opened his closet door, moving everything to one side. "How about in here?"

She maneuvered herself into the closet and sat on a case. It was Terry Johns' case. He closed the door and went to see who was knocking on the cabin door, not before he saw her shoes in the middle of the floor. Quickly he picked them up and passed them to her and closed the closet door again. He unlocked his cabin. It was Colorogne's wife.

She barged into his room. Billy covered himself with his damp towel. She saw the invite to the captain's table resting on his desk there.

"Ah. I see you got your invite. My 'usband, he don't normally go to these things but he thought it would be nice if you were there tonight. So, I am just a checking."

"Well, I don't normally attend those things either. I will be delighted."

Truth be told, Billy had never been invited to a captain's table before.

"Yes, he thought it would be nice if you were there tonight. So, he told his friend, the captain, he would attend if you could be there also."

"With Mr Johns and his fiancée too?" asked Billy.

"Err yeez. Could you unclip me pleeze?"

"I'm sorry what did you say?"

"Unclip me." She indicated for him to unclip the catch on the back of her dress.

"I sink you 'ad better 'urry, Mister Billee. I don't have long. And I think you like what's you see. No?"

"Oh. Of course." How could he not like what he saw.

She stepped out of her shoes fell to the bed and lay naked on the covers there. She was beautiful. But what was he doing with Corologne's wife? Surely he could have him killed at the drop of a hat if he knew his wife was in his bed with him. Still he was not one to disappoint a lady.

It was obvious from her groans that she was enjoying the moment. So was Billy. They made heavy passionate love for ten to fifteen minutes. *Women like Mrs Colororgne don't come around every day,* he thought, *and they certainly don't come to his cabin for an afternoon rendezvous, especially with no arrangement made beforehand. Although, Terry Johns' fiancée had done just that. Oh my God!* he realised. *She's still in the closet! She would, no doubt, have heard the commotion, too.*

"Well. I'ze go now. I told my 'usband I only be gone five minutes. I better go back."

"You told your husband you were coming here?" he said.

"Oh, No. No. No! You silly man! He would kill me if he knows I go to see someone else."

He could only imagine what her husband would do to him if he knew.

She rose from the bed, slipped on her shoes and pulled her dress over herself. "You clip me up now, pleeze."

Billy obliged the lady.

"Zank you. I go now. I enjoy zat. We do it again, no?"

Mrs Corologne was out of the door as quickly as she came.

Billy saw her out and locked the door again. Diedre exited the closet. "That was close. The bitch!" said Diedre.

She wrapped her arms around Billy. The dalliance he'd just had didn't seem to dissuade her original intentions for visiting him but another knock on the door did.

"I'll get back in the closet. You get rid of whoever is at the door. And do it quickly! I don't like it in that closet."

Billy opened the door. It was the girl who had been so polite and timid with him on the first night. The real assistant cruise director.

Her blouse was unbuttoned half way showing some nice firm breasts and cleavage. She smiled at him and said,

"May I come in?"

"Oh, I don't think that would be such a good idea, do you?"

"Actually, I do. That's why I'm here."

She pushed Billy into the room. "Don't want anyone walking in on us, do we?" she said as she dropped the catch on the door.

"No. Oh, of course not," he smiled.

She opened her blouse to reveal her beautiful rounded breasts. Then she wrapped her arms around Billy, unfastening his towel from around his waist as she did so. He raised her to the bed and slowly unbuttoned her shorts. He lifted her legs as he slid the shorts down her nicely tanned limbs. Kissing the insides of her upper thighs, he slowly moved upward to kiss her stomach. Billy wasn't sure if he was ready to make love so soon again, but as she turned him over and went down on him, he knew he was and he spent a good fifteen minutes letting her know that he was ready.

Hardly any conversation had passed their lips but the rendezvous delivered all that it had promised. All that needed to be said, had already been said.

"Well, I'd better go back to work now. I'll see you tonight. I believe you're dining with the captain tonight, aren't you?"

"Yes, I am. What about you?"

"Yes. I am scheduled to be hostess for tonight's dinner." She was busy getting herself dressed. I'll see you in the Montezuma Lounge. That is where the captain meets his guests before dinner.

She kissed him and then waved from the doorway before she left him.

The door closed and as it did Diedre burst out of the closet. "Okay, it's my turn now!" she yelled eagerly. "No one else! It's my turn! No one else!" She was rampant. Any thoughts that she might have been discouraged or put off him by his antics just flew out of the window.

Her reaction was quite unexpected. She slammed the lock to the door. It closed fast and she slammed Billy onto the bed. The two pulled each other in to a close embrace. Billy knew he needed a little time to 'recuperate' so began to kiss and caress her slowly. He went down on her slowly. Her passion grew and he'd brought her off almost immediately.

Then the two had a very passionate fifteen or twenty minutes that might have run into days had it not been for an announcement on the ship's public announcement system, announcing that the ship was about to set sail from Vigo.

"Damn. I've got to go," said Diedre, "I've to get ready. Where's my dress?"

Chapter 18
Dinner and a Show

Dinner had gone quite well as far as captain's table dinners went. A little jealous rivalry between Diedre and Mrs Colorogne seemed to be creeping into the after-dinner conversation as they all sat with the captain and the other guests.

"I don't normally dine here in the passenger dining room, but the captain and I are old friends," stated Colorogne to Billy. "Robert, how long have we known each other now?"

"Oh, a long time, indeed," replied the captain.

The captain was interrupted when Colorogne's wife interceded. "Roberto," Roberto, who was Roberto? Oh of course Robert Kinsella, the captain. "Roberto came to our wedding, didn't you, Roberto?"

"I did that. A beautiful thing it was too."

"Yes, it was zee best," said the wife, "In Monaco, we got married. We didn't sail into dere. All of us we flew in. It was beautiful and very special. Everyone who wus anyone came, didn't dey, dear? Even movie stars, dey come too. Didn't dey?"

Her husband didn't have time to speak, Diedre interrupted: "Terry and I will be getting married in England," said Diedre. "That is our home. Isn't that right, my dear?" She hugged on Terry Johns' arm as he took a bite of his dessert. "We will have just a very simple wedding with only a few special guests. But we will have it home."

Mrs Colorogne hugged her husband and kissed him on his cheek.

The captain and Billy glanced at each other. "You're not married, are you, Mr Doyle?"

"Nope! I can't say I've had that pleasure."

"That is a shame. I think you would make an excellent husband, Billy," said Diedre. "Do you have anyone in your life right now, Billy?" she almost purred.

"I am sure dat Billee 'as lots of women on his arm at all times. I bet dat he 'as stragglers on his arm right now. Is dat right, my Billee?"

Colorogne sensed for some reason Billy might be getting a little embarrassed with the ladies' conversation and thought to change its direction. "I didn't tell you, Roberto, but we only met Mister Doyle this morning in Vigo. He, umm, how you say it, Terry?" He looked to Terry Johns for help to translate, which he duly obliged him with.

"Yes. We had an experience in Vigo this morning, Captain. Some ruffian came along while we were sightseeing and stole Mrs Colorogne bag…"

"Oh, my," said the captain, "and what happened?"

"Well, the man ran off with Mrs Colorogne's purse and as luck would have it, Billy happened to be passing, saw what had happened and went after the guy. He chased after him and got the purse back."

"Mr Doyle was in your company?" asked the captain.

"Not at the time," said Terry Johns. "He was approaching us from the other side of the road and saw the man snatch the bag and run off so he went after him and retrieved the bag."

"Our Billee was a real 'ero. Weren't you, Billee?"

"Oh, I wouldn't say that. I think I just did what anyone would've done…"

"I was not there!" announced Diedre.

"We were very grateful, Mister Doyle," said Colorogne, "Thank you."

"Yes, we wuz."

"Like I said, I wasn't there, but I'm sure you were wonderful!" said Diedre uninterestingly as she sipped her coffee.

Billy thought it time to give his gratitude for dinner and to make an exit from the table.

"Captain, if you would be so gracious as to excuse me. I do have shows to do this evening and with your permission, I would like to say thank you for a wonderful dinner and make my excuse to leave you all now, to go and get ready."

"Certainly. I do understand," said the captain, "Perhaps we might see you in the lounge later."

Billy stood up and gave a semi-type of bow to the master.

"We are going to your show later," said Diedre.

"Yes, we is too. Aren't we, darling?"

"We are?" said a surprised Colorogne.

"Yez we is. You sez so earlier, before you 'ad a sleep dis afternoon."

"I did! Oh, I guess I did. We will see you later then, Mister Doyle."

"Goodbye, everyone, and thanks for a wonderful dinner and wonderful company."

"Bye, bye, my Billee!" the little cruise staff girl said sarcastically.

Billy couldn't get away quick enough. The ladies were getting a little too much. He left the table and the dining room and got the elevator up to the showroom and rushed backstage.

=========

"So, I don't want any cruise ship jokes. Do you understand? I'm the only one that tells cruise ship jokes on this ship," admonished the cruise director.

Billy just looked at him. He had barely gotten into the dressing room for the show when the CD blew up at him.

Who gave this guy the sole rights to tell cruise ship jokes? Billy said to himself. After all, one of the ways of getting through to an audience is by association whether it be by everyone having experienced a particular event or circumstance or whatever. Here, everyone was on a ship and by a process of elimination that was what everyone had in common, being on a ship and experiencing all that happens on a ship. Not only that who gave this guy, CD guy, the right to tell Billy how to do his job?

"No problem. No ship jokes," said Billy. *Fuck him!* was what he was really thinking. Billy was introduced and he took over the stage.

"Good evening, ladies and gentlemen. What a friendly crowd you are. I think that is because it is a friendly ship. Is that right? I'll tell you how friendly this ship is: Have you tried the showers yet? Yes. You know, you get in there and turn the shower on and the shower curtain raps itself around you to give you a big hug. It's so friendly…" Billy was off and running.

"You see, there is a trick to using those showers. Because the showers are so small, what you do when you get in there is just soap the walls down and then spin around!"

The cruise director was side stage and heard Billy talk about the showers. He was watching and pulling faces in distaste as Billy continued talking about the ship.

"I was talking to the 'Crisis Director'." The audience laughed at the term 'Crisis Director'. "Well, that is what he's called, isn't it?" Billy new full well that the title would stay with the CD for the rest of the cruise.

"Anyway, I was talking to the crisis director about how the ship was rocking last night.

"Did you feel it move?" I said. "That patch they give all the passengers for sea sickness, what they should do is stick it on one side of the ship!"

The audience laughed at the silliness of the joke. "But there is no problem on this ship that cannot be solved by a second dessert! I don't get up till noon, so I miss the first thirty meals.

"This is not the 'Love Boat,' it's the 'Food Boat!'

"They start you off at six in the morning that gives you the energy to go to the dining room for a full breakfast. And just in case you're still hungry, you can go up to the deck to have an open breakfast. There is morning coffee and cookies which keeps you going till a full lunch is severed at noon in the dining room and again, if you haven't had enough, there is the served open deck again for you to fill up on burgers, fish and fries and even more dessert.

"Afternoon tea and cakes supply you through till the late afternoon. Now there is no organised eating for a couple of hours, so what you do with the fruit in your cabin is your own affair. Now you're warmed up, and just in time for dinner at six. There's dinner for two hours, then they give you a show, knowing full well that midnight buffet is only a short while away.

"Everyone has pizza and visits the poop deck to poop and then get ready for breakfast to start all over again They expect you to eat here!"

Billy was doing very well. He was associating with his audience. It wasn't the type of material that he would ordinarily do, but the cruise director had annoyed him and he knew he wouldn't be back on this ship anyway.

"But I was talking about the ship rocking last night. One guy was feeling a little hung over. He was leaning over the rail on deck. I said, 'Are you feeling a little weak?'

"He said, 'I'm throwing it as far as I can!'

"I have a nice cabin. It's low down though. I called the purser on the phone…it was long distance…!!

"I said, 'Purser, I've got a leak in my cabin.'

"She said, 'What you do in your cabin is your own affair!' Some of them can be a little snooty though.

"I said, 'Can I have a room with a view?'"

"She said, 'Don't close your door.' Can you believe that?"

"And did you see the old man on deck? He was crying, I said, 'What's wrong?'"

"He said, 'I just got married to the most wonderful woman. There is nothing she won't do for me. She cooks my favourite meals. We make love all the time. She is so wonderful.'"

"I said, 'That's great, but why are you crying?'"

"He said, 'I've forgotten where my cabin is.'"

The audience loved the show and Billy was thriving on their response. The cruise director, on the other hand, was livid. Billy used every cruise ship joke he could think of. For a moment, his killer instinct was seeping through his stage character. Would he get as much of a thrill if he killed the cruise director? No. It couldn't get better than this. He was killing the audience.

"And people ask silly questions when they go on a cruise. I know I do. I think we just leave our brains at home. I'll show you. Here are some of the craziest questions ever asked by a passenger on a cruise ship."

Billy took out a piece of paper from his pocket. "Oh no! He isn't doing that? No, he won't do that? No. No!" He could almost hear the cruise director say.

"Silly question number one: 'Do the crew sleep onboard?' – No, folks, we fly them in everyday from Guatemala!

"What do we do with the ice carvings when they melt?"

"Are the things in the shop for sale?"

These may be old lines but many were laughing as if it were the first time they had heard them.

"What time does the bus leave for the walking tour?

"Does the ship produce its own electricity?" Billy paused and then put the punch out, "No, folks, we have a large extension cord that we plug in back in Miami!

"Is it fresh water or salt water in the swimming pool?" He paused again for the punch. "It's sea water, that's why it always sways when we're at sea!

"What time is the midnight buffet? Really!"

Billy continued to exhaust as much as he could about ships. If the cruise director wanted to do any cruise ship jokes during the rest of the cruise, he would have to work for the laughs.

Just about then, the ship jolted a little and made a small tilt. Billy was quick to catch onto the moment. "Oops! Just hit an iceberg folks. Don't worry," Billy calmed the people down. "I guess we just hit the Gulf Stream. What? We're not in the Gulf Stream! Okay, I've got good news and bad news folks. The good news is we're making excellent progress and we're on time. The bad news is that we're lost."

"I'm just kidding. We're not making that good for time. Listen, I'll tell you what we should do. If you all go down to your cabins now and flush the toilet, and if we all do it at the same time, we'll hydroplane into Miami in about ten minutes."

The audience laughed and clapped. His time on stage just seemed to roll on by...

"Well, I think I've talked about the ship enough, don't you think?"

Some in the audience replied, "No, we want some more."

"Well, how about you all come back for the second show tonight. I'll do a different show and I'll talk about some other things. I think I've said enough about the ship to upset the crisis director. How about a round of applause for your staff. They're wonderful people.

"Ladies and gentlemen, I do two things for a living. I work on ships and I work on television. So, you've guessed it. I work a lot on ships. See you another day! Goodnight, everybody."

Billy got a big accolade and cheers as he walked off the stage. It seemed that the CD could do nothing to even put a dent in his likeability.

"Ladies and gentlemen. The fabulous Billy Doyle! What a wonderful act. Terrific!" The CD shook Billy's hand, then gave him a hug before he left the stage. It was almost as if they were best friends. The fact that the audience loved Billy had nothing to do with the appearance of friendship at that moment. The captain was even laughing and applauding might have influenced the CD a little.

Billy had done his shows and did more than a few ship jokes during his act. Ship jokes and comments from a comedian are almost expected on a cruise ship. The fact that the cruise director had told him not to do any only encouraged him to do some.

Later, Billy went to a small lounge for his customary scotch and soda. He wasn't expecting to see anyone there, but he found the captain was sitting in a corner with Colorogne and Terry Johns. He was grateful that the ladies weren't around. Terry Johns signalled for Billy to join them. Doyle ambled over and as he did he caught the tail end of a conversation regarding Colorogne's baggage being taken ashore in Miami.

"All will be arranged. I will talk with the customs people and your luggage and your men can be the first off the ship," said the captain, "Ah, Mister Doyle, a very good show. It was very funny. I enjoyed it. Please, please join us." He called a waiter over to bring Billy a drink. Billy asked the waiter for a scotch and soda as he sat down in the company.

"Yes, it was a good show, well done, Doyle."

"Where are you from, Mister Doyle?" asked the captain.

"I'm from Manchester, sir."

"Really, that's splendid. So, what are you, City or United?"

Colorogne had no idea that the captain was asking Billy which soccer team he supported back home in Manchester in the UK. Doyle himself was surprised to be asked.

"I'm a Manchester City supporter, sir."

"Oh. That's too bad!"

"Why are you a Manchester United Fan?" he replied.

"I am. All my family have been United supporters for many years. I've been United supporter since I was a kid," he proudly boasted.

"You're not from Manchester are you, Captain?"

"I am that. I'm originally from Stretford, in Manchester."

"I would never have guessed. You don't seem to have an accent of any kind."

"Well, I have been gone from there for a long time now."

Terry Johns thought Colorogne deserved some sort of explanation as to what the two were talking about. "Raul, they're talking soccer. They both come from Manchester in England and it is almost a custom when Manchester folk meet to ask which team they support. Soccer is almost like a religion in Manchester. It's the same in Liverpool, England. Whenever Liverpool people meet, they also ask which soccer team they support. Is it Liverpool Football Club or Everton Football Club?"

"Ah, soccer, of course. You mentioned Manchester United. I know of Manchester United. Dey is very famous!"

"Yes, but Manchester City are the better team," said Billy.

"I don't want to fight you, Mister Doyle, but you know we are in the Atlantic Ocean, right now," charged the captain.

"I think I'd better shut my mouth and keep quiet," laughed Billy at the thought of him being thrown into the ocean for being a Manchester City supporter.

"I like soccer. It is very popular where I come from. It is just beginning to take off in America though," said Colorogne.

"Yes, it is," said the captain.

The conversation was good and jovial and passed for a good hour or so, ending when the captain chose to retire from the company and go to his quarters. The men also thought it time to finish their evening too, but not before Colorogne insisted the men all had one last drink.

"Mister Doyle, Terry, he tells me you do work for him? Right?"

"Well…"

"And dat you might do some work for me?"

"Well, what is it you have in mind, Mr Colorogne?"

"I have already told Terry, but I tell you now. I have many business interests. Some are in places I am not allowed to visit. So, I 'as to get peoples to go to dese places for me." The man sat up in earnest in his chair.

"So," said Colorogne, "I need someone to take a couple of things to Curacao and Aruba in the Antilles and also some to Cancun in Mexico. I want to know if you wouldn't mind doing dat for me."

Colorogne had gotten straight to the point. "Terry, here, he says you would do dat for me. Especially as you soon are to go on a ship dat stops at dose places. So, you will work for me too, like he does?"

"I'm not a drug smuggler, Mr Colorogne," Billy answered.

He laughed, "I know you're not and it's not drugs I'm asking you to take."

"No?"

"No. It's money. Yes. It is time for me to pay monies to my some of my business people that I finance. I have to rely on friends or associates that I can trust implicitly."

"And you trust me?"

Billy thought, *If the man only knew!*

"I have no reason not to trust you. There are not many people I can trust and I am a very good judge of character."

"How do you recognise that?"

"For a start, we only met a couple of days ago. You are a—"

"A comedian!" Terry Johns interceded.

"Err. Yes. I don't believe a comedian would usually have any interests in my sort of business."

"I will pay you very well. You 'as da means to transport dis money for me in your baggage."

Questions abounded in Billy's mind, *What if he was discovered smuggling in the money? What if it was discovered I was transporting money for whatever reason? What would happen? How could I explain it?*

"Next week, you join a cruise ship dat sails to some of da places I need my money to go to. You will not touch any of da money. It's a lot, so dere will be people watching it at all times, especially when it is not wid you. Like when you perform your shows and dey will watch it when you as it wid you."

"I still have to carry it on and off the ship!" he exclaimed.

"No, dat will be arranged. It will be delivered to your cabin when you board and in da ports where it is to be delivered, someone will take it off fors you. All is easy. Da way I likes it.

"All yous do is mind da cases on da sip."

"As easy as that?"

"*Si.*"

"Why me?" Billy knew he was going to do the task. He was just pumping Colorogne for as much information as possible.

"No one knows you. No one cares about a comedian. I'm sorry I means that in a nice way."

Billy recalled Smythe telling him there would never be any backup for him. He was nervous about the job but knew if he was to infiltrate this organisation, it had to be done. He had to make a start. He didn't know how much money he would be looking after but it would certainly involve more he was ever likely to own in his lifetime.

And, so it was all arranged, so quickly and so quietly. He would hold the money in his cabin till drop offs to several designations were arranged. All would take place once the Meridian Star sailed out of Miami the following week Terry Johns would give him details of the destinations for the deliveries.

Billy retired to his cabin, only to find a beautiful South American lady in his bed who should have been in her own room awaiting her husband. "Oh. The life of a comedian!"

=========

By the end of the cruise, the three men and the two ladies had become good friends.

Over breakfast in the Colorogne suite, on the ship, Colorogne asked when Billy was due to join the S/S Meridian Star.

"Sunday," he answered. "I fly tomorrow evening to Panama, stay the night there and join the ship the day after."

"So, what do you have planned for tomorrow afternoon, Saturday? Before you fly?" said Colorogne.

"I believe I have nothing planned."

"Well, come and see me. We're having a party tomorrow afternoon."

"It is our anniversary party," said the wife. "Isn't it, darling?"

"It is and I am 'oping dat there will be some people there that I would like for you to meet."

Billy deciphered that the people Colorogne wanted him to meet were the certain people that he was to drop off money to. He had also worked out that they would be the same people that Smythe had hired him to kill. He would no doubt have to play both sides in the upcoming game.

Colorogne's guards came into the suite and took the couple's baggage onto a trolley car.

Billy left the suite and went for a coffee at the open-pool restaurant. He took his drink and leaned against the rails on the upper deck. Drinking his coffee and looking over the shipside, he saw that the Colorogne baggage was the first to be taken off the ship. Colorogne and his wife were escorted ashore and through the customs building by the captain. He also saw that Terry Johns' case, the one that had been left in his cabin closet, was also among the Spanish gentleman's cases. It was full of money. Billy knew that. He was also sure it was Terry Johns' surest way to get it taken off the ship and through customs.

Billy watched from the upper deck as Colorogne, his wife and guards were passed through the customs building to go onto an awaiting vehicle. He went back to his cabin to get his stuff together for disembarkation. The young assistant cruise director was waiting for him.

Chapter 19
A Moon Over Miami

Billy must have thought he was on a busman's holiday. Having a day or so to kill in Miami, before flying to Panama to join the S/S Meridian Star, entranced him. As usually happens, many ships transfer to 'warmer waters' for the winter. The S/S meridian Star had completed its Alaska season and was presently transferring down from its home base of Vancouver to Miami. It would stop at San Diego before heading further south to sail through the Panama Canal, after which it would stop at Cartagena, Aruba, and then head to its seasonal home of Miami.

Doyle had been put up in the Hotel Splendour in South Beach, Miami, for a night before he would fly on to Panama the following afternoon. He would then pick up the ship in Gutan Lake, Panama, the following morning. It was a usual trip for entertainers that were hired to supplement the extra entertainment required for the additional sailing time that re-position cruises demanded.

He leaned out to watch Colorogne, Terry Johns and their lady companions disembark.

Doyle considered why such a wealthy man would take a transatlantic crossing when he could afford his own ship transport. It had to be the smuggling of cash from the UK to Miami. For some reason, he didn't trust anyone else to do it. Cash is still king, and what was Terry Johns' reason for travelling? His case was amongst Colorogne's and that he knew was full of cash, too.

He had his suspicions of Terry Johns.

Billy had a few hours to spare before he was due to check into his hotel in Miami. He took a bus tour of the city. It was a very hot, humid day, but that didn't detract from his enjoyment of the sights it offered. He had never been to South Florida and he was fully enthralled by the place. The massively tall skyscraper buildings just mesmerised him. He loved Miami Beach and the art deco district found around Lincoln Avenue. The hustle and bustle of downtown contrasted sharply with Little Havana and later Bayside, where the bus dropped him off. He had never seen anything like this town. The five hours just sped by and he wanted to do the tour over again. He had wanted to do the Everglades tour but time was running away. He would have to save that for another day.

He checked into his hotel, the Hotel Splendour, located on South Beach. He felt as if he had won the lottery when he saw his room. Little did he know this was the normal standard for a hotel in this part of the world. Miami was not a small holiday town. This was grand on a grand scale. Before this visit, he'd just thought the movies had exaggerated, at least just a little bit.

Now he knew this place was for real. He cleaned up in his room, then went to meet Terry Johns for dinner on South Beach.

Terry Johns and Diedre showed up on time at the Flamingo Flame Restaurant. Terry Johns had arranged the reservation for seven. He ordered his whisky and soda while reading the menu and then decided on Surf and Turf for his main course. He didn't really notice what his company ordered and he didn't really care. He was still taking in the sights of this new and wonderful land, not to mention the amazingly beautiful women that were everywhere. His mind was elsewhere and although he could hear Terry Johns talking, he really wasn't listening to what he was saying. It was when he heard the name Colorogne that he sat up and began to pay attention and hope that he hadn't missed anything important.

"So, we're meeting at Colorogne's place tomorrow afternoon, around lunchtime. Are you listening, Doyle?"

"Oh, yes. Sorry I was daydreaming for a moment. Yes, I was listening. We're all going to Colorogne's home tomorrow afternoon. Right?"

"We are, around lunch time. Diedre and I will meet you there. She would like me to take her shopping in the morning. You can make your own way there I'm sure. He did give you the address, didn't he?"

"Yes, he did. You do know I'm flying to Panama later in the afternoon. So, I won't be staying for long."

"Well, I'm sure there is a good chance that Colorogne will want to talk with you privately, a little more about arrangements to drop certain monies off along your route while you're on the ship. That will be good for you because once you find out who, where and when you will make the drop-offs, you will be able to do what you were hired to do." Terry Johns had covered his mouth while he was talking. Doyle knew why.

Doyle was surprised he was opening up so much about the business in front of Diedre. He looked at her to see if she was listening. He didn't know if she knew anything about the business he was hired for or not.

"Oh, I never told you, did I?"

"Told me what?" Terry Johns removed his hand from his mouth and leaned over to quietly talk into Doyle's ear.

"Well, Diedre and I aren't really engaged."

"You're not?"

"No, it's just a cover. It's probably not a good one, either. No. I'm married and my wife is at home in Surrey in England. Diedre works for me in my office in London. She knows pretty much everything that is going on in our department so she is very good to have around."

"I'm sure she is." Doyle was surprised that Terry Johns felt it necessary to have her round at all. He really couldn't see the purpose for her being on the mission. Would it really have made any difference if he had travelled across the Atlantic alone? He already knew Colorogne. It wasn't that she assisted him in any real way. Doyle wondered what her real purpose for being on the trip was. He also wondered why Terry Johns was talking so openly right now.

Billy noticed that Terry Johns' words were beginning to slur his words. Had he been drinking, he wondered.

"I'll tell you what, Billy," said Terry Johns.

"What is that?"

"What?"

"You were going to tell me what, weren't you?"

"I was. Oh yes I was, wasn't I? Well, I'll tell you…? You know I don't feel very well."

Billy wondered if he was having some sort of attack. "Are you okay?"

"Oh, yes. I'll pay the bill."

"I've done it, dear," said Diedre.

"Oh. Good girl. Shall we go now?"

"I've called for a taxi. Let's go outside," she said.

Billy hadn't seen Diedre pay the bill. He lifted one of Terry Johns' arms and rested him against his shoulder. Diedre took the other arm and the two of them escorted him to a waiting yellow cab outside.

"See you tomorrow, old boy." Terry Johns waved as he fell onto the back seat. Diedre got into the front of the taxi.

"I'll get him to bed and I'll see you at the hotel. Hotel Splendour, isn't it? Sometimes those pills are stronger than he thinks they are," she said, tossing a small plastic bottle to him.

The cab drove off and Billy wondered how she would have known where he was staying.

He also wondered if he would ever get any sleep ever again. He also wondered why she had drugged Terry Johns. Why was she out with them in the first place?

==========

Colorogne's home was like a Hollywood mansion, something he had only seen in the movies. As expected, the party was a very elaborate and expensive affair. The home was filled with a lot of beautiful people from Miami. A lot of good-looking people were there. There were some not-so-nice-looking people, but they were the ones that were mostly employed by Colorogne and his wife. The staff were busy catering food and serving drinks, while the guards, and there were a lot of them too, were occupied patrolling the grounds and guarding doorways.

The gates were unlocked for visitors to drive their fancy cars through to park. Security knew pretty much who they were, even though they checked all guests for their IDs. A large water fountain, almost a replica of the Trevi in Rome, Italy, decorated the main walkway to the home's entrance. Numerous dogs paraded the grounds with the minders. A combo Latin band with a large horn section played lively music in the back gardens. People were drinking and dancing and having a good time as Billy ascended the steps into the home.

"Ah, welcome, my friend," Raul Colorogne greeted him as he walked into the house. "So very glad you made it."

Colorogne grabbed a glass of mimosa from a maid's tray and handed it to Doyle.

"Wow! This is some place you have, Mr Corologne!" said Billy. "It is quite amazing."

Cologne's wife, the stunning hostess sporting a very attractive long black dress decorated by a set of exquisite pearl earrings matching her beautiful necklace, sashayed over,

"We are so glad you like it, Billee," said Mrs Colorogne, "If you want, I shows you around, no?"

"That would be very nice of you, Mrs Colorogne." What else would he say? The truth was he wasn't really interested in sight-seeing the house but was anxious to meet the men that Colorogne had in mind for him to do business with. Fortunately, Terry Johns and his 'fiancée' walked over and disrupted the conversation.

"Hello, Billy. How are you doing?"

"Good, thank you. How are you doing, Mr Johns?"

"I'm sort of wearing off a hangover. I don't know what I had to drink last night, but something wiped me out."

Diedre just smiled.

"So I was just about to show Billee my home. But I think I like to dance first. Come, my darling. I take you, Billee, you come wid me."

How could he resist such a beautiful creature? She was absolutely amazing. He followed her to the dance floor where the eight-piece dance band played some Latin swing with salsa music. She wanted to dance and he moved as best he could. She made it easier for him and helped lead him around the floor. The other dancers were invisible. Everyone was watching and wondering who was dancing with this exotic creature.

"Are you 'aving a good time, my Billee?"

"Yes I am, indeed. Thank you."

"Zee party is just starting now. You know, my Billee, I would like for to see you again, you know what I say?"

How could he resist this gorgeous woman? "That would be nice but when are you going to have some time for err, let us say, when are you going to have some time for just yourself?"

"As Raul, he always say, 'I must make time'. Maybe later, I make some time." Billy believed she really did mean she would see him later.

"Oh, not too later though," she laughed.

They danced until the music stopped and then she said, "Thank you, my friend. I better play at being zee 'ostess for a little while now." She left him near a barman who was carrying a tray of drinks. Billy took one from his tray. He had hardly had time to take a sip from it when Terry Johns' girlfriend who had been jealously watching him dance with Mrs Corologne came over to him.

"I see you've made yourself quite at home!" she spited.

"When in Rome… you know how that goes."

"I do and I think you should be careful, Mister Doyle. You don't want to get caught doing something you shouldn't be doing, do you? It wouldn't be nice, for anyone."

"Oh, I don't think that is going to happen, my dear."

"Well, I wouldn't be surprised. I see you've already attracted quite a bit of attention for yourself."

"No?" He smiled sarcastically. "Well, maybe just a little." He laughed. "You're not jealous at all, are you, my dear? Well, you shouldn't be. And anyway, you have your company, or do you?" Billy looked around and saw Terry Johns talking to two gentlemen with Colorogne.

"And who is that that Terry is talking with? Over there."

"That is Donald Beauchamp and Dr Frederick Dietz. They are from the Antilles. Beauchamp is a banker in the Antilles and Dietz is a doctor there too. Dr Dietz and his family assist in the distribution of stuff to South America, while Beauchamp owns the main bank and other interests in Aruba. He is also the finance minister there. They are all heavily involved with Cologne's business."

How on earth does this lady know so much about all this business? Surely, Terry Johns would not be so foolish as to tell her everything.

Speak of the devil! Terry Johns suddenly appeared and gave his 'fiancée' a big hug.

"So what are you both planning now?" Terry crept up into their company.

"Billy was just asking who it was you were talking to."

"Oh, come on, I'll introduce you. Come on," he said, "Mr Colorogne just asked me to bring you over to them."

Terry Johns' walked Billy over to Colorogne and his company. "Gentlemen, may I introduce a friend of mine, from England. This is Billy Doyle."

Billy shook hands with the gentlemen as he got the introduction he was hoping for. "We met Billy on the cruise ship from England, last week," said Colorogne. "Zee one we got off yesterday."201

"Nice to meet you, gentlemen."

"And did you know Billy when you were in England?" Beauchamp asked Colorogne.

"Well, not really, although it does seem like we may have known each other a long time."

"And what is it that brought you to America?" asked Beauchamp.

"I work on the cruise ships."

"Doing what?" asked Dietz.

"I'm an entertainer. I…er…I tell jokes."

"Oh, good tell us a joke," said Beauchamp laughingly.

This was one thing that most comedians hated, that any time you met or were introduced to someone and they found out what you did, the first thing they would say to you would be. "Oh, you're a comedian; tell me a joke." It is a strange concept that people think that is all comedians do, even in their spare time. One time he told a really obnoxious person what he did for a living and the person said, "Tell us a joke then."

Billy let off and said, "Why is it people always say that?"

The man said, "What do you mean?"

Billy answered, "Well, if someone said they were a plumber, you wouldn't say, 'Oh can you fix my pipes for me?' or if they said they were a proctologist, you wouldn't bend over and say, 'Oh can you look at this for me!' and point to your backside."

Fortunately, Billy refrained from this diatribe and smiled and said, "Well maybe, I will later." And tried to change the subject, "And how do you gentlemen know Mr Colorogne?" Of course Billy knew the answer but wanted to get into conversation.

The two men suddenly went quiet and closed up.

"We're all business associates," said Colorogne.

Billy thought Mr Colorogne must be pretty close to these gentlemen as he was normally known to be standoffish from most people. Colorogne's driver, the one who'd picked up Billy yesterday morning, came up to Colorogne and whispered in his ear.

"Gentlemen, excuse me a moment." He left the group and walked with the driver a few yards and confided with the driver out of everyone's earshot even though everyone was silent and tried to hear what was being said and remained quiet.

Mrs Colorogne walked in on the company. "How iz everybody doing?" she said.

"All is good, my dear," her husband had returned. "Gentlemen, I'm sorry to say that Juan will not be able to join us today after all."

"Juan, which one is Juan?"

"Juan Dibralta, my dear. He is from Cancun. He does send his best wishes, though."

"Oh, yez."

"Mrs Cologne, we don't mean to be rude, but we do have to leave in a moment. Thank you for your party. It was wonderful. Thank you," said Beauchamp. It appeared that the fact Dibralta was not going to be at the party might have meant that the other two gentlemen had no reason to be there."

"Well, first I have some papers and things I need to give to these gentlemen and then I'll see you out. Gentlemen, this way please." He started to escort the men to a side room and turned to Doyle, "Oh, Mister Doyle, would you like to join us, please?"

The men nodded and bid their farewells to Mrs Colorogne and walked with her husband.

Doyle followed behind and left Terry Johns with Mrs Colorogne who was a little peeved that 'her Billee' had been taken away from her.

Colorogne explained to the men who Doyle was and that he would be responsible for getting money to them in the coming weeks. They obviously already knew what to do with it. He would be bringing the money in via the ship because it would not be expected. They in turn knew what was expected of them. They did, but Billy didn't and it wasn't mentioned.

"We know you know what you're doing," said Beauchamp. "It was a shame that Dibralta was not here this afternoon. But soon we hope. I think we may have come all this way for nothing."

"I hope, too," said Colorogne.

The men left, escorted by Terry Johns to their vehicles.

Well, that was one way of breaking up the party, thought Billy. He too would take his leave soon. Colorogne looked very agitated. Was it the fact Dibralta hadn't turned up for a meeting? Mrs Colorogne came and led her husband to the dance room to gig with her. Billy was left to look at the Miami skyline which looked amazing. He sighed as the nice warm air breezed across the pool.

"So, what do you think of it, Billy," said the fiancée pointing out over Miami.

"It's very nice. Kind of like Moss Side, Manchester, with a beach!" he joked.

"Really!" said Diedre.

"So, did I do something wrong?" asked Billy.

"What do you mean?"

"In there, just now. I'd barely met those two guys with Mr Cologrone. He just whipped them away and before you knew it, they were gone."

"No. They are close business associates of Colorognes' and Terry Johns' and they knew they would leave soon. They weren't to be staying for long in the first place. That phone call or message that the manservant gave to Cologrone would probably have come from Juan Dibralta in Cancun to say he wasn't coming to see them. There is a lot that is going down right now and everyone is keeping very quiet about what is happening with the things in the Caribbean.

Everyone is nervous."

Everyone else might be keeping quiet which certainly wasn't the case with Diedre. She seemed to know just about everything.

"And what is the situation in the Caribbean? Why are they all nervous?"

"Oh, you know who is going to take over and be the big boss. You know that, Billy."

No. He didn't. Hopefully, he would soon.

"You seem to know pretty much everything and involved in their business, Terry's and Cologrone's, I mean."

"I told you before I just notice things."

"And does Terry Johns tell you everything?"

"Oh, hardly! But like I said, I do pick up on a lot of stuff. Like Terry had suggested to Cologrone that you drop off some money to some people in some of the islands for some services," she sounded like Smythe.

Terry Johns returned. "Is everything all right, honey?" she said to him.

"We'll talk about it later. Come on, let's dance." She led her 'fiancé' to the floor.

For now, Billy was left alone to enjoy the party. He played pool with a couple of Miami Dolphin players and a known Latin actor, of whom, he didn't know but he was obviously famous to everyone else, which made Billy's attraction even greater to the women present. He kept his own counsel as much as possible, but it was difficult. The women were beautiful and he was attracted to them. His unknown charm made him all the more appealing and that hadn't gone unnoticed with the two women he had previously escorted on the ship.

It wasn't the sort of territory he was used to and although everyone had seemed very friendly to him, he knew it could all turn on a dime and could become very nasty. He remained sensible.

"What is it that I am supposed to do for you?" Billy asked Terry Johns when they were alone.207

"I'm sorry?"

"What is my job with you? What have you told him I do for you? I would like to know."

"Mr Colorogne believes that you work for MI5 but you often do work on the side."

"For you?"

"Well, sometimes for me, sometimes for yourself."

"I'm like a mercenary. Is that what he thinks?"

"Look, right now, he thinks you're the 'Bee's Knees', so, don't spoil it. We have a mission to accomplish! And we want to finish it!"

"You're right. I've got to catch a plane. I'd better make for the airport. Please give my thanks to everyone."

He looked out over the skyline when a voice whispered, "Hi I'm Melanie. What are you up to?" A brunette had interrupted his thoughts.

Are all the women in Miami so gorgeous? he said to himself as they began to dance…and dance…and…

Chapter 20
Sail Away

Billy felt his vacation, albeit two days, had ended too soon. But he had a job to do. He took a cab to the airport to pick up his plane to Panama. A two-hour flight and there he passed customs and immigration to pick up his ride to his hotel.

He remembered getting into the car at the airport. The ship's agent – although now, he wasn't sure if it was the ship's legitimate agent – was waiting holding up a sign 'DOYLE' written on it. Billy introduced himself and the agent picked up his case and took him out to the car park to supposedly drive him to a hotel for that night.

It was some hours later that he got to the hotel. A man had suddenly jumped into the car and sat next to him just before it left the airport. Billy didn't have time to ask what was happening before a cloth, full of chloroform slapped across his face. The next thing he recalled was when he came around in the damp and dingy room.

That was yesterday. He'd had a quiet night at the hotel in Panama and had an uneventful ride to Gutan Lake. It was a long two-hour drive out from the city in a rickety old truck. Billy learned from the experience that traveling entertainers didn't always have the best means of transport at their disposal. Billy was left at a small flotilla dock at the water's edge and accompanied by a couple of Panamanian locals. His knowledge of the Spanish language was very limited so it was a very long hours' wait for the ship to come into view. It was a relief when it did. Billy had begun to think that if there was ever a place he was to disappear, never to be discovered again, this was it.

As it happened, the locals were there to sail him out to the ship as it passed by. They would lift him and his case aboard the ship. At first, Billy was in disbelief that this is how professional entertainers were accustomed to picking up a ship in the Panama Canal but it was a fact.

All aboard and Billy was shown to his cabin. He thought he'd certainly made an entrance as the decks were filled with passengers watching as he climbed aboard the ship.

He was made to feel more welcome aboard this ship than his previous encounter on the S/S Britannia Aries. The cruise director left him a message on his cabin phone to welcome him aboard and invite him to his office when he had the opportunity. His case arrived only minutes after he'd entered his cabin. There was a knock on the door. Billy opened it.

"Your luggage, sir." The room steward walked in, "I put it in your room, sir."

"Thanks." Billy offered him a few dollars.

"No need, sir. All taken care of, sir, pleez have a good cruise."

"Thank you," said Billy.

The room steward left. Billy closed the door behind him. Billy was tempted to check the case but only opened the closet door to make sure it was still there.

Billy left his room to search for the cruise director. "Hello, I'm Billy Doyle. I'm the comedian."

"Great, come in. Welcome aboard. Is everything okay for you?" The CD stood up to shake hands and greet him. A healthy looking young man in his early thirties greeted him.

"Err, yes thanks."

"Well, let me know if you need anything. And you're with us for four weeks after we get to Miami. Right?"

Billy nodded.

"Wonderful! Well, we're not going to put you on tonight. I've got you scheduled for Tuesday if that is okay with you. It's two shows. We have Valarie Engles, the singer, opening for you. She'll do about twenty/twenty five minutes and then you close the show with about thirty-thirty five minutes. Does that that sound okay for you?"

Is that okay for me? Billy thought. This is professionalism. How unfortunate that the standards of professionalism and concern can change so much from ship to ship. He was thinking back to the last ship.

"Yes, sure anything you like."

"Good, well, I said it will be two shows Tuesday and then a reprise show next Saturday of ten minutes if you don't mind. That's when all the entertainers do a sort of goodbye-type thing. Well, listen you just enjoy yourself. And let me know if you need anything. I'll get someone to show you around and get you acclimated as it were. Nice to meet you, Billy. Have a good time. I'll call Danny now."

Steven, the CD, paged 'Danny. Could you show Mr Doyle around the place for me?

Thanks.'

Night and day, Billy thought. *It really was Night and day.*

"Hi. Welcome aboard. I'm Danny Mason, the assistant CD. May I take you around the ship and show you what's what?"

"Please do."

Billy was given a guided tour of the ship: from the luxurious showroom to the staff dining area, to the pool, to the gym and given daily schedule and the ship's itinerary. There was also a letter welcoming him aboard given him.

Billy lay on his bed expecting some sort of disturbance, any sort of disturbance, but it never happened. He lay back watching television. The sports channel had a football game on, an American football game. He thought he recognised two of the guys playing. He was sure he'd played pool with them yesterday. Lazing on the bed, he dozed off to be awakened by the announcement that first seating dinner was being served. He'd been informed he could dine at the staff dining room so he made his way to meet some new colleagues there. He was to be as welcomed there as he had been by the cruise director in his office. He might not tell any ship jokes on this cruise.

Later, after dinner, he watched the ship's production show. There was something far more professional about the way the cruise director ran things here. The people enjoyed him. He wasn't aloof with the folks. His staff appeared very relaxed around their work. He just got the job done with the least amount of fuss. It was all a pleasant experience to be on this ship. That night he slept alone.

Chapter 21
Cartagena

Billy was up early the following morning. As soon as the ship had cleared customs and immigration, he got off the ship and took a taxi as to a street called Calle Montrez, where the sports bar was located. It was not in one of the most desirable of areas in the world, let alone Cartagena. It was still early in the day and the town hadn't woken up yet. There wasn't much traffic or people around. There were a few women sweeping outside of their homes and some young boys playing soccer on the rugged grass in this derelict part of the town, and that was it to be seen.

He found the bar he'd been told to go to. It was a street corner bar with an entrance on one side. The doors were open. Cautiously, he went in. A man, he assumed to be a barman, was slumped over the bar as was another whom he thought was a customer. He moved closer. Both men were motionless. He tapped the customer on the shoulder and the man slipped over and landed on the floor. He was stone dead as he landed on the floor. Blood oozed from his neck onto the stone floor. Billy saw that the man had had his throat cut. It was a massive cut and not from an ordinary knife.

There was no sign of a movement from the barman either because there was a machete sticking out of his side. Broken glass and broken beer bottles littered the floor behind the bar. He heard a groan from a back room. When he entered, he saw an elderly man groaning and barely alive. He was bleeding badly from his chest that bullet wounds had penetrated. Bullet holes littered the walls of the back room and the door to it. Yet the area was so quiet. The town was a hush. Maybe shootouts were the norm here and no one paid attention.

The old man's eyes watched slowly as Billy entered. Fear was dripped from them. He tried to raise the old man up on his seat. The man couldn't move. He was almost unable to talk either. He was almost dead. He pointed to the bar and uttered the name Gonzale. Gonzale was the name of the man he had met in Panama a couple of days ago when he'd been commandeered from the airport in Panama.

"Yes, Gonzale. He sent me here," said Billy. *"Tengo dinero, para usted."* (I have money for you.")

Billy lifted the wad of money that Gonzale had given him from his bag. The old man was fading fast but raised his finger and pointed to a jukebox against the bar wall. And said in broken Spanish, *"Detras la machina."* ("Behind the machine.")

Blood poured from the old man and he fell back backward into the chair and died.

Right now, Billy was in South America and he'd become involved in something very sinister. His life was more important and he needed to get out, and get out quickly. He crept around, almost expecting someone or something to suddenly jump out at him. He guessed the bar had only recently been ransacked.

Possibly someone had been looking for the drugs but he didn't know. He knew the perpetrators may return at any moment. What had disturbed them? Or had they found what they came for? Billy wanted to get out quickly.

He had no idea what he was looking for but went to the jukebox, the machine that the old man had pointed to. Maybe something would be behind the music box. He moved it from the wall. There was an old bag rammed inside the back of it. He took out the bag and found packages of wrapped cocaine. This was what he was supposed to pick up.

Police sirens sounded. They were coming down the street. He grabbed the bag and found a backdoor entrance. He ran as fast as he could down a back alleyway onto a main road. He stuffed the packet of cash that he was supposed to exchange for the drugs into the top of the bag, then threw the bag over his shoulder. People suddenly appeared all over the streets as police cars sped towards the bar. Billy ducked into a side street café that was just opening. He sat down and ordered a coffee. He pushed the bag under the table and watched the road and its activities. He needed a get-away and he needed it quickly. He didn't look like he belonged there. The police would surely soon be looking in his direction. He must get out.

A taxicab came down the road. Billy almost jumped into the road to flag it down, not knowing if it would stop for him, but it did. He jumped into the back of the cab.

"The port *por favor*," said Billy.

"*Que?*" questioned the cabbie.

"La Puerta. The boats. *Los Barcos, por favor.*"

"Ah."

The driver sped off and dropped him moments later at the port. He walked to the dockside, not having any idea how he'd get the bag and the money onboard. He thought of just dumping it, but knew the unknown contact in Miami and the one in Panama might not be too pleased at him for doing that.

He picked up his contact phone for Smythe in England and explained the situation. Smythe asked where his location was and told him to wait there for some assistance. "Someone will be there in about an hour. Just hang fast." Smythe was about to hang up, "Oh, Doyle. Get rid of this phone."

"Sir?"

"Traces. We don't want any traces back here."

"Oh, right, sir."

While he was waiting, he was watching how people behaved around the dockside area.

He was becoming quite paranoid. If the police took him in Cartagena, he'll probably soon be dead. If he upset the dealers, he'd definitely be dead. And if he got caught with the drugs on the dockside being dead would be a lot better than a lifetime in a Columbian jail.

He noticed a telephone sales booth in the port landing area. He went over and as best he could translated that he wanted to buy a telephone and one that could use to phone to the states.

The salesman's English was just as bad as his Spanish but they managed to do the sale. He was going to 'hedge his bets'. Corologne had told him to give him a call when he got back into Miami but he wasn't scheduled to be back for another three days. He didn't know if Corologne was involved. Had he set up the kidnapping in Panama and was testing him out? Either way, he had nothing to lose by contacting Colorogne. If Colorogne wasn't involved, he would probably want to be now.

His thinking was interrupted when one of the stevedores, a short Spanish guy who looked a lot cleaner than the other stevedores, came up to him.

"Mister Doyle, I take your bag on now."

Billy could only assume that Smythe had set something up for him. He didn't say a word and was nervous in case the man was working for the police or immigration. What could he do?

He wouldn't hand the bag to him because that would show a transaction was taking place, so he just pointed to the bag he was carrying that was at his feet.

The man picked up the bag and walked away. At least he wouldn't be charged with any smuggling, he thought. He watched as the man walked over to where the other stevedores were loading supplies to the ship and threw the bag into the middle of large boxes on a pallet. He watched a pallet truck pick up the pallet and drive it onto the ship by the same man. He saw the man who had taken his case to his cabin lift the bag from off the pallet and walk away.

Billy had finished his arrangement with Panama. He boarded the ship by the crew entrance and several minutes later, he found the bag on his bed in his cabin.

Smythe was efficient. That was for sure! But Billy still had to get this stuff off the ship in Miami. He went on the top deck and phoned Colorogne.

Colorogne didn't answer, but his wife did.

"Oh, 'ello Billee."

"Can I speak with Mr Colorogne, please?"

"I am very sorree, Billee, he iz 'avening a massage ahora. Can I 'elp?"

"Well, I have a little situation I think he might be able to help me with."

Just then, Colorogne came on the phone. He sounded gruff. He wasn't sure if it was because he'd been disturbed or he was concerned his wife was flirting with someone. Billy explained what had happened in Panama and the experience at the bar in Cartagena. It appeared that Colorogne didn't know anything about it but let him know he would have someone meet him at the port when the ship docked in two days' time.

"What about the drugs?"

"What about the drugs?" Billy realised he was talking on a phone that may have surveillance on the other end.

"I have a friend in Miami who works for customs. Check through with him."

The thought of being caught smuggling drugs in any country is not a sound prospect in anybody's book. He didn't like his chances of being caught in customs. *Don't get caught. If you do, you're on your own,* Smythe's words came back to him.

Remembering how Colorogne had taken his money into Miami, he hoped the same customs official would be on the dockside checking this group of passengers. Carrying a bag of cocaine and the consequences for doing so was a huge concern.

For three days, Billy contemplated how he would get the drugs off the ship in Miami. He wondered what the chances might be of passing through with the same customs official that Colorogne had when he had sailed in from England. This sort of operation was new to him. He was new to Miami and he was new to drug smuggling.

The shows had helped pass the time a little. He'd not thought much about them but had just performed them with as much enthusiasm as was necessary. He had other things on his mind, and to be caught smuggling could have dire consequences. A million thoughts were racing in his mind for three days until the ship docked in Miami.

Billy had to take the chance though. He disembarked with a group of passengers on the Miami port day. He took a customs declaration from the purser's desk onboard and filled it out.

Then he thought to take another form. He wrote in big letters the name 'COLOROGNE' on the second form.

When he came upon the customs official, whom he thought was Colorogne's associate, he handed him the first declaration he had filled out. The official looked at it and said, "What's in the bag?"

Billy almost panicked that the bag might be searched. He reached to his pocket and pulled out the other form, "Oh, just a moment, sir." Billy handed him the second paper with the name on it, "Sorry sir." The official looked at and read Colorogne's name and said,

"Okay, have a nice day," and signalled for him to go through.

"I have a taxi for Doyle," shouted a man as Billy walked out of the customs building. The man took Billy to a car and carried the bag for him.

The man had barely opened the trunk when two men hustled the man into the trunk of his car with the bag. They then jumped into the car and ushered Doyle into it. They drove away, one driving and one in the back seat. "We're going to see Mr Colorogne. He is expecting you," the driver said. After his abduction at Panama Airport, he was apprehensive about his new companions and kept an eye out for another chloroform attack. Some fifteen minutes later, he was in Coral Gables.

==========

"My darling Billee, 'ow are you?" said Mrs Colorogne as enticing as ever, as she greeted him.

"Come in Billy. Good to see you," shouted Colorogne from the palacious living room.

"And you too, Mr Colorogne. Quite a relief to be back, I might say." The two men shook hands.

Terry Johns entered from the swimming pool. He escorted his beautiful assistant who had just been swimming into the room.

"So, you had a little inconvenience I hear?" said Terry Johns.

"Somewhat."

"Well, you iz safe 'ere now. Zat is dee important thing." Colorogne's wife handed him a mimosa.

"Quite."

"So, do you know what it was all about?" asked Terry Johns.

"I was hoping someone here might be able to tell me," he said.

"Soon, I'm hoping, soon," said Colorogne.

As he spoke, one of Colorogne's servants came to the poolside and indicated that the driver wished to speak with him. Colorogne walked over to the driver.

"So you join another ship?" inquired Terry Johns' assistant. Would that the two men knew he had bedded both of their mistresses? What would happen?

"Actually, I've already joined. I picked the ship up in Panama. I'm on the Meridian Star for four weeks. I'm looking forward to that. I've never been to Mexico and Aruba. It should be fun."

"Hopefully not as much fun as you've had recently, though," Terry Johns smiled.

Colorogne returned to the room, "Well, it seems it was all nothing my friend. It appears some people wanted to set up their own business on the side. But they didn't think about that they might be interrupting already established business. They do now!"

"How do you mean it was all nothing?" asked Terry Johns' girlfriend.

"Well, it has all been taken care of, or it all will soon be taken care of. Some people should not get involved in other people's business."

"Certainly not," said the girlfriend. Billy thought again, what the heck was she doing there? She was too presumptuous and she obviously knew about the situation; well, they all did.

Cologne must have told Terry Johns after Billy's phone call to him and that was why he was there and he would have told his girlfriend.

"Anyway, the situation has been taken care of. No one else will be doing that in the future, that is for sure."

The other man who had picked up Billy in walked in with the old bag.

"And you have a supply of coke and some money?"

"Yes, that is true. Now we can all relax."

"Well, I would love to stay, but I have to get back to work." Billy was inferring that he had to return to the Meridian Star.

"Doing shows on the ship is work?" snubbed Diedre.

"The very best sort of work," replied Billy.

"And the most exacting," supported Terry Johns.

"Oh, no, you can't leave, Mister Billee. You just got here," said Mrs Cologne.

"I'm very sorry, but I must."

"Very well, my boy. You goes. I knows too dat you have a busy scheduled ahead of you, so I sees you soon." Cologne was referring to Billy's job of passing money off to the arranged contact in the islands. He handed Billy an envelope. He assumed it to be the addresses where he was to make money drop offs on his next voyage.

Billy would have liked to have stayed. He was relieved that the pressure of getting the drugs through customs in the morning was all over and that fortunately he hadn't been stopped coming back into Miami and avoided any consequences. Except now, he had similar escapades ahead of him in that he had to make payments to Cologne's associates. It was something else that needed consideration.

"Are you sure you 'ave to go, my Billee?"

"I'm sorry. I do."

"Vell, perhaps we take you to the ship. Diedre and I are going shopping aren't we, my dear, and we can put you at da ship."

"Yes, we could do that," said Diedre. "You could always come shopping with us too."

"Thank you, but no."

"Okay, my dear. Billee does not want us to be around. So, you and I, we go."

"I'm on my way!" Diedre got up to leave with Mrs Cologne. She'd wrapped a bathing dress around her. Mrs Cologne helped her. The two women appeared a lot more friendly than they had at the Captain 'Roberto's' dinner party.

The two women addressed their goodbyes to the gentlemen and left.

"Okay. I'll be off then. I'll be in touch within the week."

"Oh, before you leave, if you pleez, I vill text to you details of what you are to achieve is in da envelope and do dis week."

"That will be good."

"Okay. Sergio, my driver, will take you back to da ship. If dere is anywhere you need to go on da way, just you tell him and he take you. Next time, Mister Doyle." The two men shook hands. Terry Johns stood up to acknowledge him a safe trip.

Chapter 22

So I Was On This Cruise Ship, When ...

The Meridian Star was all set to sail for its Western Caribbean itinerary. It was planned to do an Eastern Caribbean cruise one week and a Western Caribbean cruise the second week. This week the ship was to take in Cancun, Aruba, Curacao and the Bahamas. The first stop was the Bahamas and they were due to dock early the following morning.

Billy wasn't scheduled to work until the night after that when they would have spent half the day in Curacao. Billy's plan was to check out Frederick Dietz address early after they had docked in Curacao. He was hoping that he would complete his mission in two weeks when the ship would repeat the same schedule. For the first evening's cruise, Billy had a couple of martinis in one of the lounges and listened to the trio. They were very good and the music was very pleasant. He had never visited any of these exotic ports but was keen to explore them.

His plan was to survey the land and then make a plan to succeed at his mission. He knew he would work alone and no one would be around to assist him. He also knew that he had to cover all his steps. For instance, he told himself, if there was any sort of inquiry, nothing must link him to any wrongdoing. If he were to take a cab to one of the destinations, police investigation might lead back to him through the cab driver or drivers. The fact that he might give a designated instruction, as to where to go that the usual passenger didn't go to, might be incriminating.

Still, he would need transport to get him to the places. He could hire a car but that could give a possible trace back to him. The only place to get a cab would be outside the port, where passengers had been dropped at their destinations or were on their way back to the port to pick up more trade. Even this could lead to some identification.

It was while he was walking around the straw market in Nassau that he saw a group of people, passengers probably from another ship, riding around on scooters. That would be what he will do. He'll find the nearest bike shop and hire a scooter when they get to Curacao. If he could, he'd do it with a group. And he would use a scooter for his transport.

And that is exactly what he did, the day after, when they were docked in Curacao. In broken Spanish and English with a little French thrown in, he mingled with a handful of people and bartered for a scooter. The people couldn't tell where he was from, especially when he paid for five scooters in cash. No one complained. And he got the other guys to sign up for everything. All he did was pay for the party.

He had already mapped his route to Frederick Dietz's place before he got off the ship. It should only be a twenty-minute ride. He set off following where his co-riders were going and then veered off in the direction of Dietz's place. While on his computer, he had also checked out Dietz. Dr Frederick J. Dietz was a renowned surgeon and noted for his work on facial reconstruction. His wife was a general practitioner.

It took less than twenty minutes to ride over to the doctor's place. The cool ocean breeze hindered the heat from burning his white face as he pulled up towards the large house.

He carried on driving past it when he saw a number of policemen running into the home.

The police outside looked to be questioning what looked like bodyguards who presumably worked at the home. Billy stopped for a while to see if he could see what was going on.

"Excuse me. sir, I'm sorry but you can't stop there. You'll have to move on," said a young police officer.

"Oh. Sure. Sorry, Officer. What is going on?" Billy faked an American accent. It wasn't a good one but hopefully it might have fooled the young officer.

"A police investigation, sir,"

Billy saw two body bags being carried to an ambulance on the driveway.

"Wow! Somebody dead! Who's dead?" asked Billy.

"I can't say, sir. Please move on." The officer was called over presumably by a senior officer and ran over to the other side of the driveway. He and another policeman guided the ambulance out of the driveway and onto the road so it could drive off. As it did, other officers closed the gate and began to put yellow 'Do not cross Police' tape up around the house.

Billy made it look like he was about to leave on his scooter. He needed to find out more.

An old car pulled up outside the gate and Billy watched as a little chubby man, probably in his early forties got out. He spoke with a strange accent, probably an island type of accent, as he showed a card to a policeman and asked if he could go inside.

"No. This is a police matter. I'm not to let anyone in."

"Well, can you tell me what's happened?" asked the man.

"You'll have to read about it in the papers."

"But I am the press, Antoine. You know that."

"I also know I'm not allowed to let you in, even if you are my cousin!"

"Well, give me something, Antoine. You're like my brother for fucks' sake! I got a call that there's been some shooting. Is that right?"

"Yes."

"Is it the doctor?"

"Yes. It's the doctor. It's the doctor and his wife. Mr and Mrs Dietz. That's all I can tell you, you're going to have to go. I'll see you at dinner tonight."

"And they've been shot?"

The policeman looked over his shoulder to see none of his superiors were watching him talk to the cousin.

"Yes. They were shot. Dr and his wife are dead."

"Got the gun?"

"Yes. We got the gun and a wallet was left with someone's driving license in it and some cards. That is all they have so far." A senior officer was walking in their direction, "You gotta go. Quick, scoot away!"

"Thanks, Antoine. See you at dinner."

Billy had heard the conversation and thought it best if he disappeared. He motored on his scooter in the opposite direction and made back towards the port. He pulled his cap back down over his face and kept his sunglasses on as he handed one of the operatives the machine. He pretended he was going to use the bathroom and would return to sign for the scooter but made a getaway through the front door when some people came in the shop.

No one would have recognised Billy. Once back onboard and checked his pass into the ship's officer on the gangway, he discarded his cap into a trashcan and put the sunglasses into his pocket. He took off his shirt and put on a different one and went up to the pool deck, dropping the shirt onto a lounge chair and went to the bar for a coffee.

Billy sat in a sun lounger and surveyed the few people that had stayed onboard the ship and contemplated what had just happened. So, the first of his potential assassinations had been taken care of, but not by him. Whose driving license was in the wallet? Why had Dietz and his wife been killed and by whom? Would he find out?

"Everything okay, Mr Doyle?" said the cruise director, strolling around Billy's deck chair.

"Yes, thanks. What about you?"

"Perfect. Beautiful day, isn't it?"

"Isn't it just? People would kill for days like these." If only the cruise director knew exactly what he was saying at that moment. "Are you not going ashore today?"

"No, thought I would just idle around the ship."

No need to tell anybody anything, he thought.

"Enjoy it. See you later."

"You too."

Billy recalled what Smythe had told him about being a successful agent slash assassin:

"First and foremost, there is no right or wrong." There was no time for the usual training that agents or assassins were given, Smythe had informed him. All the training he got was from a couple of bits he'd been left from a brief lecture at what used to be the Saxon Restaurant back home in Manchester. "In our business, you must erase every trace, become anonymous and leave nothing behind." Doyle thought he had done that.

"Remember," Smythe had told him, "don't take an interest in people outside of work."

He didn't think he'd done that really, but maybe? No. He wasn't serious about any of his female encounters. "There is no such thing as trust," his boss had told him.

Now, that is true, thought Doyle. *I don't even trust my boss.*

Chapter 23
Again?

Billy did a forty-minute show that evening. It didn't go as well as he hoped but for the most part it was acceptable.

"I couldn't tell what he said," said one old lady to her husband as they were leaving the showroom.

"I thought he was very funny," said her husband.

"Well, you would. I don't like it when people make jokes about women."

"I didn't hear him say any jokes about women."

"What about when he said, his wife asked the minder if she could hire the donkey and the donkey minder said, 'Yes, there's a little screw under the saddle'?"

"That wasn't about women?"

"No!"

"No, oh I thought it was."

"No."

"Well, I guess I liked him then. I did like the singer. She was good. She should have sung longer."

"She had nice legs."

"You were supposed to be listening to her voice, not looking at her legs."

"I couldn't help it! She had really long legs."

"That's you, that is. Let's go to the midnight buffet. What time is the midnight buffet," and they both laughed as they walked towards the dining room.

Billy was right behind them as they walked down the stairs and had a chuckle. He wasn't going to the buffet too. He'd had a long day and was tired. He had to get ready for Aruba the following morning.

============

Billy had only met Frederick Dietz and Beauchamp for a few moments at Cologne's party. He didn't like either gentlemen, but then he hardly knew them. He thought them to be obnoxiously quiet, almost to the point of being rude. They didn't trust anyone. That was probably the reason why they had been in business for so long, Terry Johns' fiancée, Diedre, had informed him. They were link up men with the Messilican Syndicate in South America. Though many had tried, no one had been able to do away with them. Probably being middlemen had offered them protection in the US from Colorogne and from the big boys in the cartel.

They ruled their businesses with an iron hand. Their employees more than likely worked for them out of fear rather than any other sort of allegiance. There were always people that surrounded them and a slight lapse in security would mean death to anyone who hadn't avoided any sort of situation.

Beauchamp was originally from the island of Aruba, Antilles. His main headquarters were at his home in San Ferlini in Aruba but he also had a place in St Thomas in the Virgin Islands. He had been head of the bank there for a number of years now.

Frederick Dietz and his wife were native residents of the Antilles but originally came from the French island of Mystique in the Caribbean. Both were doctors but had their hand in so many different types of business. They were popular in this part of the world.

Juan Dibralta was quite different. He was a quiet but evil man. He could have dinner with guests while having someone tortured in a back room. Rumour had it that he'd even had someone roasted alive and then served them to his guests as a special delicacy. He had no feeling for anyone and enjoyed a reputation for being evil. His mansion, off the coast of Cancun, was supposed to be impenetrable and heavily guarded. Very few people were ever invited as guests and even fewer left his property.

His visit to Colorogne's party would have been an extremely rare occurrence. He was a very cold and very private person. Beauchamp and Dibralta had been invited to Colorogne's to discuss expanding the business and were due for further discussions with the cartel. But he didn't show up at the party.

Only a fool would think the power track from the cartel could be shifted but there was plenty of room to manoeuvre and there was money for everyone. Still even at this grand level, egos came into play and no matter how much it could be denied, everyone wanted to be boss, except Colorogne. Unlike most gangsters, Colorogne really did not enjoy his position. It was something he had grown into out of necessity as a young man. He grew up very poor and had just wanted to provide for his family and one situation had just lead to another until one day he found himself running a very large business that he was unable to get out of.

Though Colorogne seems to have gotten into the middle of something, he never wanted to be involved in and now he was at the centre of all operations and was trusted by all the major players. No one seemed to know when, but a meeting was to be scheduled of all the major players soon. The boss of the cartel was stepping down and wanted to appoint a new charge and avoid a scramble for power between rival sources once he did. Dibralta wanted the position, but because of his loyalty, the trustworthy Colorogne was favourite for the job.

In the meantime, Billy had still had two assignments to carry out. Why he did not know, but that wasn't what he was paid to know. He just had two people to kill Beauchamp and Dibralta. Dietz was already dead.

As he got off the ship early in the morning, he decided to walk to a nearby hotel where he would hire a taxi to take him to Beauchamp's place. It was a relatively modest place, quite unusual for someone in his position. Beauchamp was a local politician in Aruba. It was almost a family position that he inherited from his father. Everyone in Aruba knew him but no one knew that his sideline was that of shipping drugs from Columbia to South Florida. His family had owned a number of bars and brothels on the far side of the island and he'd been left them when the family passed away.

Business was good all around for Beauchamp. He was shrewd and was a good man for the cartel. Of late, he'd been taking his money from Aruba and investing it in property in South Florida in the form of several of the large hotels and condos that were shooting up in Central Miami.

Billy got a taxi from the hotel to Beauchamp's place. It was located at San Ferlani on the outer west bank of the island. There were no guards around the house. Maybe there was a security camera system. As he walked around the house from the beach side, he could see a man, whom he thought to be his target, sitting at a dining table and eating.

An elderly lady served him breakfast. Billy climbed through the garden to get closer. He knelt down to observe. As he did, a pistol rested against his temple. He turned to knock the gun away but as he did a rifle was pointing directly at the other side of his head.

Two men lead Billy into the house. He had no choice but to follow as directed.

"Ah, Mister Doyle, I think it is, if I'm not mistaken."

Billy nodded.

"Yes, we met at Senor Colorogne's house last week, if I recall. Please join me. So what brings you out to Aruba? You know you didn't have to sneak around the back to get in. I do have a front door. You know what a front door is. It isn't a new invention. You knock on it or ring the bell and sometimes someone opens it for you to enter. Quite ingenious, really, don't you think?"

His sarcasm was wasted. All the time he spoke he kept reading the paper. "Come, Mister Doyle, sit down and have some breakfast. Come, come."

Billy did as requested or rather as he was told. The old lady poured him coffee. Her dark skin showered a hardened face with lines that spread like an old dividivi trees that adorned the beach ahead of them. "You like breakfast?" she said.

"Of course he would. Bring him a full breakfast."

Billy knew Beauchamp's hospitality was only temporary. He was in a situation and he wasn't sure how he would get out of it. Beauchamp waved his minders away and folded his paper.

What could Billy do to save the situation? There were probably other minders that were secluded so it didn't look viable to suddenly make a bolt for the door and run. He wouldn't disclose his intentions and reasons for being at his home, although Beauchamp had probably guessed.237

"So, tell me, Mister Doyle, why are you here? Did Colorogne send you?"

"No. I—"

"You came of your own accord? And the reason for your unexpected visit is?"

Billy didn't say anything. He was dumbstruck.

"Have you come to kill me, Mister Doyle?" He put his newspaper down on the table.

"People seem to come by a lot these days for that reason. Why, I don't know?"

A car pulling up in the driveway was heard through the open windows. "Ah, a friend of yours is here to visit also. That's good. I seem to be very popular this morning. They're early too, which is good."

Two more minders, appearing from nowhere, were in the hallway. They went out through the front door. Beauchamp was expecting the visitor.

The old lady brought breakfast to the table and placed it down for Doyle.

"Thank you, Maria. I have to leave shortly Mister Doyle, but I would like you to not be hungry. How you say, 'It is never good to die on an empty stomach. Eat up'." Beauchamp laughed.

A gunshot hit Maria as she turned to go to the kitchen. Beauchamp got up, pulling a gun from his lap under the table as he did. But he wasn't quick enough to return fire and two bullets hit him through the chest. He went down, motionless in an instant. Another shot fired, this time directly towards Doyle who dropped down onto to the floor to miss it.

It barely missed him. Doyle heard the shot as the bullet flew passed his ear. He grabbed hold of Beuchamp's gun that had fallen to the floor and fired in the direction of the gun peering around the corner of the hallway. He couldn't see who was firing at him, just a hand in a glove holding a gun.

Another bullet missed him and ricocheted off a stone pillar. He moved around the floor consistently firing towards the hallway as he did. He dropped behind the couch for shelter. He waited, hoping he could get a full view of the shooter to return fire. Whoever it was not going to show themselves. Doyle lay behind the couch as the shooter took the moment to leave.

Realising whoever it was leaving, Doyle ran after them. Two minders lay on the floor dead in the doorway and the car, a mustang convertible, sped off as quickly as it had arrived.

Who was it who'd come in shooting? Obviously someone Doyle knew but who? They were gone and away. Doyle saw a passport on the driveway. It was a passport belonging to Terry Johns. *So Terry Johns was the shooter?* He thought he should pick it up but didn't.

Time to get out, he thought. He was thinking he might take one of the fancy cars but that might cause too much attention to him if he did. He picked up a bicycle that was leaning against a wall and peddled off in the direction of the hotel. Not for long though, because the car that sped off was coming back in his direction and it was speeding directly at him. There was no traffic on the road. In fact, nobody was around as the Mustang sailed straight in his direction. He could see it getting faster and faster towards him.

He hit a brick or a curbside, he couldn't tell. He didn't have time to check. Either way, his bike was jolted and it threw him high in the air. He landed under a dividivi tree and the car sped past him.

The car stopped yards away and made a quick U-turn. He could see it was going to come at him again. He lifted himself up and began to run through the sand. Fortunately, a school bus came into view and he ran in its direction. The driver must have seen the bus and thought better to just drive away.

So, someone wanted him dead? Who? Could it be Terry Johns? Terry Johns' passport was on the driveway. Doyle made his way to the ship as best he could on a trashed bicycle. More people were in view as he closed in on the hotels and the port area. He'd had enough for one day and spent the rest of it on the pool deck sunbathing with the occasional margarita.

So far, two of his assignments had been killed, but not by him. Something was very strange but he could not work out what it was.

Chapter 24

Just a Few Questions

Billy was about to get ready for dinner when there was a knock on his cabin door interrupted him. Opening it, he found his room steward and a policeman.

"Mr Doyle, the captain wants you to go to his cabin please."

"What's it about?" He looked at the Aruban policeman, "This looks like it might be serious."

"He just wants for you to go to his cabin," said the room steward.

"Okay. Let me just put my shirt on." He guessed the policeman was there as an escort, too.

"Mr Doyle, this is Inspector Bourgois of the Aruban police force," were the words that the captain greeted him with as they entered his quarters. Billy shook hands with the gentleman in a shirt and tie. "That will be all, Manuel," the captain signalled for the room steward to leave their company.

"Mr Doyle, this is Inspector Bourgois of the Aruban Police Department," the captain continued to speak, "Well, Inspector, perhaps I'd better let you take it from here."

"*Merci,* Capitan," said the inspector, walking forward. The other policeman, who had accompanied Doyle from his cabin, stood by the doorway. "Senor Doyle, we have 'ad a couple of incidents on our islands and we would like to ask you a few questions."

"Certainly. Anything I can do. What is it?"

"Yesterday in Curacao, there was a murder. It 'appened when the ship was in port. Where wus you when da ship was docked?"

"I think I was on the ship. It's always pleasant onboard when the passengers are ashore. Very quiet. You know, I enjoy the peace and quiet."

"You were onboard all da time?"

"No. I believe I got off to walk around for an hour or so, shortly after we docked. Just around the docking area. It was very hot, I remember that. I had a show last night and I didn't want to get tired. So, I believe, after I had walked around the port area I then came back onboard the ship."

"Did you go anywhere near Mount Crescent or that vicinity?"

"I'm sorry I don't know where that is. This is my first time in this part of the world."

Billy knew that was where Mr and Mrs Dietz had died, but he wasn't going to let the police inspector know he knew of it. To the best of Billy's knowledge, no one had seen him and it would be highly unlikely that anyone could have recognised his riding the scooter. "Never leave a trace!" Smythe had told him.

"Can I ask what this is all about?"

"Monsieur Mount Crescent is where Mr and Mrs Dietz live. Do you know those people?"

"No, I don't. Should I?"

"I'm not sure."

"Dr Dietz and his wife, they are doctors in Curacao. He is, and his wife, are, I'm sorry to say, they are dead. There was an incident there and they are both dead."

"And that is why you're questioning me?"

"*Qui, monsieur.*"

"But I wasn't anywhere where I would have seen a murder, if that is what you are asking me?" Billy was trying to work out why the police had been led to him.

"We did find a driver's license."

"I don't think it was mine."

"Why do you say that?"

"Because I have mine here with me. Here." Billy took out his wallet and showed the inspector his documents. "Here's my crew pass too."

"And your passport?"

"The purser's office have that. They took it when I checked onboard when I first joined the ship."

"No, Monsieur, it was not your driving license."

"Well, whose was it?"

"Do you know a Monsieur Terry Johns?"

Billy thought the inspector might be trying to catch him out with a mistake. Perhaps he could have been arrested for the dismissal of Beauchamp had he done the deed. What was going on, he wondered.

"Er, no, can't say that I do. Who is he?" If he wasn't supposed to reveal his identity under investigation, he was pretty sure he wasn't supposed to reveal one that belonged to somebody else or their information.

"He is an Englishman," said the inspector.

"Well, I too am from England and I do know a lot of Englishmen, but this one err 'Terry Johns', did you say? I don't know him."

"Terry Johns."

"Terry Johns? No, I can't say that I do know him."

"Apparently, you sailed on a cruise with him."

"I did?"

"The Britannia Aries that did a transatlantic crossing from Southampton in England to Miami. It happened about a week or two ago."

"Sorry, I may have met the gentleman, but I don't recall. I meet a lot of people. Inspector, what has all this to do with me?"

"We found your boarding ticket with Terry Johns' driver's license at Mount Crescent.

"That is why we are questioning you now. Do you know how your boarding ticket to Britannia Aires happened to be with Terry Johns' driver's license yesterday?" Billy hadn't noticed the ticket when he left the license.

"I'm sorry, I don't know, I have no idea." Someone was setting him up and it was probably the same person who killed the banker Beauchamp that morning. But who and why?

In his mind, he was trying to work out a series of things. Only Smythe back in England would know he might have been to Mount Crescent. Only Colorogne, Terry Johns and possibly Diedre in the US would know that and what his intentions were. Although, Colorogne wouldn't know he intended to do the killings. He couldn't imagine any of them setting him up. Still, he was new to this sort of game. Was he being used as some sort of fall guy? No one to trust. "Don't trust anyone," was another of Smythe's advisory bits.

Did Smythe confide with Terry Johns what he had planned for him? If he had confided, what would Terry Johns have gained by killing Beauchamp? And Terry Johns would not have been so careless as to leave his driving license on the scene of a crime. Speaking of which, the police inspector hadn't mentioned the shooting in Aruba yet. No sooner said,

"Well, I have some more questions for you, Monsieur." The inspector looked right into Doyle's eyes.

Doyle returned the look at the inspector firmly at his face, inferring he had nothing to hide.

"This morning we had an incident here on this island, Aruba, where another man, actually a permanent resident of Aruba was killed."

"Two men are dead in two days?" Billy looked surprised, even shocked.

"Well, dere are more than that?"

"Pardon?"

"Let me come to that. It appears there was some sort of shoot-out at Monsieur Donald Beauchamp's home this morning. Monsieur Beauchamp was our minister of finance as well as head of the bank here. We haven't done any blood work or finger printing yet, but we would like you to come with us."

Billy knew he mustn't get off the ship and be incarcerated in Aruba. It could take some time to get it all cleared up with the authorities.

"Look, I understand your situation but I'm supposed to be working. Just to leave the ship on some sort of wild goose chase isn't going to achieve anything." Doyle pondered the thought to the inspector.

"Were you at 'Mount Crescent' yesterday morning?"

"I don't know where that is. Where is it?"

"It is zee 'ome of Doctor and Mrs Dietz. Were you dere yesterday morning?" Billy knew again, they had no evidence to link him to the shoot out today, or the murders of Dietz and his wife yesterday. Even so, he was beginning to feel uncomfortable.

"Don't know it. I do not know of the gentleman or the place where he lives."

The inquiry was beginning to get tiresome. "Look, I'm hired to work on this ship. I have a show to do. If I come with you, I won't be able to do the show. If I don't do the show, I don't get paid. I'm sorry some people are dead. But it's not my fault they are dead. You have no reason to take me from my place of work without an arrest warrant and there is no reason I should be arrested."

"We're not arresting you, Monsieur. We just want you to help us with our inquiries," said the inspector. He walked around the room for a moment to recollect his thoughts.

"It's getting late. I'm sure the ship will be sailing soon. If I come with you now, I'll miss the ship and not work and not get paid. Are you going to pay me for missing my show and apologise to the passengers if I do miss the show?"

"Mr Doyle is right, Inspector," interrupted the captain. "You really shouldn't be taking any of my crew off the ship without just cause. If you like, you or any of your other inspectors are welcome to cruise with us to follow up on your inquiries. I will just have to contact the home office to let them know the situation."

"No. No, you are right, Captain." Doyle could sense the inspector didn't have anything to connect Doyle to their inquiries, other than his boarding pass from the Britannia Aries and that wasn't much at the moment.

"You sail to Mexico, now, is that right, Captain?"

"Yes. We have a day at sea and dock at Cancun at 8:00 am the following morning."

"Perhaps we can follow-up then. Mr Doyle will not be leaving the ship while we are at sea," he smiled. "And can I ask that Mr Doyle, he stay on your ship when you get to Cancun?"

"I see no problem with that, do you, Mr Doyle?"

"No, Captain." Was he to disagree?

"Okay. I will let you know if different, but I may be visiting to see Mr Doyle again in Cancun. Till then, you keep him here, please."

Doyle knew he could probably argue the matter, but there seemed little reason to.

The inspector and the policeman left the captain's office. Billy Doyle was about to do the same.

"Oh, Mr Doyle, may I have a word please?" Once the room had cleared except for Doyle and the captain, he moved up to Doyle. "Mr Doyle, I don't know if you are involved in this mess or not, but I really do not take kindly to this sort of happening on my ship. It does not look good for the company when we have police inquiries and it certainly doesn't do me any good. If you are involved in anything, I want it to stop right now. The inspector asked to see your passport, which I had brought from the purser's office. It is over there right now on my desk. If you are involved in something that you shouldn't be, when I turn around, I suggest you grab your passport and jump ship and run for it.

"I would prefer reporting that to the authorities here than to sort things out with Miami and the company there. Otherwise, you stay on the ship until the police come back to see you in Mexico. Is that understood?"

The captain turned to walk out to his deck and look down a get prepared for the ship to set sail.

Doyle left the office, leaving his passport on the captain's desk. He rushed to his cabin to get his phone and called Smythe to see what was going on.

"You pick the damndest time to call me, Doyle. What do you need?"

"Sorry, sir. I know that there is the time difference but I wanted to clear some things with you." Doyle explained to Smythe that he'd gone to do the job at Mount Crescent yesterday and what had happened there and then told him of the shootout today in Aruba.

"And you're just letting me know this, now?"

"Well, I was just going to see how things worked out first. And, well, actually there's more."

"And what is that?"

Doyle then went into the full story of the police coming to the ship and asking him to stay onboard when the ship docked in Cancun and that he thought there might be a possibility of him being arrested.

The sound of the ship getting ready to leave the port of Miami and the horn blowing was almost drowning out his conversation.

"I doubt that is going to happen, but it could hold things up. Give me a call after you're spoken with the police in Cancun and see what progresses from there. Doyle, keep me informed. I'll check on things from my end."

"Sir, before you go. I need to ask you what exactly does Terry Johns know about my business out here."

"Well, he knows that you're working for us and that you needed the connection to Colorogne and anyone else out there. He knows you had work to do for us and with you cruising around the islands, he would pretty much know what you were up to out there. I don't believe he would know you were out there to kill anybody, why?"

"Why would his driving license have been left at Frederick Dietz's house together with a copy of my boarding pass for the Britannia Aires?"

"I can't answer that. I had better let him know."

"No. Don't do that. Let me see what happens in the next few days."

"Well, I'm sure he will have a visit from the police soon. He should be warned what to expect."

"Give me until I've talked to the police again in Cancun."

"It kind of puts a kibosh on your plans for now, I'm guessing," said Smythe.

"Not sure. Already got two down, even if I didn't have anything to do with either."

"You don't think someone is setting you up, do you?" Smythe queried. "It sure sounds like it."

"I'd wondered about that. You don't think Terry Johns did the killings and negligently left his driving license at the scene? Do you?"

"I doubt it. He's not that sort of person to be so negligent. No, I think the driving license and your boarding card were left by someone to incriminate him. In fact, probably to incriminate the two of you. But I'm not sure why someone would do that. In fact, you'd better get rid of this phone as soon as we've finished talking now. Don't want any traces and that. Don't worry though, I'll get another one to you."

The two talked for a good twenty minutes more and everything was just as vague and unsolved as when Doyle had first called him. Doyle left the conversation feeling frustrated.

Smythe had told him he would see what he could do back home, but to just 'play dumb' when the police returned.

There was nothing to be done in the interim. Doyle took the phone and threw it in the ocean as the ship sailed out of the harbour and out to sea. Then he went to his cabin to dress in his evening clothes. There was nothing to be done for now except just relax and enjoy the cruise. He had a couple of nights off before he was supposed to work again.

========

"I have to tell you, Monsieur, that we are still concerned as to why your boarding pass to the Britannia Aries ship was found at the death scene of Dr and his wife? And, we would like to know why you say you 'ave no connection with Terry Johns?"

"Because I don't!"

Billy was having his breakfast at the open deck café when the police inspector walked over to disturb him. The ship had just docked in Cancun and it hadn't yet been cleared for the passengers to leave.

"Monsieur, I think you knows something and you are not telling me. I am informed that I cannot take you back to Aruba for any questioning until I have further information. Will you walk with me awhile please?"

Billy left his breakfast table and the two men were strollied along the deck. They stopped when the police inspector halted and looked down at passengers walking down the gangplank to a tender boat to take them ashore in Cancun. The early morning sun was still rising, readily inviting the hot day that was ahead. *The policeman must have gotten up very early to take the police boat over from Aruba to Cancun*, thought Doyle. It was no vacation for the inspector. He knew something was afoot. Doyle was convinced the detective had to know that Dietz and Beauchamp were involved in things other than banking and the medical profession and local politics.

"I've told you all I know, Inspector," said Doyle.

"I will need to talk to you again, I'm sure. We do need to solve why your boarding pass was at Mount Crescent. It is a problem that concerns me."

"I have no idea, sir."

"No. Perhaps you don't. But I am sure you know something that will be of help to us. Maybe I will talk with you again later today. I have to see someone in Cancun today, while I am here. Actually, 'is name is Monsieur Juan Dibralta. Do you knows the gentleman?"

"Can't say I do, Inspector. Who is he?"

Doyle knew exactly who he was.

"Monsieur Dirbalta is a business man, of sorts. He lives in that house over there." The inspector pointed to a large house on a very small island in the ocean way.

"That looks like a castle more than a house!"

"Indeed, it does appear to be some sort of fortress. And you don't know 'im?"

"No, I don't. I just said I don't."

Billy was not going to admit his name had been mentioned at Cologrone's home a few nights ago, nor admit that he had plans was to kill him.

"I really am sorry I can't help you, Inspector. I am as ignorant of this whole situation as you are."

"I do not knows about that, Monsieur. Well, anyway, we are going over to see Monsieur Dibralta now." Billy wondered how the inspector had gotten Dibralta's name involved in the inquiry. "Mr Doyle, I need to ask you to stay on the ship. I know I will have more questions for you soon. I go now."

The conversation was very quickly interrupted just as it was finishing. A massive explosion blew up at the fortress. The two gentlemen watched as flames flowed into the air from Dibralta's home. Suddenly, there was another explosion and passengers screamed as did many local inhabitants. Doyle thought he saw a rocket sail across the sky to the fortress before the second explosion. From his military experience, Doyle thought the air missiles to be rockets equipped with explosive warhead. Everyone saw a motor boat speed away into the ocean.

Perhaps the rocket came from the motor boat.

"I 'ave to go, Monsieur. You will be 'ere because I need to talk to you. Later!"

Doyle watched the inspector run down the stairwell and through the doors. Moments later, he ran down the gangway and jumped onto the awaiting police boat which sped in the direction of Dibralta's home.

Billy was just as unaware of what had just transpired as the inspector was. Once again, there was nothing he could presently do. That is, other than to finish his bacon and eggs from the buffet.

=========

The police inspector didn't return to the ship that day. Billy just assumed that he had other things, other than a preliminary inquiry that was going nowhere, to attend to.

Although he had never been to Mexico, Billy thought it best to do as told and stay on the ship. Should Dibralta have escaped the explosions, which seemed unlikely, he now knew where he lived and if necessary would take care of the business he was hired to do in the near future.

He also had a show to put together for the farewell show the following evening. He listened to passengers talk about the explosions until later in the day. Different stories were spreading around quickly. "It was a movie that was being made!"

"Drug wars. That's what it was. Happens every day in Mexico!"

"It's the start of a civil war down here!!! They haven't had one in a while. Last one was when the Union Army were down here!"

"It was a party that went wrong. Glad I wasn't invited."

Chapter 25

Well, That Was a Short Cruise!

After the second show, he was on his way to his cabin and was stopped by the cruise director.

"I'm sorry about this, Billy," said Steven, "but I have to inform him that you are to disembark in St Thomas in the morning." No one was around to hear the conversation on the stairwell. "The company thought it might be best to fly you to Miami from the Virgin Islands."

The cruise director was very awkward in his reasoning. After all, he knew little if anything about what was going on.

"It's nothing to do with your shows, Billy. They were great. The company just feels uncomfortable about the present situation and the police being involved. They feel it might reflect something with the passengers and they don't want to risk it. When the ship's agent boards first thing tomorrow, he will have your flight ticket and take you to the airport. I'm sorry about this."

Billy felt he had been fired. He understood, though, but never expected it. He was also relieved that he would soon be away from circumstances he seemed to have little or no control of. He wanted to get back to Miami to find out exactly what was going down. He also knew to expect the unknown.

There was no shipping agent to meet him at Miami International Airport when he arrived.

He carried his suitcase from baggage claim. He had all but forgotten that it still had Cologrone's payment money in it. He carried it thought the gate and was making for the taxi stand. He wasn't stopped for inspection.

"I have a taxi for you, Mister Doyle. Come with me."

The man took the case and Billy followed. The case landed in the back seat.

"Get in!" commanded the man.

Billy just went with the flow. The car raced from the airport. Billy recognised where they were going. They hit I-95 South and then cut off towards Coral Gables.

Colorogne and Terry Johns were waiting for him as he entered the house. Colorogne fed his dogs and then got a manservant to take them away.

"So you 'as been gone just a few days, Billy, and a lot 'as 'appened. Wouldn't you say?"

Colorogne was very serious.

"I guess so," was all Billy could say. He didn't know quite what was in process here.

"I will say so," said Terry Johns. "What do you have to report?"

"I…I don't know."

"What do you mean you don't know? You were there when everything went down." He was stern. "I would like for you to tell me what 'appened please." Corologne was agitated. He was very concerned to say the least. He had a look of anger and disappointment and curious not as to what had recently occurred but what might just happen now.

Billy was nervous not to say anything he shouldn't, and yet, aware not say anything that he should. And he had no idea if he was in the middle of one big set up and if one or both of these two men before him might be responsible for that. He was brought out to throw confusion into the cartel's business but he hadn't done anything and there certainly was confusion. He was confused about the way things were too.

"Well, as you know I went on a cruise and there were some murders in a couple of places. Three of your colleagues are now deceased. The police questioned me about the murders. I saw Dibralta's home destroyed yesterday." Billy looked straight at Terry Johns and wondered if he knew his driving license had been found at Mount Crescent. "I believe I'm in the middle of some sort of set up and I don't know why. I actually have nothing whatsoever to do with what has gone down there, this last few days."

"You don't?" queried Corologne.

"I remember that Mr Beauchamp and Dr Dietz were at your party the other day. Now they are dead. I never saw who did it and I know I didn't do it."

"Did you see Dibralta's house attacked?" asked Terry Johns.

"It was a hell of an explosion. I don't know if Dibralta was killed or not. I'm sure he was. Somebody sure wanted those three men dead and I had nothing to do with it." This was true but it was still Billy's intention to kill all three.

"I met Mr Beauchamp and Dr Dietz here. If I recall Mr Dibralta wasn't able to make the party. I do not know why. Why would I?"

"And what 'ave you told the police."

"Only what I knew and that was nothing. He wasn't going to mention about Terry Johns' driving license and his boarding pass."

"And why did they want to talk to you?"

"I honestly don't know. Just as I don't know why all this went down."

"It is very strange that they did think you might know something, Billy?" said Terry Johns.

"Yes."

"I think you know a bit more. And you're not talking."

"Such as!"

"I'm not sure. Anyway, you are 'ere now. I'm not sure what to do. Perhaps I should let my men take you and find out. 'Ow did you go on wid our marketing plan?"

"I'm sorry? What do you mean marketing plan?"

"I mean, where is my money dat was put on da ship for disposal?"

"I'm sure your contacts on the Meridian Star have that taken care of that," said Billy.

"So, we have gone nowhere. Or rather, you have gone nowhere?" was Terry Johns' response.

"Anyways, I 'ave someone for you to meet soon," Corologne got up from his chair to pour himself a glass of milk.

"Oh, who's that?"

"Dibralta?" said Terry Johns.

"Dibralta?"

"*Si*. Senor Dibralta."

"So he didn't get killed in the explosion," said Billy.

"No, 'e escaped da explosion."

"He is here soon. He wants to meet you, Billy."

Colorogne's wife entered.

"Ah, my dear. You look gorgeous as always." Colorogne kissed his wife on her cheeks.

"Zank you, darlink. Hello Billee, 'ow are you?"

"My dear, where are you off to?"

"Diedree and I are going shopping."

"Again."

"Of course, darlink. Do you want anythink?

"Just to see your beautiful face again."

"You're so sweet."

Terry Johns' girlfriend entered. What on earth were they doing here in the middle of this conversation? Billy was astounded.

"Hello Billy," Diedre smiled at Bill and then turned to Mrs Corologne, "Are you ready, sweet?"

"I am. We'll see you soon. Bye, dear." She kissed Corologne, stopped to look at him and then strolled for the front door. Diedre hugged Terry Johns. It was a cold hug, Billy thought. She too strolled to make her exit.

"Now we 'as to talk before we meet wid Dibralta," said Corologne. "As you may or may not know, Billy, Dibralta or myself are in line to take over the business of running the cartel. I do not know exactly what you do know. But Dibralta, I know, wants the leadership more than I do. You are new here and now I am not sure what your involvement really is.

"I am not one who wants the leadership but I am the one that most of the other associates would like to run da business. Dibralta is not too popular wid da odders, and he sees dat we should be going in different directions. So, I think it really is da time he and I, we should talk, like a man to man. Our leader is not a well man and the organisation wud like for to arrange 'is successor as soon as is possible…and as smoothly as possible. No fighting, ya know what I's means, Terry. I know you is here for to help me but it is time soon for you to go back to home."

"Go home?" …

A loud explosion sounded to the rear of the house that almost blew Billy and Terry Johns out of their seats,

"What the f… was that?" said Terry Johns.

Colorogne ran to towards the doorway to see, pushing the emergency protection switches for the windows and doors. One of his security men ran in.

"Mr Colorogne, I believe we are being attacked!"

Another explosion, caused by a bazooka fire, shot straight through the living room.

"Who would be attacking you?" asked Terry Johns.

"I don't know, but we should find out."

A spray of bullets hit the protector screens.

Billy ducked down behind the sidewall of the large living room to see what was happening. He barely made it there through the bullet fire. He saw a rocket launcher in the yard being set, to fire towards the window. He dived onto the couch and slid to the floor as it exploded just outside the house.

Security guards were running everywhere. One man got shot running by the pool holding his rifle for action. Two others fired back in retaliation. Chaos ensued both inside and outside the house. A rocket blew right through the back screen, shattering the bulletproof window.

Another security guard came running in. "Mr Corologne, they have broken down the Southside entrance and men are coming over the wall near the Venice Brook. There is a lot of them. Do you want me to get the helicopter ready?"

"Yes. And as quickly as possible too."

"Did I visit too soon?" Billy said light-heartedly.

The first security guard came running back in. "The helicopter has been immobilised, sir. I suggest you arm yourself while we try to fight it out."

Colorogne moved to the wall cabinet and pushed a button on the side of it. The cabinet slid away to one side to reveal a large closet with weapons hanging on the walls. He picked up an A-47 and put a hand pistol into his pocket. Then took a box of shells.

"Have you ever used a gun, Mr Doyle?"

Billy followed him to the room and grabbed a semi-automatic and a pistol too. He threw a gun to Terry Johns who caught it and checked it to be loaded, then made towards the screen doors and started firing out. Billy grabbed a couple of grenades off the closet table and joined him.

Gunfire crowded towards the front door. They could hear that the offending attackers were closing in on the house. A couple of the security guards came in the side entrance firing back at men that were forcing them back. They were coming up through the front yard. One of them went down as a bullet shot straight through his temple. Another one dropped as bullets pelted through his body.

The enemy were closing in fast on the house and gunfire was accelerating. Gun smoke was now rampant in the air. Billy ran to where the sliding glass doors used to be before they'd been blown off. He ran out to the deck behind a garden wall and lifted the pin from one of the grenades and released it into the air disrupting some of the offending attackers as it landed on them and blew them up.

As Billy was shooting at the on-comers as fast as he could, Colorogne covered him from behind. It had been some time since Doyle was shooting for his life and that was in Afghanistan with organised troops alongside him. Corologne followed closer up behind him, shooting at the foe. He was a good shot and his semi-automatic was doing itself justice.

Terry Johns was defending the side entrance inside the house with the security guards and seemed to be winning until the front door suddenly blew up and dark black smoke entered the room. The two security guards fell as it exploded which left the area wide open for the attackers to move in.

Terry Johns turned and fired his gun in the doorway, bringing down as many of the enemy as he could with his semi-automatic.

Meanwhile Corologne and Billy were holding their own on the back deck. Billy's gun locked. He was out of bullets. He threw the gun to the ground and took out his pistol. He moved himself further forward and saw a guy on the roof about to fire at Colorogne. Billy discharged his gun immediately and the man fell from the roof disabled. Colorogne saw the man fall and nodded in gratitude to Billy.

The attackers began to retreat as Colorogne and some of his men and Billy fired fiercely at them. It was a desperate battle for survival. It was almost of military proportions. It was certainly not what anyone expected. "Always expect the unexpected," was another of Smythe's sayings. Who was it and why were they attacking?

The back of the property went momentarily quiet and eerie. Gunfire was dwindling at the front of the house. Terry Johns had been shot in the leg and it was bleeding badly. The attackers had gone silent at the front.

The house looked bombed, and it had been.

"So, how much is property like this going for?" joked Billy as he looked at the devastation.

Colorogne just grimaced.

Billy grabbed a tablecloth and tore it up and tied a strip of it around Terry Johns' leg and pulled it tight to stop the blood circulation.

"We need to reload. I'm thinking they will be back in a minute," Terry Johns sweated.

Colorogne and what was left of his security guards grabbed what they could from the armoury closet. They prepared themselves for another probable attack.

"So, who is it that you've pissed off, Mr Colorogne?" asked Billy.

"I do not know. Do you 'ave any ideas, Terry?"

"No. None that I can think of, but someone is obviously upset with you."

"Where are the dogs?" Colorogne ran to the back and looked out in the yard where he could see three helpless animals lying motionless on the ground. "I'll kill the bastard that did this!" he yelled.

Billy grabbed another semi-automatic weapon from the armoury closet.

A single gunshot sent another of the security guards to the ground as attackers shot their way through the front door and hurtled themselves forward. Their fire received a similar greeting from the other guards. Terry Johns fired above them and a bullet ricocheted off a steel wall ornament and sent one of their soldiers down. Another guy fell over him as he went down and his gun went off against another. The front hallway was beginning to just litter with bodies.

Terry Johns, who was not far away from the group, slid across the floor with his gun aiming towards where the back patio was or at least used to be. He fired his gun at more would-be intruders. They, in turn, returned fire at him and he caught a number of bullets across the chest.

Billy rushed from the closet as did Corologne and the two disintegrated the remaining onslaught of forces coming from the rear.

Yet another explosion came in through the front and blew the couch clear through the air, out of the house and onto the back porch.

"Good job, we came out for some fresh air," Billy joked again as the furniture piece landed behind them in the back yard.

In the excitement, neither of them man had noticed a helicopter land in the front yard.

They did though as the rear end of the house porch blew up from incendiaries that it dropped.

One sent both men backwards, landing them on the couch. Corologne's gun left his hand. Billy went to fire his but again this one had jammed.

Before they realised it, they were surrounded by a handful of attacking forces. Their support had been immobilised and they were trapped as they both sat on the couch overlooking the pool area.

"It's Dibralta," sounded Corologne.

"I thought he was dead," said Billy.

Senor Dibralta walked towards the house and up the steps to the porch.

"I'm sure you did. And believe me I would have been had I not been in my cellar at the time of the attack. What was your intention, Mr Corologne? Why you want me dead? Not to mention Beauchamp and Dietz." Dibraltra stood holding a machine gun on the two men. He looked like a greasy Latin general and was surrounded by him me.

"I didn't want you dead, Juan."

"Oh, come now, you go to all that trouble and you didn't want me dead? Yes, seeing is believing is what I am thinking. You wanted me dead and that is why you attacked my home yesterday."

"I assure you I had nothing to do with that. In fact, we were discussing what happened yesterday before, well, before you arrived here. I tell you I had nothing to do with it. I give you my word."

"I don't think your word means very much, Senor."

"What I want to know is, well, I want to know a lot before I kill you. What I want to know is why? I thought we had a good relationship going and all was working well. Why did you want to cross me?"

"I'm telling you I didn't, I don't, mean to cross you. I'm as much at a loss at this as you are. I have no idea who set out to kill you yesterday. And I have no idea why."

Corologne knew he was about to die. "But someone wanted to destroy our system. That is why they went to kill Beauchamp and Dietz and you. But it wasn't me."

"If it is not you, then who?"

"I don't know. I'm guessing whoever it was would have been coming after me soon too."

"I'm sure you know. And who is this?"

"This is Billy Doyle. He was the one that was bringing money to you and the others."

"I kill him!" Dibralta raised his gun to aim at Billy.

"Whoah! Look!" said Doyle. "I was with a chief inspector of police when your place was attacked. I saw what happened from a distance. I was on a ship in Cancun, but I had nothing to do with it. I'll tell you what. Oh it doesn't matter, you wouldn't believe me."

"Ha ha. Try me."

"Well, I did see a motor boat sail away just after the second explosion at your place. When I saw you just now, I thought, well, maybe it was you in the boat and you'd escaped. That's all."

"No, I told you I escaped later when I came up from the cellar. But you wouldn't have known that I hadn't been killed Mr Corologne, would you, you son of a bitch!"

"He had nothing to do with it, Dibralta!"

Obviously, Doyle knew his task was in part to get rid of Dibralta, but someone had beaten him to it the attempt. But who? And why?

He still wasn't sure if it was Corologne's doing or not. Corologne would certainly have had no idea that was Billy's original intention. He could have assumed at first that Dibralta had been killed. The way things had moved just recently inferred that he had nothing to do with an attempted killing.

"What about Terry Johns?" Billy considered. "But again why?"

Terry Johns knew Billy was assigned to do work out in this part of the world. Was he using Billy just to add more confusion to everything? Thing just did not add up. And if it was Terry Johns, had he considered if he got it wrong, would he have known he'd gotten himself into this situation? And right now, he was lying motionless and bleeding to death.

No, things just did not add up. He couldn't make sense of it and a gun was pointing in his direction.

"We'll take your gun, Meester Doyle." Dibralta indicated to one of his henchmen to remove it. "And if you're not going to tell me what this has all been about, I see no reason to keep you around any longer. Goodbye, gentlemen."

Dibralta raised his gun and coldly aimed it at Corologne, but before he had a chance to shoot, Terry Johns had strengthened himself up and fired a bullet right through the middle of Dibralta's head, killing him instantly.

Dibralta's men immediately fired endlessly at Terry Johns lying on the floor.

One of the men ran to Dibralta and said, "Dibralta *es morte! El hombre es morte! Vamos, vamos*," and they dispersed. With Dibralta dead, the attackers no longer had a leader and no one seemed interested in taking up his position.

Colorogne and Doyle sat motionless on the couch, looking at the mess all around them.

"If Terry Johns had done that in the first place, there wouldn't be this mess to clean up now."

The two men sat there exhausted both physically and mentally.

"Shall I bring you your coffee now, sir?" asked Colorogne's manservant who appeared unscathed by the whole scenario.

Colorogne just laughed.

"So, who did it?" asked Billy.

"Did what?"

"You know, the killings in Aruba and Curacao and then try to kill Dibralta?"

"I don't know," said Colorogne.

"I thought you had set it all up," said Billy.

He leaned forward and reached to take a pistol from behind his back. Corologne took a pistol from a pocket in the arm of the couch. They stared at each other. Then put the guns between them.

"No, it was not me," said Corologne, "I thought maybe it was you or someone who had hired you to do it."

"Who then? Who?"

"I have known Terry Johns for a number of years now. I do not think it was him. But you and him, you work for the same people in England, do you not?"

"How do you mean?"

"Don't take me for a fool, Mr Doyle. You both work for British Intelligence? I kind of suspected all along that you did. Everything seemed so…comfortable… and convenient, the way it all worked out for how you come to be my associate. I thought maybe you have plans for to get rid of me and I told my people that, that is why they watch you."

"No, I had no plans to kill you, Mr Colorogne," said Billy.

"You had no plans? What about now?"

"Still no plans?"

"I don't know what it is going on."

"Me neither." Billy really could not fathom out the situation.

They both sat back on the couch. The manservant brought out a small table and placed the coffee on it.

"Could you bring the 1957 Cognac, please, George?"

"Yes, sir."

"So now what? How are you going to explain this?"

"To whom?" said Corologne. "I don't have to. There is no one to tell this to, well, not here anyway."

"Oh, how is that?"

"It looks like my business dealings are at an end here. Perhaps that is what you were sent for, to finish my business here?"

"In Miami?"

"Well, in this part of the world that is for sure. Certainly, all my connections are done with now. Isn't that what you wanted, my friend?"

Billy didn't answer.

"Now, 'ow you say, I've to pay the piper. Thank you, George. Just put the bottle down." Colorogne took the bottle and poured some brandy into the two glasses next to the coffee pot. "Cheers."

"Pay the piper, is what we say."

He handed Billy a glass.

"Cheers." Billy sipped the cognac. "That's good."

"It is one of my favourites. The very best."

"So, what do you mean you 'have to pay the piper'?"

"For the longest time, people have thought that the world's drug trade and illicit business was run from South America, dictated to by the Mexican and Columbian cartels. But no. The people that control any business are never the figureheads, the leading persons. And I have to inform you it is not me either."

"What are you saying?"

"What I am saying, my friend, is our business is directed from somewhere else. The owner of Walgreens or KIA does not run their own business. The bosses at MacDonald's and Burger King, they don't run the whole company. They 'as franchises that are run independently but have a big corporation pulling da strings. They have bosses they have to repay to and their bosses 'ave to repay to their bosses. No one, or rather very few people actually know who the real bosses are. The real bosses control all da strings. They control everything from the politicians and the businessmen down to the floor cleaners, speaking of which, I must get the cleaners in here."

"What are you trying to say, Mr Colorogne?"

"I joke. I'm not getting cleaners in here!"

"I don't understand."

"I joke, Mr Doyle. You not understand comedy? I wouldn't get cleaners in here now."

"I meant what, or rather why are you telling me this."

"Look, Mr Doyle, let's not play no more games. I look around me now and I see my business here is over and I must answer to my bosses. I tell you this because, now, I know I am finished. I'm guessing at best you take me somewhere and I be arrested. If I'm lucky, I make it to England or wherever it is you take me. It is more than likely that I be killed before I get to wherever it is.

"I would like just one thing now before I am done away wid. I would like to see my granddaughter in Bogata before I go. Her parents, dey wus killed some time ago and I 'ave her looked after in St Theresa's Chapel in Bogata. It is a nunnery. I put her dere some years ago. I pay for da nuns to take care of my granddaughter. I buy dem da whole nunnery in return for dere 'elp. I could never bring my granddaughter into dis 'orrible world."

Billy did feel some sympathy for the villain. Certainly, it did appear that his empire had crumpled. Billy still didn't know quite why and by whom though. His reasons for being sent out to Miami had been achieved. Though he hadn't done the deed himself, the situation had been sent into such disarray, there was no business left. Corologne had little or no future left and the other leading players were now out of the picture.

The moment with Corologne brought a closeness to the villain he never thought could happen and he felt for the man.

"You know, Billy, if I may call you Billy? I never wanted this."

"I'm sorry?"

"It was never my intention to set out to have this 'ow you say, 'Empire'."

"No?"

"No. All of it came by accident. I tell you now. It makes no difference whether you want to believe it or not. I was a young boy in Rence, a small town in Bogata. My family had a small farm dere. And like a lot of people." Corologne took a sip of his cognac. "And a lot of people in Bogata in dose days, da bad people come and tell you to grow things. You know like cocaine, even though they know it is bad.

"Even though it is bad, they do it because there is nothing else to do. American money goes into the making of drugs worldwide. Did you know? I'm sure you did. Even governments finance it. And if you don't do what your governments tells you to do, they might kill you or take away your land.

"My father for many years fought against all these evil forces until one day we find him dead in da fields. I was young, very young. My mother she tell me to run away. I leave her and my sister because she knows they will kill me too. I live in da mountains there for long time. I learn to…

"Survive?" said Doyle.

"*Si*. I learn to provide for my family although I cannot see dem. They say I am wanted man. Gradually, I did what I had to do and I do what I not supposed to do. But even though I do okay, I can never go home because I shamed my father's wishes."

"Is your mother still alive?

"No. My *madre es muerto*. Holy mother of God!"

"My mudder y fadder dey is dead. *Mi hermana*, my sister dat is, and *mi abuela*, my granddaughter dey live in da nunnery. I get money to them and I always think I will see them but I know I never will. I, 'ow you say, 'Make my bed'. No one knows but only you now. I ask dat you give dem dis wid my love." Corologne took a necklace from around his neck and handed it to Billy.

"I believe you have come now, and dat you have to take me away, true? *Es verdad*?"

Billy just looked at the man who had lost everything.

"Yes. But soon it will be all over. And I be glad too. For so long, I fight. And keep fighting and I do bad things. I like for you to 'ave some information. Perhaps I can put a little right in the wrong I 'ave committed.

"You 'ave another drink, Senor." Colorogne poured two more drinks of cognac.

"Yes. Thank you."

They raised their glasses and just as quickly threw them to the ground. Billy saw a familiar gloved hand. The one he had seen at Beauchamps' house in Aruba. The hand was holding a revolver and was pointing directly at the couch. He dived to the floor taking his gun in his hand with him and fired.

Corologne had thought he saw a reflection in his wine glass of a woman walking towards them carrying a gun that looked as is if she was about to fire. He grabbed his gun leaned forward and fired too. As he did, he shot his wife dead.

Billy ran to his assailant. It was Diedre, Terry Johns' fiancé. She was barely breathing.

Blood was curdling from her lips. She smiled at Billy. "We almost did it, didn't we?"

"Yes, you did."

Now everything fell into place. And it was all so obvious. The two women had conspired if not to carry out the deeds together but to throw Billy's and Terry Johns' plans into confusion.

That was why Diedre was always around and knew so much. Who else had such close contact to the business at hand? Of course! Why didn't he see that? It was so obvious.

Mrs Corologne's plan in all this was to take over the cartel. By getting the potential heads to fight each other, she could just walk in and take over everything.

"So, the two of you had this all planned? All along?"

Diedre shook her head as she looked up at the two men. "Yes, we almost did it." She coughed up more blood then passed away.

Billy looked over at Mrs Corologne lying motionless and Corologne looking down on her remorseful. He really had lost everything.

"I should have known," said Colorogne.

"How could you? It was a great plan of deception."

"She, the two of them planned this all along. I think they had in mind that you would take the blame for the killings."

"Well, and I think Diedre had all the inside information they would need from Terry Johns himself and back home in England. They must have hatched the scheme between them."

"Do you think she planned to kill me all along?" A despondent Corologne knelt down by his dead wife.

"I'm sure they did."

"And dey planned to take over the whole business. Unbelievable it is."

"I believe that was their plan. Unfortunately, they hadn't planned on Dibralta escaping his assassination attempt. That kind of messed things up," explained Billy.

"So now what? Do you kill me now?" asked Corologne.

"Not necessarily."

"You mentioned someone else was in charge."

"*Si*. But it will take a long time for dem to build the empire up again."

"And you know who they are?"

"*Si*."

"I have a proposition for you."

"You 'ave no means to keep me safe, Senor. So I don't think you can make propositions."

"You never know," said Billy.

"Well, before you tell me your proposition, I tell you an idea I 'as.

"I 'as a proposition for you. Before you take me back for interrogation or whatever it is you are to do to me, if I can give you the name of the people who run zee ole thing. You make it, so I can see my family for just one more time. I give you my word. I want nothing else now I vill even take you to the people who run all of it – the drugs, the trafficking, guns, da women, all of it."

Billy began to think if he were to get rid of the big noise, perhaps there might be a way out for Cologne. The truth was Billy was thinking more of himself than Corologne. Even if, with Colorogne's help, he could swing it and wipe out the whole corporation, Smythe would never agree to any arrangement whereby Corologne would get to see his sister and his granddaughter in exchange for the information. Still, he could go along with a plan and use the granddaughter as a negotiating tool with the Spaniard.

"What do you say?"

"I have to contact my bosses."

Colorogne said, "Well, let's make it quick. They won't be pleased to hear about what 'as 'appened 'ere. The sooner I get to talk to them the better."

"Where are they?

"A long way away."

"Where?"

"Hong Kong."

"Damn! I thought you were just going up to Palm Beach!"

=========

Chapter 26
I Like Chinese

Billy spoke with Smythe who said he would arrange for Billy to stay undercover and would keep a close surveillance on Colorogne.

Smythe fully understood Colorogne had little left under the circumstances to negotiate with.

"I'll need two false passports for us," said Billy. "Just in case we have to get out of China some other way. I'll let you know when we'll need them."

"That can be arranged," said Smythe, "I only hope you know what you're doing, Doyle. I've made all the other arrangements you asked for."

Smythe must have some big theatrical contact to arrange showbiz gigs for him. He had arranged for Billy to do a show in Hong Kong at the Marriatta Hotel. It was an annual event for British ex-patriots who lived in Hong Kong. Usually, a big name entertainer was hired to do this job. The agency, or at least Smythe, had built up Billy's credentials for the job to Marriatta buyers.

"How are we going to do this?" Billy asked Corologne.

Colorogne had contacted the powers that were in China and told them where he was staying, which was also the Marriatta Hotel. The two of them had separate yet adjoining suites.

Billy had given his word to Smythe that he would be watching out for Corologne and would bring him in when the job was done and they had scooped up the bosses in China.

Smythe had no option but to sit tight and hope it all worked out.

========

Billy and Corologne had made agreements before they got on the flight over to Hong Kong. In exchange for the head of the cartel and its collapse, Billy would personally ensure that Colorogne would get to see his sister and his granddaughter before he was taken into custody.

They would arrange to go from the airport in Miami separately. They would check in separately. They would have no contact with each other whatsoever. To all intents and purposes, they were traveling separately to Hong Kong and for different reasons. To most other people, they didn't know each other.

Smythe had concocted the plan, in as much as he could. The truth of the matter was that it all really lay in the hands of Graham Ling, the head of the Medellin Cartel that was run from China. The fact that China was one of the countries in the world that had really strict punishments for drug crimes had gone a long way to curtailing the traffic of drugs and its associated businesses in that part of the world. In Ling's mind, he was running a business and not the business of drug trafficking. No drug business was done in China. But, it was just run from China.

It was agreed that two of Smythe's men would travel from the airport with Colorogne. Colorogne's faithful manservant would be allowed to travel with him too. From the airport, they would check in at the famous Marriatta Hotel into one of the suites, which would adjoin Billy Doyle's suite.

As a protection for Doyle, another of Smythe's men, under the guise of a representative from the booking agency, would accompany Doyle. The accompanying man would have a separate room in the hotel but would really stay in Doyle's room.

Colorogne would contact Mr Ling upon his arrival at the hotel and arrange a meeting with a time and place. Smythe wanted everyone to be wired but Billy said that would be too much to risk and anyone that got within a hair's breath of Ling would be searched. As Corologne had said to Billy, "You'll have to trust me on this one." Ling would want to meet with Corologne to get his contacts and transaction information from him.

"Well, I want full contact, full communication all the time on this one. Do you understand, Doyle? I don't want to find out about things after," said Smythe.

"You got it, boss."

"We have enough back up and security in the hotel if and when we need it, but I understand we don't want to crowd Ling. As far as he knows, Colorogne is the only one that is looking to talk with him. In truth, Colorogne is a sitting duck. I'm sure Ling is far from happy the way things have gone for him this week."

"I know," said Billy, "I'll let you know what happens."

"You'd better. Oh, and, Doyle, do keep your distance. If Ling gets a whiff of your scent, you'll be a dead man."

"I know."

Billy was getting tired of Smythe's matronly persistence. He knew he'd brought Smythe within range of the Mescillican Cartel and so far that was an achievement. But, this was a very big fish. He knew they were close but all could just close away so quickly if they weren't careful.

Billy held back the hotel limo, just to make sure Colorogne and company had their ride taken care of. He then jumped into the car. The supposed agent drove and Billy sat in the side.

The driver introduced himself as Julian, Julian Ladish. "But you can call me 'Jo Jo'," he said he was English and came from Hackney near London.

"Were you born there?"

"No," said Julian. "My father was from there but my mother was born here in China, in Canton and until my youth, I was educated in China. I did go to Oxford University though. I studied English Literature and took some special courses in physics and industrial studies."

Billy wasn't sure if what he was saying was true or was he just reciting his cover.

"And now you're my representative from the theatrical agency?"

"That is right," the 'agent' responded. "They call me Jo Jo there too."

"And what do you know about English entertainment, Jo Jo?" asked Billy who was trying to see how he would cover himself if the subject were likely to arise.

"Oh, I know a lot. That is why they put me on this assignment. That is why I am here, now."

"Such as?" Billy questioned him.

"Well, I have watched a lot of television in England. I do enjoy the sit-com shows. I have been to the theatre in London many times and have seen many, many concerts there. I also enjoy visiting the pubs and the clubs."

"There aren't as many of the clubs as there used to be," Billy interceded.

"No. That is true. There are the arena type shows which do well for comedians like Michael McIntire and Peter Kay. Oh, and there are the comedy clubs in England too, which I enjoy; many Americans do well in England. People like Kevin Hart and—"

"And what sort of audiences does the Marriatta have?"

"I don't know. The agency hasn't told me. Perhaps we can ask at the hotel."

"I'm sorry?"

"I tell you what I know, not what I don't. We are almost there. I think I will valet park the car."

The 'agency rep' pulled up behind Colorogne's limo. Billy saw the manservant and the security guys walk into the foyer as they pulled up. The 'agency rep' clicked open the trunk and a doorman lifted Billy's case on to a trolley and wheeled it in. After they had left the car to be valet-parked, the two of them entered the reception area of the hotel.

Billy took his time going into the hotel. He didn't know who might be watching and following Colorogne. A woman and her husband were ahead of him in the reception line. From their accents, he guessed they were American.

"Ah, Mr Doyle. You're in one of our suites on the fourteenth floor. Here is your key and your case will be taken up to your room right away. I believe Mr Johnson, our floor manager, would like to see you first though. I'll just call him. I won't be a moment."

The receptionist had barely put the phone down when Mr Johnson appeared out of thin air.

"Mister Doyle, I'm so glad to meet you and welcome to the Marriatta Hotel. We hope you have a wonderful stay with us. Anything we can do to make your stay with us absolutely delightful, please let us know at once. Is there anything we can do for you now?"

"I wouldn't mind seeing the showroom, if I may."

"Not at all. Follow me please." Mr Johnson led the agent's rep and Doyle to the elevator and took them up to the eighth floor.

"Oh, this is Julian Ladish, Sorry, this is Jo Jo from the William Morris Agency. He's my representative from the agency, the variety agency that is."

Billy suspected the two may have met before.

"So wonderful to meet you, Mr Ladish. And you are staying with us too?" said Mr Johnson.

"He's in a room near me I believe. Is that right, Mr Jo Jo?"

"Yes. I'm already checked in. I was here earlier in the day."

"Wonderful. Here we are. Just to your right, through the large doors and here is the showroom."

The party walked into the exquisite showroom. Waiters were busying themselves, preparing for dinner. It was a grand place. The décor was exquisite and no expense had been spared. This was indeed a very plush gig.

"Do you have a big crowd tonight?" asked Billy.

"Actually we do. We sold a lot more tickets in the last few days as soon as people got to hear you were coming. Apparently, you're quite a star back in England I believe." Billy didn't know who had sold him on that line?

"And what is the procedure?"

"Well, we have cocktails at seven. Dinner is served at 7:30 and show time, that is you, ha ha, at nine."

Two musicians walked by. Billy guessed they were musicians because they were carrying instrument cases.

"Oh do you need the orchestra, Mr Doyle?"

"Maybe just for a play on and play off, please."

"Tony!" Johnson signalled to one of the gentlemen, the one who was carrying the saxophone case. "Tony, this is Billy Doyle, our headliner this week."

"This is Tony Marchet, our bandleader. You can tell him anything you need."

"Nice to meet you, Tony. Actually, I don't need much. Just play me on with something bright as soon as I'm introduced. Once I hit the mic, you can all leave the stage, but please be quiet as you can if you don't mind. And come back fifty minutes later. I'll do about ten minutes once you're back on stage and when I say goodnight, then if you just play me off to something bright again."

"And that's it?"

"Yes, I think so. Why?"

"No music or nothing?" questioned Tony.

"I don't have any music with me."

"We can fake something if you want?"

"Okay, how about 'My Way' in Eflat?" Billy remembered Harry Tomkin's version from White House Inn."

"Perfect," said Tony.

"Okay, I'll give you a cue and the piano just plays the intro round and round till I start singing."

"And that's it?"

"That's it. Thanks."

Tony left. It appeared that they band might be about to be doing their own rehearsal.

"Our lighting man isn't here yet," said Mr Johnson. "We didn't expect you for another hour. Is there anything special I can tell him you need or do you want to come back in about an hour?"

"I just want the lights full up when I come on stage and dimmed when I start to sing the song at the end. And that's all. No need to come back later, don't you think?"

"That's fine," said Johnson.

"I'll take you to your room. Follow me, sir." He led them to the elevator and pushed the button for his floor and opened the door to his room. "I believe your room is further down the corridor, Mr Ladish."

"Oh, okay. See you soon, Mr Doyle. Have a good show, sorry shows." Jo Jo walked down the corridor to his room.

Mr Johnson opened the door to Billy's suite, "And this is it, Mr Doyle." Sprightly, Mr Johnson entered the room. He was excited to show off the facilities. There was an arrangement of flowers on the table, some candies, nuts, chocolates and a note reading 'WELCOME MR DOYLE TO THE MARRIATTA HOTEL, HONG KONG.'

======

The bathroom was about three times the size of his back home. Johnson showed the large veranda that held a couple of chairs, a table and two canopy beds. "Oh, and the wine bar is here, full with hopefully, whatever pleases you." The bedroom, with its king-size bed looked so enticing against the old oak furniture enclosing the room.

"If there is something special you would like, please let me know."

"I'm good. Thank you. I think I'll get a shower and sort my stuff out for my show." Billy went to offer Mr Johnson two twenty-pound notes.

"Oh, no sir, it is my pleasure. Mr Doyle, I will leave you now. Please ring if you need anything."

"Well, thank you. I'm much obliged."

"Have a wonderful show this evening. I'll get to watch it tomorrow night."

He left, pulling the door behind him. Billy's suitcase was standing behind the door. He lifted it to the bed and was about to unpack. A knock on the door to the adjoining room interrupted his unpacking.

Billy turned the key and opened it to let Colorogne and his manservant into his room.

Colorogne cautiously came in and looked around. "I've spoken with Ling. He says he will probably come here tomorrow night for dinner and the show, but who knows, he never keeps to a schedule. I expect he'll want to get this business over as soon as possible, so I expect to see him sooner. I have thumbdrives with all the information I have on it. I have already given your people in England a copy of it."

Colorogne and his man were walking around the room, looking for bugs and devices as he did. He wandered out to the veranda. Doyle followed him.

"I know he'll want the thumb drives before they gets how shall we say, 'misplaced'," said the Spaniard.

"I'm sure he will. He doesn't want to lose what is left and he doesn't trust you? You know that."

"I think it's more that he doesn't trust the situation. Ling and I have been colleagues now for a number of years. Lesser people would be searching for a deal with anyone to save their skins in this situation. And he certainly doesn't want that, certainly not before he gets the thumb drives."

"And you have the thumb drives with you?"

"I have the originals. As I said, your people have the copies."

"Of course."

The two men re-entered the suite.

"Are they in your safe, in your room?"

"No, that would be too obvious and I think Ling would know that so I doubt if he would break into my apartment to get to my safe. They are safely tucked away though. I think it best if I'm the only one that knows where they are. You'll just have to trust me a little."

Billy felt Colorogne was melting away. He'd lost his empire, his wife and no longer had any power. The only thing that was keeping him going was the possibility of seeing what was left of his family again.

There was a knock at Billy's apartment door. Colorogne hid behind the wall edging the veranda and his manservant stood against the wall behind to the door.

Billy opened the door. It was Jo Jo.

"Come in, Jo Jo." Billy looked outside of the room to see if anyone else was around. He could see Colorogne's security guards stood by the suite door next to his. He closed the door behind Jo Jo as he came in.

"Jo Jo, let me introduce you to Mr Colorogne." Colorogne suspiciously shook Jo Jo's hand. His manservant startled Jo Jo when he realised he was stood behind him. Colorogne had seen Jo Jo at the airport when Smythe's security entourage met up with him and Billy.

"Jo Jo is a representative from the variety agency that booked me here at the Marriatta. By the way, are you coming to the show this evening?" Billy asked Colorogne.

"I might. I just have this feeling our..." He kept looking around expecting to find some listening device.

Jo Jo said, "We don't have any plans on how we are going to carry out this mission. What are your ideas, Mr Doyle?"300

"I think we'll just go along with the flow and see where it leads us. I'll stay with you. Mr Colorogne has his company, but I think it is important that everybody keeps in close contact with each other but not so much as to raise any suspicions. Do you know what Mr Ling looks like?"

"No. Nobody does, not even Colorogne. Even though they have done business together for a number of years, they have never met each other. What about you?"

"No. No one knows what he looks like here either."

"There are no records or photos of him on our files in England either."

"So, we really are going in blind!" said Jo Jo.

"Okay. I'm going to get some sleep before I have my dinner," said Colorogne, "I will see you gentlemen later." With that, he walked to the adjoining corridor, opened the door and left with his manservant close in attendance.

"I'm going to clean up, Jo Jo."

"Okay. Oh, I nearly forget, I have a phone for you. It's for England but Mr S says to only call when you have some news. I see you later, but I be hanging around outside if you need me."

"Okay."

Jo Jo left the room, first checking the corridor was clear to do so. He nodded to the two security guards standing over the suite next door.

=======

"Good news!" said Mr Johnson, greeting Billy as he entered the dressing room, "Actually great news. We almost have a full house this evening and tomorrow night, too. Tonight, we have a lot of British and ex-British patriots, you know British people who either reside in China or work full time over here. Some of them are very important people, even the British governor to the island is here tonight. They are all excited to see you. They have heard so much about you." Mr Thomas was very excited.

"Tomorrow we have the British 'get together'. It is an annual thing that has been happening here for many years. It is always a great night and the people are so very enthused about it. You must be very popular in England, Mister Doyle."

Billy was wondering if maybe Smythe may have over sold him just a little. If Johnson's gushing was any indication, and it did look that way, Billy was concerned if all the adulation might not be a hindrance to the main business at hand. Then again, it may cause a distraction for Corologne to carry out his business.

"I told the people that were asking about you that you were big on television in England just like BRITAIN'S GOT TALENT and FAWLTY TOWERS. That is right, is it not?"

Billy had never appeared on television; well, certainly not on variety television and really did wonder how Smythe and the agency had managed such propaganda. He just smiled as he walked to the side of the stage and peered through the curtain.

The orchestra were playing some dance music. The waiters were clearing away dinner plates and preparing for the tables for the show. There was no bar but waiters were amply supplying drinks where needed. The room was heaving with excitement. The anticipation was breathtaking and Billy could sense it. He too was getting enthralled in it.

"Tomorrow, we will have mostly British people for the annual event. Many are retired British Army and Navy people. There are not as many of those as there were once were, but many English people stayed here with their families after 1997."

"1997?" queried Doyle.

"That was when Hong Kong was returned to China and became independent from Britain," said Jo Jo. "We have lots of British business people and their families that lived here too."

Doyle took a breath and walked toward the curtain, behind which was the stage.

"Have a great show, Mister Doyle. We are looking forward to it," Jo Jo put his thumbs up to the entertainer. "I'll go and find somewhere to sit," he said.

"Will you be all right?"

"Fine, thank you." Doyle was a little pensive.

Jo Jo left the room grabbing the arm of his female escort who was waiting for him outside the dressing room.

Chapter 27
It's Showtime!

Billy looked in the mirror to hand-smooth his hair back. A drum roll started up, the lights dimmed and a smooth voice came onto the microphone:

"Ladies and gentlemen. Welcome to the Excalibur Showroom here in the beautiful Marriatta Hotel. It is with enormous pleasure that we bring to you the amazingly talented comedian from England, Mister Bille Doyle!"

The orchestra struck a massive fanfare that would normally herald something or someone of great stature. The applause and the cheers were tumultuous. Billy entered the stage to a thunderous reception usually only afforded the greats. Someone had really sold him well.

Billy bowed to the throng as he entered, masterfully walked up to the microphone and the conductor cut the band and left all up to Billy.

"So were you expecting someone else?"

The audience laughed not knowing why, but they laughed. They were out for a good time and he would give it to them.

"Good evening! What a thrill it is to be in Hong Kong, which is a sort of Blackpool with rice."

Billy knew there were a lot of British folk in that night and thought it wise to acknowledge them with some local British references from the start and get them on his side. It seemed the whole audience related. The fact he'd mentioned Blackpool was reminiscent of the days when Blackpool was considered to be a premier holiday resort for the British. They laughed which inferred that many of the audience hadn't been to that seaside town in years. If they could just see it now, he snickered to himself.

"An amazing place, this Hong Kong. Four million Chinese and I still can't find a decent laundry!"

The stage curtains slowly closed to leave the stage alone to him. "Oh, how's some appreciation for this wonderful orchestra..." the audience responded as Billy outstretched his arm to the band.

"The band is very religious. They only drink on two occasions. When it's raining and when it's not.

"They're leaving now, because, well, it's the only chance they'll get to go to your rooms and go through your things. And, ladies, I do hope you've left your jewellery in your rooms to make it worth their while!"

The crowd laughed as they were applauding the musicians. The musicians laughed too.

The curtains were almost closed and the comedian confided to the audience:

"You know the last time I saw curtains close like that, the casket had just gone through them."

Billy turned to the audience and took the microphone from the stand. "Well, I guess before I get into the show proper, I should find out where everyone is from. Do we by any chance have anyone in from England?"

A loud cheer went up.

"Where are you from, sir?" he referred to a gentleman who stood up waving his arms.

"Bradford, Yorkshire," the man shouted in a very broad Northern English accent.

"Bradford," said Billy. "I know it. Bradford, that's near England, isn't it? "You can't be from Bradford. You're White!"

"If you're from Yorkshire, where's your turban?"

The audience laughed. Billy knew it wasn't the most politically correct of lines to say.

Bradford was a known area in England where the population was very much of Asian origin. But it didn't matter. This audience had been around before the invention of political correctness and they were out for fun.

Billy bantered with the man for a few moments. "Okay, where are all the Scottish people?"

Another big cheer went up.

"So, who paid for you lot to come in tonight?"

Another politically incorrect reference to Scotsmen for having a reputation for being a bit mean regarding their money habits.

"Do you know the difference between a canoe and a Scotsman? A canoe tips!" I can say that because I'm half Scots…through a friend of my fathers… Do you know why Scotsmen keep their money in a sporran? … It's so that if they get robbed, they'll enjoy it! It was a Scotsman who started the Grand Canyon in America. Yes, he dropped a nickel down a rabbit hole and went after it!"

Billy spent over forty minutes ad-libbing lines to where people had said they were from.

He had the light man switch up the house lights while he was in the audience. He noticed that a group of Chinese gentlemen had come into the room and sat at a reserved table. He wondered if the gentleman, looking important in the nice suit and tie might be Ling. The Chinese gentleman did look the part and those around him gave the impression that he was of some importance.

He began to move and work his comedy in that direction. The group understood the humour and laughed,

"My wife is Chinese. We just had a baby. We call it Wot Went Wrong! They say, every third child born today is Chinese. Thank Goodness I've only got two kids."

Billy began to play more to the Chinese guests and they enjoyed it. He saw Jo Jo and his lady sat at a table just behind them with Colorogne and his manservant. Jo Jo nodded. He believed Billy had located Ling.

As Billy turned, he saw another Chinese man at a small table sat with another man. An old lady and her nurse or nanny were also sat with them. The man looked very serious. He smiled but he was serious.

Billy slowly moved further in that direction. As he did, the table filled with the Chinese folk suddenly went quiet. They didn't look in that direction but their reaction inferred Billy might be sailing a little too close for comfort. Billy turned to another table.

"A Chinaman says to this Englishman – from Bradford, 'Why is it that the British always win the last decisive battles in history?'

"The English man said, 'Well, before the battle we always pray.'

"The Chinese gentleman said, 'Well, we pray too.'

"The Englishman said, 'Yes, but not everyone understands Chinese!'."

The joke gave a breathing space to the table, especially as Billy moved to another part of the room and passing Jo Jo, he whispered, "Over by the post!" Jo Jo acknowledged that he had seen where Ling really was.

Billy stayed on stage for over an hour-and-a-half. He kept glancing at the table of Chinese folks who seemed to get back into his show. They didn't leave, nor did Ling. Hopefully, they were just temporarily jaunted. It was obvious to Doyle and Jo Jo, the well-dressed man and the group of Chinese gentlemen were just a foil for Ling.

The show ended. Jo Jo and his female accomplice left to follow the Ling table when it did.

Meanwhile, Billy was accosted by a throng that wanted to more than meet him. It was arranged that he would have dinner with all of them during his stay in Hong Kong. The governor would personally take him on a tour of the province. The small bastion of British military would fly him around Canton. And the British Navy were to take him into the China Seas. What better hospitality? And what a wonderful way to see the Orient.

But despite the adoring crowd, Billy had a more immediate predestination and couldn't falter from it. After many whiskies and socialising for what seemed longer time than his act had taken, he finally made his way back to his suite. Jo Jo and Cologne and his minder were waiting for him.

"Still no word from Ling?" Billy asked Colorogne.

"No. I'm thinking we'll be meeting tomorrow afternoon now. Might as well get an early night now. I'm beat." Colorogne left the room with his manservant trailing behind.

"You might as well call it a night too, Jo Jo. I'll see you in the morning."

"Are you going to bed now, Mr Doyle?"

"I think I might go to the top of the hotel. I think I'll take in a view of the lights in the harbour. I'm still hyper from the show. It might help me come down a little."

Jo Jo left the room. The Spaniard and his minder had already disappeared. Billy cleaned up and changed into some lounge clothes. He thought he would take advantage of the 'down time' and he took a trip to the top of the hotel. The evening air might be a little cooler up there, too. Billy passed Colorogne's room and the security guards on the way to the elevator. He acknowledged them as he passed. *All is quiet for the time being,* he thought.

The elevator stopped at the top floor and he got out. He saw the old lady who had been sat with Ling. She was sprawled out on the floor. Her nurse or attendant was a little panic-struck and was thinking the worse for the old lady.

Doyle knelt down next to the old lady. She was motionless but her eyes moved.

"Is everything all right?" asked Doyle as he got to her.

Her nurse spoke in Chinese and Doyle couldn't understand what she was saying. He took the nurse's bag and placed it under the old lady's head. Then he started to unbutton the collar of her tunic.

The nurse screamed at Doyle and tried to stop him.

"It's so she can breathe," said Doyle, pushing the nurse off him. "Is she on any medicine?"

"Medicine? Pills?"

"Ah, yah." He was beginning to get through to her companion because she reached into the shopping bag and held up a few packets and a bottle of pills and pushed them at Doyle.

Doyle looked at the pills. While he was doing so, the companion pushed a plastic pillbox in front of his face. It was a pillbox that had the letters for each day of the week on it. He opened the box up at today's day. The compartment still had today's pills in it.

"It looks like the lady hasn't taken her pills today," he said, "and these packets with the needles in them have insulin in the syringes?"

Fortunately, there was an ice machine in the hallway. It was easier for Doyle to go to the machine to get some cold water in a cup and bring it to the old lady than it was for him to signal to the assistant. He sat the old lady up. The lady's companion helped support her head as Doyle fed the old lady the pills and some water to wash them down with.

The old lady rested. Doyle looked through the insulin packets. "I'm guessing she didn't take her insulin either," said Doyle.

He tore one of the packets open and set up the syringe. "I think we should call the house doctor to make sure though," he was talking to himself.

Two men came through the sliding doors that led outside. They too spoke Chinese and that didn't help Doyle. They were two from the Chinese table in the showroom. They 'mambo jambo'd' in Chinese and pulled guns on Doyle. Doyle was kneeling down next to the woman and her companion as they pointed their guns to his head. Doyle just held up the packet, showing that he was only trying to help the old lady. The two men spoke in Chinese again but it was just mumbo jumbo to Doyle. One of them stood back and made a call on a walkie-talkie.

Moments later, another man came through the doors escorted by the man Doyle assumed to be Ling.

Doyle remonstrated, "Look, let's phone the house doctor. This lady needs her insulin!"

"Ah, funny man. What is it you're doing?" said Ling.

"I just found these two ladies here. This one," he indicated to the old lady, "had passed out. I'm guessing she hasn't taken her insulin or her tablets and her body has had a reaction. I think we should call for a doctor."

"You're right." The man, he thought to be Ling, knelt down next to the old lady. "This is my mother." He spoke to his mother in Chinese. "I don't think she has taken her medicine. Do you know how to do it?"

"Sure, but I think we should get the doctor."

"Let us try first." He gave the package back to Doyle to proceed.

Doyle pushed the sleeve of the lady's tunic up her arm and injected the insulin via the syringe into her forearm. Doyle was calm but inside his heart was rushing. He was praying that what he was doing was the necessary procedure and he was doing it correctly.

Luck would have it, it was. Gradually, the old lady slowly came around.

"I still think you should call for the doctor."

After a few minutes, the lady started to look better and her colour returned. She grabbed Doyle's arm and said thank you in Chinese.

"Are you going to call for a doctor?" Doyle asked Ling.

"There is no need. We will get her home and my doctor will take care of her there. Thank you for your help. It was a good show tonight too."

"Thank you."

"We take care of her now. You can go."

Doyle didn't want to lose any opportunity that he might have, having just met Ling.

"Well, I'll help you take her to her room." Before any argument could arise, Doyle lifted up the old lady in his arms, "You just show me where we're going."

"We're actually going outside."

"We're going outside?" said Doyle.

"Yes, I have my helicopter outside."

"You're not staying in the hotel?"

"No, we are not. I only live a short distance away."

"Well, I'll just follow you. Show me where your transport is."

Doyle carried the old lady. Her assistant picked up the bag and carried it, scurrying behind them. Ling's men stepped to one side as he and Doyle walked the old lady through the doors.

"And this is your helicopter?" said Doyle. "Wow, that is quite something." Doyle had flown in helicopters many times when he was in Afghanistan, but none there had gold plating to decorate it.

"I like it," said Ling. The smile was the first one that Doyle had seem him make.

He carried the old lady to the steps of the copter. One of Ling's men picked her up from him and took her inside the aircraft. He assisted her companion up the steps.

"There you go, young lady. Goodnight," smiled Doyle.

Doyle moved to one side to let the men ascend. He couldn't think of anything he could achieve right now. He certainly had no idea how he might do anything. He reached out his hand to Ling, "I'm hoping your mother is all right now. Goodnight, sir. Just make sure she takes her insulin in future."

"Yes, I will."

They shook hands Doyle walked away as the helicopter's propellers spun and the entourage boarded. Doyle watched the helicopter's propellers spin as he stood against the railing on the side of the building. In the background, the glorious lights of Hong Kong sparkled magnificently below him. He turned to look and admire the harbour view. A cruise ship was sailing by. Passengers were on the deck. What the view must have been like for them to take in as they sailed by, he could only imagine.

"Excuse me, sir," a voice said. It was Ling who had climbed back out of his copter. One of his guards stood by his side. "What was your name again?"

"Doyle, sir. Billy Doyle."

"So you are also a medical practitioner as well as a funny man?" Ling smiled again.

"Hardly. I've just been in similar situations before."

"Well, I didn't thank you. Which I would like to do now. I have been in quite a rush with things this evening. It was my mother's birthday today and we, well, we kind of treated her to dinner and the show for it." So that was the reason Ling didn't meet with Colorogne upon his arrival this afternoon.

"Like I said, I would like to thank you for your consideration. Is there anything I can do for you, Mr Doyle, sir?"

Doyle was somewhat taken aback and really unsure how to conduct himself. "No, I don't think so. But thank you."

The moon shone across the mountaintops and for a moment, Doyle thought he even saw a shooting star. It may have been the reflection from one of so many beautiful lights.

"You like our view?" asked Ling.

"It is amazing. It really is. I've never seen anything like it!"

"Yes, we like it too, but I'm afraid, we take it for granted."

"I think everyone does when something is on your doorstep all the time. It really is very nice though."

"Well, thank you again, Mister Doyle. I do appreciate your help."

"Not at all." The two men shook hands again. Ling departed to the copter with his security guard lagging behind him. Ling began to climb the steps and paused to have a word with his guard. The guard walked back to Doyle.

"Mr Ling said he would like to take you on a tour of the harbour in his helicopter if you like," said the man.

"No, thank you, you have to take the old lady home."

"No, you don't understand. Mr Ling would like to show you the lights." He was a bit firmer. "We will bring you back here afterward."

Doyle walked over to the helicopter. He crouched down a little to avoid the helicopter's propellers and leaned up the steps towards Mr Ling inside the helicopter. "I really do appreciate it but you have more important things to take care of," he shouted over the sound of the engine.

Doyle was faking but hoping Ling would not take no for an answer.

A few minutes later, they were flying over the lights of Hong Kong Harbour. Very few people in the world have or would ever experience such an event. Ling enjoyed showing him points of interest. Doyle was excited. He just wasn't paying attention and just enjoyed the view.

The sound of the propellers were hindering hearing anything Ling was saying.

The old lady's companion tapped Ling on the shoulder and spoke in Chinese to him, "Mr Doyle, my mother says she is feeling how you say a little queasy. It might be best for us to take her home before I bring you back to the hotel. Is that okay with you?"

Doyle couldn't believe his luck. He could never have planned it. He was to gain entrance to Ling's fortress. One more step and this too, to get his contact base, his list, his organisational contacts. And he had hoped Cologrogne would be doing that, but what will be will be.

The copter turned towards the hills of Kowloon. Now the lights gradually faded. There were now no lights. It was dark and very shaded as they made their landing at Ling's mountain home. A nurse and a doctor greeted the copter and the company. The old lady was lifted into a wheelchair and wheeled away. Ling kissed her on the cheek before she was taken. Doyle thought she raised her hand to acknowledge him.

"Will you show Mr Doyle into the house?" Ling said to the very attractive Chinese lady waiting by the helicopter ramp.

"Yes sir," the reply obviously implied she was not a wife of Ling's but more a servant.

Either way, this young woman was very easing on the eye. Her hair pinned back, the bright red lipstick and the split skirt were reminiscent of the femme fatale of an old spy movie. "Mister Doyle. You please you come this way, please," she said.

Doyle followed her and the man that was sat next to Ling during the show. Massive paintings decorated the walls of the home and together with the classic sculptors and other décor inferred a lot. Much money had been spent on the collections. Doyle was not a connoisseur but anyone could appreciate the wealth that dressed this home.

"What would you like to drink, Mr Doyle?" the woman asked him as she delved behind the bar in the living room.

"Oh, I guess I'll take a whisky and water if I may."

"And you'll have your usual, Mister Chooppin?"

"Yees!" the man mumbled.

The lady poured the drinks and handed them out.

"You're not having one, my dear?" asked Doyle.

"No, I don't drink," she replied.

She mixed another drink just in time for Ling to pick it up from her as he entered the room.

"It is quite some place you have, Mr Ling. I don't think I've seen anything like it before. Not even in the movies," said Doyle.

"Thank you. I am indeed flattered. And you are from England, I believe."

"Yes, I am. Manchester, to be precise. It is in the North of England."

"Yes. I do know Manchester. For a while, I was actually studying economics at Liverpool. That is an interesting place. I once went to a soccer game there. Do you like soccer?"

"Love it."

"Do you play it?"

"I only wish."

The other man interrupted, "I like soccer. I used to play."

"Professionally?"

"Yes, I had trials for Chelsea Football Club."

The conversation was idling away when the doctor entered the room to talk with Mr Ling. The two of them couldn't be heard as they were confiding in each other for a few moments.

"Would you like another drink, Mr Doyle?" said the girl.

"Oh no thank you, Miss…?"

"Sonne," she replied.

"Sunny? As in Sunny weather?" Doyle thought she was being humorous.

"Well, not quite. It is Sonne Daie. And that is my real name," she said.

Mr Ling turned to his guest. "Mr Doyle. My doctor has informed me that my mother isn't too well this evening. I'm going to spend some time with her for a little while; well, until she sleeps at least. Now I did promise to return you to your hotel. It is entirely up to you. My pilot can take you back now, but you are indeed most welcome for to stay the night here and then we take you back in the morning. It is up to you,"

Again, Doyle couldn't believe his luck.

"Well…"

"It is getting late and we have some excellent accommodation for you here if you would take up my offer."

"I don't want to impose."

"Not at all, it is my pleasure. Please feel at home. Anything you want, Sonne will make it available to you."

"Well, how can I refuse?"

"Good. I will wish you a good night. You too, Chooppin. Sonne, please take care of my guest." He left the room.

"I'm going too," said Mr Chooppin.

"So, I show you to your room. Mister Dolyee."

"You can call me Billy."

"Billee Doylee," said Sonne, giggling.

"Come with me please," the young woman said.

He followed her to a large bedroom. As she turned on the lights, numerous colourful fish were seen swimming in glass tanks in the walls that surrounded the room. The glass windows gave the impression that the room rested on the ocean bed. Exotic fish like the candy baslet, the Clarion angelfish and a peppermint angelfish adorned the windows. They were all extreme collector's items.

"Do you like fish?" Sonne asked.

"Mostly for dinner. But…Is that a platinum arowana?" Billy said.

"I believe so."

"Wow! That is worth well over four hundred thousand dollars!"

A bottle of scotch and bottles of iced water in an ice bucket lay on his bedside table. Soft music caressed the room and the soft plush carpet invited him to remove his shoes.

She showed him the large bathroom with tub and shower. A change of nightclothes and dressing gown lay along the huge bed.

"I leave you now but I will be back soon to see you are all right and that you have everything you need."

She closed the door in the sexiest way a door has ever been closed to. She turned to smile as she pulled the door behind her. He had no doubt there were cameras set in the room probably watching him but he saw little point in getting upset about it. He would get a shower and get ready for bed. No one would ever believe he was spending the night in such a place.

It seemed barely minutes before Sonne returned. He was in the shower when she moved into the bathroom. She slid open the shower door and slipped in naked next to him. The two caressed and water ran over their bodies and they intermingled. The two continued their lovemaking into the night, on the large bed, and fell asleep in each other's arms.

========

Billy awoke early in the morning. He didn't know the time and he didn't care. This was a place and a moment to enjoy no matter what else was happening in the world. He looked at the fish in the wall as he reached to the bedside table to pick up his wristwatch. One large Neptune grouper appeared to be looking at him through the glass and saying, "What time are you going to get up? Come on get up you lazy…" He knew he was just imagining it. He enjoyed the moment and rested back on the bed and watched the fish rotate their places in the water.

Sonne was gone. He didn't know where and it didn't really matter for the moment. He noticed his clothes were cleaned and ironed as they hung over a laundry rack at the foot of the bed.

Had she spent the night with him because she wanted to or was it part of her job to keep an eye on him for Ling? It seemed a reasonable thought. After all, he was little more than a stranger to Ling's world. His rest period didn't last long. He sat up in bed as she appeared with a coffee tray that she placed on the side table.

She was dressed and ready to face her day. "Breakfast is being served in the kitchen, when you're ready for some," she said. He looked at his watch which told him it was moving close to 7 am. Soon it would be time for him to rise, but for now, he would enjoy the aquarium creatures a little longer. Not to mention the sweet Chinese creature that climbed back into his bed. His night wasn't over yet.

Chapter 28

It's Just Another Day!

It was around eight when he strolled into the kitchen, fully dressed, with Sonne.

Chooppin was sat at the kitchen counter eating a fishplate. A chef was preparing food and placed a tray of food for him to sit opposite Chooppin.

"For me?" inquired Doyle.

"Ya, ya," the chef replied. "You eatee."

Doyle sat down and looked at the massive plate of food for him. "Good morning, Mr Chooppin."

The man grunted and then spoke in Chinese when he saw Sonne walk into the room.

Doyle began to eat at his food. Sonne replied to Choppin in Chinese and then looked at Doyle. The two of them spoke Chinese for a few moments until Sonne turned to Doyle and said,

"Mister Doylee, Mr Ling will not be joining us today."

Doyle wondered what might be keeping Ling away from his company.

"Oh, I'm sorry to hear that. I do hope nothing is wrong."

"No. Not really. Well, yes there is I'm afraid. Mr Ling's mother passed away during the arrangements to be made. It is very sad the lady had a heart attack during the night and he has family business to take care of. He is sorry he will not be able to accommodate you."

"Well, in that case, I will make my way and get out his so that he may be left alone to sort things out. Please give me him my condolences and I hope we can meet again at another time. Is there a taxi I can call?" Doyle knew it would be highly unlikely for a taxi to drive over the mountain to Ling's place.

Sonne again spoke Chinese to Chooppin. While the two conversed, Doyle listened but had no idea what they were saying. Chooppin got up from the counter, having finished his food, and left the room.

"We will take you back to the hotel when you are ready, Mister Doylee. Mr Chooppin will fly us after you have had your breakfast."

"I don't want to put you out. I should get back as soon as Mr Chooppin is ready to fly me to the hotel. I think it would be best for everyone to leave as soon as possible."

"We go now, but, your breakfast?" A large fish with huge bulbous eyes out stared at him from his plate.

"No, that is fine. I'm ready now." Doyle didn't like the way the fish's eyes were staring off the plate. Perhaps it might have been a friend of the grouper he had been watching earlier.

Doyle got up from the table. He hadn't brought any clothes and was ready to go. She escorted him from the room and outside the building to the helicopter Choppin had waiting for them.

Chapter 29
Now the Fun Starts?

"So where 'as you been?" said Colorogne as Doyle walked into his room.

Colorogne and his minder were awaiting him.

"Oh, I just went to see some parts of this beautiful island."

"Doyle, I 'as a meeting with one of Ling's assistants this morning."

"One of his assistants?"

"Yes. Ling cannot see me and 'is sending a man to meet me. I think he will want the thumb drive from me. What shall I do?"

Doyle was nonchalant and for a moment kept his thoughts to himself.

"I was supposed to meet with Ling himself. But now he's not showing. I don't know why," said Colorogne.

"Well, it could be that Mr Ling cannot meet with you because he has to take care of some family business."

"What you say?"

"Mr Ling's mother died this morning and I believe he has family stuff to sort out."

"'Ow you know did?"

"Because I spent last night at Ling's home in the Sintree Mountains."

"'Ow? 'Ow you do this?"

"I met Ling last night and we got talking and well, let's just say I spent the night at his place. He was very hospitable, too."

"I don't understand." Colorogne looked at Doyle very suspiciously.

"I am sure you will get chance to meet Ling eventually. You can use that as an excuse not to hand over the thumb drive until you see him. I do believe having the thumb drive in your possession is the only way to keep you alive. When are you supposed to be meeting his assistant?"

"Shortly. In fact, in about ten minutes in the candescent lounge for coffee."

"Well, you go down there and meet his assistant. I won't be far away."

Colorogne started to leave for his appointment.

"By the way, you haven't seen Jo Jo this morning, have you?" asked Doyle.

"No. No, I haven't." Colorogne left the room.

Doyle grabbed his cards and his phone from the desk. A message on the phone read, 'Goods arrived. Exit time?' It was from Smythe and he wasn't sure what it meant.

He erased the message and left for the lounge to watch after Colorogne.

Colorogne was shown to a table where Chooppin and Sonne were sitting. He and his minder joined them. Doyle watched from across the room.

From the distance, it appeared as if their conversation was getting overheated. It looked as if Sonne was doing all the talking and even pointing her finger down on the table. Colorogne remained calm as Doyle hoped he would.

"Ah, Mister Doyle, how are you this morning?"

"Are you ready for your tour of beautiful Hong Kong?" Mr Johnson said, seeing him sitting alone.

"Mr Johnson, I had forgotten all about that."

"Well, Mr McKenzie, the ambassador, will be here soon to show you the sights. I know he is very excited."

"Wonderful." Maybe Doyle had taken in too much whisky last night but he certainly had forgotten he had an appointment with the ambassador and dignitaries to show him around Hong Kong today. "I am looking forward to it, too."

Billy turned for a moment to see how Colorogne's meeting was going. It didn't seem to be going well.

"Tell me, Mr Johnson, have you seen Mr Jo Jo this morning?"

"No, I haven't. Shall I have him paged?"

"No, there will be no need. I'm sure he will show up soon enough."

Suddenly, the conversation at Colorogne's table had gotten very difficult. Sonne suddenly stood up and began to leave. She shouted at Colorogne in Chinese. Maybe she was cursing. It probably was. She left. Chooppin was close behind her.

Colorogne sat back in his chair, like a man defeated and puzzled as to what had just happened. Doyle knew full well what had happened. His glamorous bedside partner had revealed the witch in her, which had been let loose upon the Columbian.

"Did she tell you why Ling couldn't meet with you?" Doyle asked him when they were back in his room.

"Yes, but I don't know if that was the truth," said Colorogne.

"She said, she would translate my message to him."

"Good. Well, that gives you a little time. I'm pretty sure though Ling will make his presence known sometime today, even though he has to take care of family matters."

"Have you seen Jo Jo yet?"

"You asked me that before?"

"I'm getting a little concerned that he hasn't shown."

A knock on Billy's door showed a hotel clerk was there to take Billy to the foyer in the main hallway to meet with the ambassador and his party.

"Look I have to leave," said Doyle. "The ambassador and his company are showing me around Hong Kong. If you see Jo Jo, tell him to get in touch with me right away. As soon as possible."

========

Doyle's escorted tour of the island was very enlightening to say the least and the exotic lunch and other dining were quite something. But his concern over Jo Jo and how he and Colorogne would get the information from Ling distracted from the enjoyment of the tour. Although he was enjoying his time, other thoughts impeded his enjoyment.

A text came on his phone:

'Received Goods.

Get Out Now!'

Again, it came from Smythe but Billy couldn't quite understand it. It did say 'Get Out Now' and he understood that.

"A lady friend from back home?" laughed the ambassador who'd seen him read his message on the phone.

Doyle smiled, "No. But I do have to get back to the hotel soon. I'd better get to get back to the hotel to get ready for the show." He erased the text.

What goods had Smythe received? Perhaps Colorogne had gotten info to Smythe while he'd been out. Better get back to find out.

He was puzzling about the text all the way back to the Marriatta. 'Get Out Now!' Does that mean drop the show? He was confused. Hopefully, Colorogne could help enlighten him.

Colorogne couldn't. He hadn't heard anything from anybody. Doyle told him of his text from Smythe.

"Are you sure it's from your head office. I haven't spoken with Ling or anybody yet."

"Yes, I'm pretty sure. Where is Jo Jo?"

Where was Jo Jo? Why was his contact missing? Something was definitely wrong. What had happened to Jo Jo? Ling had no idea of any relationship between him and Colorogne? Other than Jo Jo, no one knew. Jo Jo had been hanging around him all the time. Where was he now?

Billy and Colorogne walked together from the elevator to their respective rooms.

"Just a minute," said Billy, "Where's your security guards?"

There was no one watching Colorogne's room.

Billy stealthily opened Colorogne's door. The two security guards were seated deathly quiet in the lounge chairs. They were dead. Behind them in an upright chair was Jo Jo. He looked a sight. Blood all but covered his face and he was tied to the chair by his hands and legs.

Billy rushed to him and took the gag from his mouth. Two of his teeth fell out with the cloth as Billy pulled it away. His face looked as if it had been used as a boxer's punch bag. His eyes were swollen. The right one was completely shut. He untied the ropes and his right arm dangled. Jo Jo screamed in agony as he was unleashed.

"What happened?"

"Ling. It was Ling," said Jo Jo. "But I did it."

"You did what?"

"I did it." Jo Jo was excited but passed out in pain.

"What did he do?" said Colorogne as his manservant searched the bathroom and other room for accomplices.

"Nothing," he signalled to Colorogne.

"What are you going to do, Billy?" asked Colorogne.

Billy went to the phone and called for Mr Johnson. He asked Johnson to be discreet but bring up the doctor and a nurse. I have someone in the room that has been severely hurt.

Mr Johnson was in Colorogne's room in an instant. "Oh, my God! What happened?"

"Mr Johnson, I need your utmost discretion. This man has been unnecessarily hurt. I don't wish for anyone else to know of this business. It would be very unfortunate if it were to get out, not to mention that it could cause quite a bit of trouble for me. Most of which you don't want to know about."

"Oh, I can't bear to think what it would do for the hotel."

"So, can we get the doctor to sort Jo Jo out. Is there somewhere we can take Jo Jo?" Billy was busy cleaning up Jo Jo as best he could. He moved out of the way when the doctor and the nurse came into the room for them to attend to Jo Jo.

Johnson went to the phone and called for someone to bring up a trolley bed and get a hotel car ready to go to the hospital."

Colorogne said, "I think you should get him to a hospital as soon as possible. This man is in a bad way."

Billy looked at the Spaniard. "I'm thinking this is Ling's way of warning you, Mr Colorogne, but what do I know?"

The doctor administered some smelling salts to bring Jo Jo around who came to.

"Jo Jo, listen to me," Billy knelt down. "What happened?"

He mumbled as best he could, "Ling's men. I followed you last night, to Ling's. I stay there when you leave this morning. I did it." Jo Jo screamed as the doctor tried to apply a temporary splint to his broken arm.

"You did what?"

Jo Jo tried to spit, Billy put the towel to his mouth as he did spit and a thumb drive slipped from between his lips.

"What is this?" asked Billy.

"It's what we need. I did it." He started to pass out again. The doctor gave him some more salts. Then he gave the patient a morphine injection.

"His arm is broken," said the doctor, "and his fingers here are broken."

"Can you patch him up quickly?"

"Patch him up!" questioned the doctor. "Help me get him on the floor. Be careful both his legs are broken. I'm sure there are internal injuries. Let's lay him down on the floor. I cannot patch this man up here. We must get him to the hospital and the sooner the better!"

"I believe the people who did this to him will be back soon."

Jo Jo came around again. He nodded, as best he could, "Yes, they come for Colorogne. They find me in their computer room this morning looking through their things. Ow!"

"But I did it. I get stuff to Smythe."

"You contacted Smythe?"

"I told you. I did it."

'RECEIVED GOODS' of course that was Smythe's message. Colorogne had no idea what he was talking about. Neither did Johnson.

"We need to get him to a hospital," said the doctor.

"I agree," said Billy. "Let's do it."

Moments later, Jo Jo was being stretchered to the elevator, taken down and out of the rear entrance of the hotel to the hospital. Billy grabbed some cash from his desk and handed it to Johnson. "Mr Johnson, please take this and do whatever is necessary to get Jo Jo well. Oh and please keep all this quiet. It's important."

"I will, Mr Doyle. By the ways, dere are two odder gentlemen in a chairs dere that need taking care of."

"This is not the sort of thing that this hotel usually specialises in, you know," said the hotel manager.

Showtime was fast approaching. There was less than an hour to get ready. He thought it best to contact Smythe before the show to let him know of the situation. He also knew that Ling and his entourage would soon be on their way back for Colorogne Smythe's conversation with Doyle went something like:

"Yes, our contact out there was able to transmit all we needed from its sources this morning. I suggest you finish the assignment and 'get the fuck out of Dallas as soon as you can'. I'll get passports to you at the airport. Job done, Get out now!"

Billy assumed that at present Ling still knew of nothing that linked Billy to Colorogne but how long would that be for? He also assumed that Ling would not have known Jo Jo had gotten information to Smythe, at least for now. He also knew the saying 'to Assume only makes an Ass out of U and Me!'

"Listen, Colorogne. Ling will be on his way back here. I'm guessing his people would have been sorting out Jo Jo while he was taking care of his mother's situation. Once his people have let him know what had gone down, he'd be on his way here for you. I'm thinking it best if you stay close to me."

"Still don't trust me?" said Colorogne.

"Don't be fucking stupid, Colorogne! Do you want to stay alive? Stay within my sights."

"Are we leaving now?"

"Soon," said Billy. "Get your stuff ready. Both of you." Billy looked over at the manservant. "Get ready to get out quick. We're going as soon as I've done the show." Billy didn't know how they were to escape Ling and his people. He did know there would be a lot of confusion when people were leaving after the show. That would help a little. Maybe Thomas could help him with some transport to the airport? "Stay around here. I'm going to do the show. Come down there when you're ready."

=======

Billy went to his room and threw on his suit. He felt he'd run a marathon and now he had a show to do. He took a deep breath and thought how they were to escape.

Mr Johnson came running in the dressing room. He was flustered.

"Mr Doyle, the show will have to start a little late tonight. There are so many people. We have a full house and we have had to fill the dance floor with tables and chairs to accommodate. That means dinner has run later and in turn cleaning up after is taking longer. I'm thinking it best to begin the show about thirty minutes later. Will that be a problem?" said Mr Johnson.

"I guess not," replied Doyle. "Did you take care of Jo Jo's situation?"

"He'll be at the hospital now and in a private ward. It won't be long before the police begin to be asking questions though."

Doyle would much rather have gotten the show over and done with as soon as possible in view of the circumstances, but at this moment, the dressing room was probably one of the safest places to be. The band playing their music in the background and that was helping pacify the waiting customers.

"WHY ARE YOU STILL THERE, Mr Doyle?" Smythe shouted down the phone. "As I messaged you earlier, Mr Doyle, we have the information we needed." Smythe didn't let Doyle get a word in. "Our agent Jo Jo did a superb job!"

"Your agent?" asked Doyle.

"Do you know if he got out? I mean, was he able to get away from Ling's people?"

"He did. So he sent you Ling's details. How did he manage that?"

"Apparently, he jumped on a helicopter to Ling's place with you last night. Not sure how he did it. His message was a little distorted, I guess being Chinese and all that. Who knows?"

Billy listened, but the background music had crescendoed for a moment or two and was drowning out the phone.

"Yes. Jo Jo wired us all details. I guess he would've have been in Ling's computer room when he retrieved everything and was able to transmit it to us. I believe he was going to copy everything to a thumb drive in case we didn't get it. But tell him we did get it. Have you been in contact with Jo Jo?"

"Yes, I have," said Doyle. "I left Ling's home first thing this morning."

"You stayed the night there?"

"Yes, but that is not important. I left this morning but I had no idea Jo Jo was at Ling's place at the same time. I saw Jo Jo a little while ago. He was in a very bad condition though."

"How do you mean?"

"He had been worked over, pretty badly."

"Ling caught him then?"

"Looks like it."

"But he got out?"

"Well, kind of. Yes he did. Right now, he should be in the hospital being repaired. I think he's in good hands."

"I'll get some people over there to make sure he's covered," said Smythe.

"Does Ling know you're involved?"

"I don't think so, but I'm sure he will soon."

"We need to get you out, Doyle."

"I haven't completed the mission just yet. Still need to get rid of Ling."

"You need to get out ASAP. Do not waste any more time. Get out NOW!"

"I still reckon I've got a little time to get Ling first."

"Doyle. I need you out of there now! It's no longer safe for you there. Get out!"

The band were playing the old standard 'For the Good Times'.

I think I may be in the best place for the time being, Billy was thinking being on stage might just be the safest place to be. Should Ling discover he had a connection with Jo Jo, he would send his men after him, not to mention if he discovered that all his information had been discovered and wired to Smythe in

England. Ling and his men were hardly likely to cause a gunfight in a crowded showroom.

They would wait until later for him though.

"Someone tried to open the door."

"Got to go. Got a show to do," Billy said into the phone. "Oh, the passports. I need a passport for me and for Colorogne. We will be at the airport later."

"Colorogne?"

"We had a deal. I'm going to uphold that."

"I'll get them to you at the airport. Just get there someone will contact you."

Smythe hung up. Someone tried the door again. Billy shouted, "Just a minute, please."

He took the sim card from the phone and dropped it in a garbage can, then threw the phone behind a stage curtain. He opened the door. Colorogne and his cohort rushed in.

"Mister Doyle!"

"What are you doing here?" said Billy.

"I zink we have trouble coming. I believe I saw some of Ling's people come into zee 'otel. We have pistols but zat is all."

"Where are those from?"

"Da men dat were watching my room. Dey is dead so I thought we take what they 'ad." Corologne's manservant tapped his hand on his jacket to signal he had a weapon too.

"Well, you can't use them in here. There are too many people around here. Ling won't come after you, after us rather, with all those people around. You'll have to blend in with the crowd. But listen, keep your eye on me all the time and remember no shooting inside the building. Also, let me warn you Ling's people are very experienced people. They're not your usual gun shooting thugs you find in South Florida or South America. These are skilled fighters and we have to fight them the same way."

"'Ow we's do that?"

"I don't know, yet."

Mr Johnson came into the room. "We have a lot of people that came back to see you from last night, Mister Doyle. I hope…you have a…good show." Johnson looked at Colorogne and his manservant. "Ahhggh!!"

Doyle closed the door behind Johnson and pulled him into the dressing room. "Mr Johnson, I have another favour to ask of you, if I may."

Johnson didn't take his eyes off Colorogne. He just stared blankly at him. "I believe, Jo Jo, he will sleep for some time. He was in lots of pain. What did happen to him? Do you know?"

"Never mind that for now. Is there anywhere that these gentlemen can be to watch the show?"

"But we are full."

"There has to be somewhere here."

"No seats left."

"Well, they don't need seats. How about the sound booth?" said Doyle.

"Yes, we have the sound booth." The hotel manager just stared at Colorogne. "It is not very big and they will have to be very quiet."

"That will be good. Could you take them there, please?"

Johnson opened the door. "You come with me, please." He was still staring at Colorogne and his partner. "Oh, Mister Doyle. Are you ready for the show now?"

"I am." He wasn't but it had to be done. Where else could he go at this moment?

A matter of minutes passed and he heard the orchestra strike up a fanfare and Thomas, Mr Johnson, walked out on stage to introduce Billy Doyle who walked out to a receptive room.

"Hi everyone. Nice to be with you. Nice to be here. I'm staying in a nice hotel on the other side of the island. Nice but they're overcrowded. Yes, they had to put me up in the honeymoon suite. Yes, I'm staying with a nice couple from Malaysia. The brochure advertised it as a place to see the stars at night. The hotel doesn't have a roof. I ordered a $200 suite. They gave me a bowl of rice pudding. In this place I'm staying at, there are two Austrians, a family from Israel and an Italian…and in the other bed!"

Doyle watched as Sonne Daie and Chooppin entered the room. He knew they were looking for Colorogne. Billy looked to the sound booth. He could see Colorogne in there. *Stay there. Keep out of sight,* he said to himself. Sonne crouched down and crept towards a table full of Chinese gentlemen and spoke to one of them. It was Ling.

Ling was in the room. Did Ling know he was involved with Jo Jo and Colorogne and in turn with the theft of his information? He will soon, no doubt.

Ling looked angry. He whispered to Sonne who looked over at Doyle. *What, no smile?* he thought. No, there was no smile. She grimaced a deathly look at him onstage. Somehow, they all now knew that Doyle was an accomplice of Colorogne's. The table of men stopped smiling and waited for instruction from Ling. Sonne left and edged her way to the back of the room. She guarded the hallway to the dressing room door. The only way Doyle could make the dressing room was from the stage. His way out of the showroom would be blocked by the audience and that would be more difficult to do once the show was over and they wanted Doyle's attention.

He was nearing the end of his stage time, what was he going to do? Chooppin and his men had found Colorogne and were escorting him and his manservant to the dressing room.

That's not for safekeeping, thought Doyle.

"Well, I hate to say this ladies and gentlemen, but I have to leave you now. You know one of the nicest things you can give a person is time. I'd like to thank you for giving me your time.

"And before I leave you, I'd just like to say, if you've enjoyed yourselves, please tell your friends my name is Billy Doyle and this is the Marriatti Hotel in beautiful Hong Kong. If you haven't enjoyed yourselves, I'm Tom Jones and this is the Sands Hotel in Las Vegas.

"I'll see you again. Goodnight." Doyle left the stage and didn't do an encore.

Chapter 30

I'm Outta Here!

"Thanks fellas," said Doyle to the band as he made his wayside stage and to the dressing room. He removed his jacket as he entered the dressing room and threw it onto a chair. People were in the room. Cologrone and his manservant were seated. Their hands were tied behind their backs with plastic ties. Sonne stood by the door, looking very striking in a deep-blue pants suit.

She wasn't smiling. She looked like she was ready for some sort of action. Ling and some of his men were stood around. They were waiting for Doyle.

"Mr Ling," said Doyle, "I was so sorry to hear of your mother's passing."

"She was old and it was her time," said Ling as he moved towards Doyle. "But that is not my concern right now. You fooled me, Mister Doyle."

"We didn't tell him, Doyle," interrupted Cologrone. One of the watchers hit him on the head with the butt of his gun.

"You just did!" said Doyle.

"So, you were responsible for Cologrone's chicanery. And I believe you were involved with the break in to my computer room this morning too?"

"How do you reckon that? I was at your place last night and you know that."

"You were, but I believe you had a helper with you, who got into my computer rooms during the night and stole information from my computers. Apparently, my men caught him trying to leave this morning. We weren't able to get our information back from him, though, and he suffered their indignation."

"I'm not sure what you are talking about, Mr Ling."

"I think your accomplice may have sneaked into my helicopter while we watched your show. That would be how he got into my house last night."

Ling came up to Doyle who stood with his back to the curtain, behind which was the stage but there was no way out through there now. He knew that. A knock on the door interrupted the conversation. It was Mr Johnson. Ling turned away and walked to one side to allow Mr Johnson to enter the room. Everyone put their guns down while he came into the room. He was pushing a food cart. A magnum of champagne decorated the centre of the cart with plates of food dressing around it.

He pushed the cart forward toward Doyle and in front of everybody. "Ah, I see you have company already, Meester Doyle." He halted the cart in front of Doyle. "I'll leave the tray for you to enjoy. If I may show you first the delights? We have some shrimp and rice dish here and some crabs here." He lifted the plate cover and Doyle saw a .380 revolver on the plate. "Also, there is dessert on the tray below." Johnson pulled back very slightly the cloth to reveal a submachine gun's handle sticking towards him.

"I hope you'll be very pleased. Enjoy." Johnson nonchalantly walked back towards the door and smiled at Ling as he did. Sonne opened the door for him. She had barely had time to release her grip from the handle when Johnson turned,

"Oh. Mr Doyle. It was a good show. And I think the people will be gone from the showroom in about ten minutes if you wish to use it for your rehearsal. Goodnight, gentlemen and lady." He left the room.

What the hell would he want to use the room for a rehearsal for when he'd finished his show? Doyle knew exactly what Johnson was inferring. They would have gotten all the customers and staff out of the room in about ten minutes. He had ten minutes to avoid a massacre of customers.

"You two, watch the door!" Ling signalled turning to the entrance.

One of Ling's men left the room to stand watch over the door outside the dressing room.

Sonne again closed the door behind them. Sonne didn't look quite so appealing when she wasn't smiling. She looked cold and serious. Maybe she was as nervous as everyone else in the room even though she didn't show it. Her beauty still shone through her cold exterior.

Tension was building. Something was going to happen soon. What and When?

Ling turned to look at Doyle again, "Who do you work for, Mr Doyle?"

"Er, myself. I'm self-employed."

"I don't think so. Who is it? MI5? CIA? Who?"

Doyle reached to the shrimp plate.

"Stand back, Mr Doyle."

"I was just reaching for some supper. Do you want some?" Doyle tried to be cool. He of course was reaching for the revolver, but Ling interceded,

"Well, right now, for you, it is no longer of any importance; who you are working for, you will not be working for them any longer. But before I kill you, I need something from you. A certain thumb drive that I think belongs to me. I don't believe Mr Colorogne has it. He was not at my house. But you were and so was your accomplice."

"Yes, and I had a wonderful time, but I have no idea what you're talking about," he bluffed.

"The imbecile that broke into my computer room this morning. Don't waste my time. I believe he would have used a thumb drive to steal information from me. I'm thinking he may have given the thumb drive to you. Where is it, Mister Doyle?"

"I don't—"

Ling pulled out a gun from his belt. He quickly turned and fired a shot into Corologne's manservant, who just slumped down, dead. It was so cold. Doyle's stalling was not going to work any longer.

"I want the thumb drive, Mr Doyle!" He obviously had no idea that Jo Jo had already streamed the info to Smythe.

The game was over. No more bluffing.

Doyle reached into his pocket. Ling pointed the gun directly at him. Doyle slowed his action down. Holding up his left hand he reached into his pocket and withdrew a thumb drive between his fingers.

"This wouldn't be what you're looking for, would it?" smiled Doyle.

He held the thumb drive up. Ling reached out for it but Doyle feigned he was throwing it in his direction. It landed in the ice bucket on the cart. As he threw it Doyle knocked the ice bucket over and grabbed the revolver off the plate. He threw himself behind the couch landing on the feet of one of the gunmen. Before the gunman fired a shot, Doyle released a bullet from his gun and killed the man.

Colorogne quickly took action and dived onto the floor for any shelter but there was nothing. He crawled as best he could to a table and crouched down under it.

Gunshots were fired from all direction but none hit Doyle, who'd jumped to his feet and held the revolver in hand to face anyone that came his way.

Suddenly a very heavy foot, belonging to Sonne, hit his jaw as her body sailed straight across the air into him. Her other foot hit him hard and knocked him backwards. Jolted uncomfortably, he dropped his gun as he landed on the food cart, knocking it over. Ling jumped out of the way as his men let fire towards Doyle.

Doyle ran over and grabbed the sub-machine gun from the cart and began firing incessantly. Fortunately for Colorogne, gunshots were firing above waist level as he dropped himself deeper down and lay on the floor.

"Drop it," said Ling. "Drop it now!" Ling was holding a gun to Colorogne's temple.

Doyle put the sub-machine gun down and climbed his way to his feet as Ling commanded.

Ling turned his attention to Colorogne while one of his men tied a zip tie around Doyle's wrists.

"I've had enough. Raul, I believe you are responsible for all this. You brought Doyle here. You came under the pretence of giving me information about our South American trade and all the time you intended to rob me." Ling looked angry. "Handcuff him!" he commanded Sonne. "In fact, cuff them both. Take them to the helipad. We'll deal with them at 'Itshometome'. That was the name Ling had given for his home. "It's getting too busy here, the police will come soon. Let's go."

Ling put the thumb drive in his pocket and left the room presumably to go to the helicopter. One of the guards tied a zip tie around Doyle's wrists and also put a pair of handcuffs on him.

Another lifted Colorogne to his feet. He looked sadly at his manservant. He knew he would soon receive the same. He had given it his best shot but knew he would not be seeing his granddaughter after all.

Sonne opened the dressing room door. The men on guard duty outside just collapsed against the door as it opened. They had been shot. *Had Johnson done this? No, he would have had some help*, Doyle said to himself.

The party climbed over the bodies and cautiously followed Ling to the elevator. For a second night, Doyle was going to get a ride in the magnificent machine to Ling's home. This time his hands had been tied with a plastic tie and handcuffs. Sonne pushed him into the elevator.

He slipped a little and knocked into her, then balanced himself against the wall of the elevator.

The wind blew cool across the rooftop. The clouds covered the moon that had gleamed so brightly previously. You could sense a storm was brewing. The lights shone as brightly still.

Had it been so long since he'd first been invited to the sightseeing journey of the harbour?

"I have to tell you, Mr Colorogne, I am very disappointed with you. You do not seem to have the integrity that I may have afforded you. I'm not even sure how you managed to run your business in South America so well for so long." Ling pushed him towards the helicopter with his gun. "String them up! Let's give them a real tour of the city!"

What was left of Ling's men led Colorogne and Doyle into the copter.

"Don't I get a goodbye kiss?" Doyle looked at Sonne's hair blowing in the wind. The girl was a looker. She leaned forward. He raised his arms looking to slide his arms over her head.

She stepped back and as she did, he grabbed her hair clip from her hair with his teeth.

"Not so fast, Billee Doylee," she said.

She walked back to him and kissed him passionately. Did he almost get to her? No. She was from another planet.

Ling was already in the helicopter and looking through the window as Chooppin started up the engine. Sonne and the men climbed the helicopter steps and pushed Billy and Colorogne into the back of the machine. Billy fell over a toolbox and almost dropped the hairclip from his teeth. One of Ling's men held up Colorogne while the other roped the copter cable around his neck, securing it with a padlock through the hook.

Doyle had no sooner been sat down when he spit out the hair clip to his feet and picked it up between his fingers. He straightened out, as best he could, the hair clip and slipped one end down into the side of his handcuffs down the side of the lock mechanism. He jiggled it and then levered the catch inside the cuffs, releasing it open. He opened the other side of the cuffs the same way.

With his teeth, he grabbed the end of the zip tie and pulled it tight. He got to his knees to give himself more room to manoeuvre. Then resting his elbows to his sides, he pushed his arms quickly forwards and snapped the zip tie with his wrists.

The guard holding up Colorogne up saw him break loose and hit him. He tried to kick Doyle down but Doyle grabbed his foot and tossed him backwards.

The man over balanced and fell backwards and out of the door as the helicopter started to ascend. Sonne got out of her seat to help the other man who was wrapping the cable around Colorogne. Colorogne thumped the man into his shoulder and sent him tumbling into Sonne. Doyle began to unravel the cable. The man was getting off the floor when Colorogne swung his foot as hard as he could into his jaw and knocked him out.

The helicopter was in the air as Sonne and Billy scuffled with each other. Ling unfastened his seat belt and turned with his gun in hand. The helicopter was in mid-air now. The door was still open and Sonne was holding Billy over the open side. Billy's hands were holding the sides as she held him back. She was about to direct one of her karate kicks to him when the helicopter turned causing Billy to release one of his handgrips. Sonne went floating past him through the doorway and out through the air to the earth below.

"What can I say?" said Billy. "She fell for me!"

Ling fired his gun at Doyle. Doyle was saved as the man Colorogne had knocked out came out of his unconsciousness and climbed up between him and Ling and took the bullet in his head. The man fell backwards and knocked Ling onto the pilot, Choopin. Another bullet was fired, this time hitting Choopin. The helicopter rocked.

Colorogne began to slip towards the doorway with the cable still firmly around his neck.

Doyle grabbed the toolbox. He found two spanners and jammed their heads into the padlock on the cable. Quickly, he forced the heads outwards to open the lock. As it did, the cable whipped across the front of the helicopter and lashed against Ling who fell further onto the steering column.

The copter started to descend. It hit a power line as it did, which caused the tail end of the helicopter to explode. The helicopter was on fire as it started to descend. Colorogne snapped his wrists to untie himself. Doyle grabbed hold of him and the two men jumped out of the copter.

Neither had any idea where they would land.

The helicopter blew up into the Chinese sky and a ball of fire descended into the harbour below. It was almost as if someone had shot a canon out to culminate the wonderful light show that the hotels and buildings of Hong Kong offered.

Doyle and Cologne had landed on a canopy that overlook one of the rooms to the Hotel Marriatta. The canopy was not strong enough to hold their weight and the cloth tore as they both fell below. They were hurt and in pain, but at least they were safe.

Chapter 31

All's Well...

Colorogne and Doyle sat down exhausted but safe on the room veranda. The police ran out through the room with Mr Thomas.

"Mr Doyle! Are you okay?"

"We're fine, thanks."

"I see you've brought an escort."

"The police will need to ask you some questions, sir."

A couple of the policemen helped Doyle and Colorogne to their feet.

"How do you feel, Colorogne?" asked Doyle.

"I think I'm okay. How about you?"

"Bit of a headache, but I think I'll live."

The two men walked through the bedroom with Thomas and the police escort. An elderly couple sat up in bed. "Is there a problem?" the woman asked.

"No. No problem, ma'am," said Mr Johnson as everyone left the room.

"So now what?" said Corologne.

"Well, I think I'm going to clean up and I'm going to have a scotch and soda. How about you?"

"Dat sounds very good. May I join you?"

"See you downstairs. Would you care to join us, Mr Johnson?"

After the formalities in reception were cleared the following afternoon, Mr Johnson said, "It was a pleasure, Mr Doyle. Will we see you again soon?"

"It certainly isn't in the plans, Mr Johnson, but you never know. Thanks for your assistance last night. It was much appreciated. I am a little curious about one thing though. When did you know there was a problem?"

"Oh, that reminds me, before you go. I have something that was delivered for you this morning." Johnson handed him an envelope. He opened it and pulled out two new passports. One for himself and one for Colorogne. And two airline tickets to Germany.

"Any reason why Germany? Do you know?" asked Billy.

"Mr Smythe said you will know what to do when you get to Berlin."

"Smythe, so you…"

"Of course. Mr Smythe told Jo Jo and me to make your visit to Hong Kong a memorable and as enjoyable as possible. You never know who is watching, do you?" Billy looked at Thomas puzzled but not for long. A cab pulled up and bellboys helped a man with a broken arm and splintered foot and numerous other bandaged parts get to the entrance to the hotel.

"Ah, Mr Doyle. I did it. I did it."

"Yes, you did, Jo Jo. Job well done. Good to see you. Thanks for the gig. See you another day. Oh."

"No need to say it."

"Somebody has to. Thanks. Both of you."

======

"So this is Germany? Where do we fly to now, Mister Doyle? England."

Doyle sat down next to Colorogne at a bar restaurant in the airport.

"So, I guess you fly me to England now for questioning?"

"No."

"So, you kill me now? I knew it!"

"I always keep my word, Mr Colorogne. I don't like what you were involved in. Hopefully, you're not anymore, but I did make you a promise."

Billy handed Colorogne plane tickets. One was for Berlin to Miami and the other was for Miami to Bogata.

Tears welled in Colorogne's eyes. "I see my granddaughter?"

"You see your granddaughter. And you might just need this. Let's just say you'll need a ride from Bogata Airport to the nunnery. I don't think you have one." Billy handed him an envelope with a large amount of cash in it. "Bringing up children is never easy, let alone the cost of doing so."

Colorogne cried as Billy got up from his seat. "And you, Mister Billy? You're not coming with me?"

"I have to go and check on a young lady and her daughter in England. And anyway, the soccer season is about to start."

Billy got up to walk away. They shook hands. Colorogne looked at his ticket to Bogata and smiled. He looked up again. Billy had disappeared. He never saw him again.

Printed in the USA
CPSIA information can be obtained
at www.ICGtesting.com
CBHW060714191223
2756CB00007B/126